HIDDEN SEAMS

ALESSANDRA TORRE

HIDDEN SEAMS

Editor: Madison Seidler

Cover Design: Perfect Pear Creative Covers

Proofreader: Janice Owen and Perla Calas

To H. John Benjiman.

"Read a book for once in your life."

PROLOGUE

I hate these events. Rooms packed with glitter and gold, everyone preening, cackling, smiling. A woman at the bar, her dress cut down to her navel, stares at me. I meet her eyes, then look away. She'd be perfect. Bent over the bathroom sink, that gown flipped over her back, feet spread, back arched. I'd take her quickly, my hands skimming down the straps of her gown, baring her breasts, and then watch them in the mirror as I fuck her. I turn and accept a glass of champagne, my heartbeat increasing, and I walk forward, moving away from her and will my dick to soften.

She'd be loud when I let loose on her. I'd have to gag her with my fingers, muffle her moans, silence her with my kiss. Her skin would flush, her lipstick smear, and she'd flex around my cock, contracting tightly before she drops to her knees and opens her mouth for me.

Jesus. I push open the bathroom door and nod to the attendant, taking the farthest stall and closing the door. My hands quick, I unzip my pants, pull out my cock, and squeeze it. Closing my eyes, thinking of her breasts, the mirror's reflection of them bouncing as I slam into her... the orgasm comes, quick and sudden, and I lean over the toilet and shoot the evidence into it.

Breathing hard, I take a moment to compose myself, a moment where I put myself back together, all of the pieces of Marco Lent shuttering back into place. Stepping out of the stall, I wash my hands and accept the hand towel.

"Thank you." I open my wallet, pulling out a fifty and passing it to him without meeting his eyes.

Back in the room, the crowd moves toward the auditorium, the woman gone from the bar, and I find Vince by the doors, his hand reaching for mine, the crowd cheering as we step through the doors and onto the press walk.

"Mr. Horace!" A camera is shoved in Vince's face and he stops, my attention grabbed by a second reporter, his microphone extended, calling my name. I turn to him, the famous Marco Lent smile in place.

"Mr. Lent, what is it like, watching your partner being awarded Gay Man of the Decade?"

I widen my smile. "I'll let you know in a few minutes."

There is another shout of my name, a dozen more camera flashes.

"How long have you and Vince Horace been an exclusive couple?"

"For me?" I laugh. "Three years. For Vince…" I make a face and am elbowed by the man himself, who clamps a hand on my shoulder and scowls at the press.

"Don't listen to this guy. Look at him! How can I even be tempted by anyone else?" He presses a kiss to my cheek and I smile, the flashbulbs going crazy, the crowd behind them cheering.

Three years. Three years, and I was dying inside.

CHAPTER 1

SEVEN YEARS LATER

I fucking hate fashion. Not the clothes, but the people, the illusion—this industry was handed down to us by the greats, and we've poisoned it with greed, inflated opinions and social standings. The garment no longer seems to matter, just the label sewn into its neck. A brilliant gown could be ruined by the wrong pedigree, banished to a Des Moines TJ Maxx rack and some cornhusker's high school prom. In this world, the designers are the gods and lives are choreographed, backs stabbed, promises and threats made, all to try to climb onto one of those almighty thrones.

I'm the worst of the bunch, and know the sacrifices more than anyone. The last ten years of my life has been orchestrated, a web of deceit and lies, all for one of those thrones.

I sit in a Vince Horace original, a tribute to the god, the custom silk-blend suit hugging my build perfectly. It should. He measured me himself, stretching out that gold and red tape measure, his glasses perched atop his nose, his eyes admiring the lines of my muscles as he worked. Now, I watch him sleep, the fur coverlet tucked under his thin forearms, the limbs slack and almost swallowed by the tubes and wires. Between us, set against gold-leaf walls and velvet curtains, a monitor beeps, his statistics displayed in quiet clarity.

It's been four days since he last spoke. Four days that I've sat in this chair and watched one of the only men I've ever loved, die.

"Are you done with dinner, sir?"

I don't turn my head to acknowledge the man or the silver plate that sits on the table beside me, the veal now cold, the greens past limp. "Yes. I'd like another drink."

"Certainly. I've taken the liberty of calling in Tony. He'll be here shortly."

"That's fine." In another situation, I would wave off the masseuse, but if there is any energy left in Vince, it doesn't need to be wasted with scolding me on the finer things in life. If he knew I was sitting here with a stiff back and tight neck, he'd bust a blood vessel, his lips sputtering, eyebrows pinching, disappointment heavy in those piercing brown eyes.

"Marco." When he speaks, my name is soft, almost lost in the clink of silver, the butler pausing, both of our heads turning at the sound. I rise, stepping to the bed and link my fingers through his, a contrast of strong against weak, tan against pale. I keep my eyes on the man's face, his eyelids fluttering for a moment but not lifting. "I think it's time."

"I know. Stop stalling, old man."

A ghost of a smile lifts one corner of his mouth, a mouth I know so well, so much wisdom and friendship passing through those lips—a decade of curses and brilliance. "Live well, Marco." He wheezes out the words, his hand tightening on mine for a whisper of a moment.

I swallow. "I love you, Vince." I know the answer before it comes, yet need to hear it one final time.

"Always, vecchio amico."

"Always, vecchio amico." I lean forward and press my lips to his forehead. "The world will miss you."

I wait for a scoff, a humble protest of something we both know to be true, but there is only a gentle sigh, a moment of peace falling over those strong features, the muscles in his face falling, my grip of his hand unreturned.

The world spent five decades learning his name, and in just a handful of seconds, Vince Horace is gone. I close my eyes and try to feel him in the room, his presence one I've leaned on as heavily as breath. But there is nothing. I lower myself carefully, my hand still in his, to my knees, my cheek against the rough paper of his palm, and close my eyes, saying a prayer that God will respect his choices, honor his lifestyle, and accept him into his kingdom. I pray, in the dim bedroom six floors above Fifth Avenue, for guidance and peace—both for him and for myself.

I stay on my knees beside my mentor, until the doctors arrive, an ashen-faced butler helping me to my feet and to my bedroom, the bed already turned down, my evening wear laid out on heated pads, a glass of ice water chilling beside a sleeping pill on the nightstand. I glance at the curtains, pulled tight, and wonder at the city behind them, the chitter chatter of news services and reporters, blogs, and Twitter. The death of Vince Horace will not be ignored. Tonight, a throne is vacant, and everyone in the fashion world will be elbowing and fighting for a chance at it.

———

I sit on the edge of the bed and work my watch from my wrist, the vintage Cartier dull in the dim light. I pull off the jacket, stepping slowly to the large closet and carefully hanging the piece up, ignoring the line of similar suits, each one a different story, a different factory, trip, or memory.

I am naked by the time I move into the bed, my eyes closing as I lay back on the goose-down pillows.

I think of the future, but only feel lost.

CHAPTER 2

SPRING

AVERY

I take the two bags of Chinese takeout and tip the guy a twenty. Pushing the door shut, I flip all three deadbolts, then arm the alarm.

Jogging up to the kitchen, I withdraw the top carton in each bag and set them on the stove. Ignoring the temptation of the food, I snag a fortune cookie and rip it open.

Wealth and good fortune are coming your way.

Ha. I smile and tack the fortune to the fridge with a penguin magnet, then pop the cookie in my mouth. Crunching through it, I pull on a set of latex gloves and return to the takeout bags.

The first Styrofoam lid pops open, revealing the cash, neatly stacked three rows high and bound in counter strips. I pull the stacks from the Styrofoam and line them up on the counter, counting as I go. Five, ten, twenty …. sixty grand in the first box. I toss the empty carton toward the trash can, pull the second out, and repeat the process until the stretch of granite is filled with neat rows of cash. I count it all a second time. Two hundred and five grand. Perfect.

The cash didn't always come with beef and broccoli and shrimp fried rice. It used to come from a little old lady, one who birthed a monster and liked to sit in my living room and talk about her medical problems. And she had a *lot* of medical problems, enough to fill entire evenings. And I couldn't complain to her employer because no gangster wants to hear that his mother is painfully time-consuming.

That arrangement died when she did. Out of every medical issue I'd listened through … it had been a steep flight of stairs that killed her. She slipped, fell backward, hit the wrong part of her neck, and died instantly.

I don't know how the Chinese restaurant guys are connected to Ralph, but I'd take a wild guess and say that they owe him money, and are paying it back through my deliveries. It works out well for me. They're on time, give me all the MSG-laden food I want, and the delivery guy doesn't speak a lick of English, so if he's got a bad hip and ingrown toenails, I'm oblivious to it.

I text confirmation of receipt and move the cash into Ziploc bags, then a duffel bag. Grabbing the food, I move to the living room. Sitting cross-legged on the couch, I pick up the remote and find the last half of a medical drama.

I need a boyfriend. I decide that as I spear a piece of broccoli and watch bored nurses getting frisky in a supply room. As much as I love having full control of the remote, and a steady diet of stir-fried dishes, it's getting old. It has *gotten* old.

Maybe I should have been a nurse. As a nurse, I would have met someone by now. Someone who wasn't a step away from being shot, or arrested. That's the problem in my business. Any good guys end up dead or behind bars. And the bad guys … I pick up my soda and twist off the top. The bad guys aren't worth dating. I did that once. Fell into his pretty blue eyes and looked the other way whenever he beat the shit out of someone. I'd like to say I was young and dumb, but I haven't exactly made strides in a better direction. I'm still here, spending my nights alone, counting someone else's money, with no plausible relationship options in sight. I could be in scrubs right now, my tired soles being worked over by some gorgeous husband with a five o'clock shadow, a baby girl sound asleep in the crook of his arm.

The show ends, and the news comes on, the top story about some dead rich guy. I turn it off and stand.

I shove the empty takeout containers into the trash, then yank the ties, lifting the Hefty out of the can. I grab the duffel and carry it all down to the garage. The Hefty goes into the garbage can. I roll underneath the Tahoe and bring the duffel bag along.

Or maybe I'll get a dog. That would probably cure this stupid yearn for a man. I reach into the duffel bag and pull out a couple of bags of cash. Stacking them inside the Tahoe's front bumper, I think of a possible dog. It'd have to be something big and scary. Maybe one of those military-trained German Shepherds. I'd want a girl, and I could name her something absolutely unscary. Like Ethel. Or Joyce. Maybe, I could get two.

I push the bags into a hidden compartment, one installed there two years ago. I'd put it in after an overzealous badge pulled me over, then felt the need to dig through my trunk, discovering enough cash to start a Mickey D's franchise. I almost lost that money, the cop confiscating it and refusing to return it until I proved a legitimate source of the cash. That had been an interesting conundrum, one I had barely wiggled through.

Now, if anyone pulls me over? They'd need a cash-sniffing dog to get these bad boys found. I place the last bundle of cash in, lock the hidden door into place, and roll out from under the truck. *There.* Money secured. I push to my feet and head back inside. Pulling the door shut, I reach out and hit the light switch with my palm.

In bed, I scroll through gossip articles, stopping at one image of some sexy playboy who just inherited a billion dollars. I skip the article and focus on the photos of him—standing on the front of a yacht, his abs on display, his gorgeous grin pulling at the ache between my legs. I put down the phone and close my eyes, imagining the sun on my face, ocean waves crashing in the distance, him pulling me down onto a towel and kissing me everywhere.

———

I unwrap the McMuffin, steam rising, and hold it in front of the air vent, managing the tight turn with one hand. I glance down at the breakfast sandwich and almost hit the two men that step out from the shadows, their guns raised, a spike strip thrown out.

I groan, and hit the brakes, skidding to a stop, and think of the money in the bumper. A man, one big enough to squash a small horse, walks up to SUV.

I crack the window and glare at the man. "Seriously?"

He lifts his AK in response, as if that will scare me. I've got bulletproof windows in this baby. Steel reinforced doors. A front grill guard that a battering ram would have trouble working through. I look forward, at the three thugs standing in front of my car. I should just gas it. Run over them and continue on my way. Let them try to shoot me. But that would cause a scene. Even in this part of Detroit, dead bodies in the street attract police. Police … and questions. Plus, there are the spike strips. I'd make it a mile before I'd be on the side of the road, trying to explain *that* to someone.

I rev my engine and the three guns ahead of me raise their scopes in warning. Oooh. Scary.

The muzzle knocks on my window and I sigh, looking over at him. He lifts a gloved hand and points toward my steering wheel. "Turn off the car."

He's white. That's my first hint. No accent, which is my second hint.

I'm on the edge of downtown, smack in the middle of Italian territory, which is my third. I roll the window down a bit more and dare him to fucking shoot me. "Call Tony."

I'm sure there are a lot of Tony's in the world, probably a thousand in this zip code. But in *this* neighborhood, there's only one who doesn't need a last name. Tony Bruno. There's a moment of hesitation in the man's face, and his eyes dart to one of his friends. I lift the McMuffin to my mouth, test the temperature with my tongue, then take a bite.

"You want me to call him?" I offer, a speck of McMuffin flying out and hitting the steering wheel. I watch his finger move along the AK's slide and I press the phone icon on my steering wheel, the voice assistance tone sounding. "Call Tony B," I call out. He steps closer and holds up a hand to his friends, telling them to wait.

"Ave. What's up?" Tony's voice comes through the speakers and I turn up the volume so that my new best friend can hear him.

"Your boys are trying to buy my car."

"They aren't my boys."

"Mmmhmmm." I trace my fingers over the stitching on the steering wheel. "Call them off."

"Let me talk to them."

I reach for my phone and turn off the Bluetooth, rolling the window further down and passing the cell through it.

The guy takes it with a snarl. "Hello?"

His eyes dart to me and he jerks his head at his goons. There is a lot of scowling, words exchanged, and whatever Tony says causes him to hand the phone back, the gun dropping out of sight. "Go on."

"What's your name?" I lean forward and give him my best smile, the one that used to earn me black eyes from prep school bullies.

He ignores the question, and I'm willing to bet he was the sort that used to deliver those black eyes.

"I'm Avery." I hold the phone to my ear, moving the mouthpiece away from my mouth. "I come through here a lot. So, we good?"

He gives an irritated nod and waves me forward as if he's a cop directing traffic and not a carjacker anxious for his next victim. I glance in the rearview mirror and take my foot off the brake.

Tony clears his throat. "I'm sorry about that. It's just business. You understand?"

I *don't* understand, the profit margin on boosting cars not worth the trouble and risk. But I'm not about to question one of my best clients. He pays his bills on time and keeps his mouth shut. If he wants to run his business like a thug, whatever. "I understand." Reaching up, I flip down my visor and touch my fingers to the most valuable piece of this car, reassuring myself of its presence. It's a photo, one taken three decades ago, a worn crease running down the middle and almost cutting my mom in half.

In the photo, she's seventeen and at a LiveAid concert. The weekend it was taken, she'd danced to Bono, fucked some hippie, then scampered back home, unaware of the tiny fetus growing in her tummy. Six months later, her parents shipped her off to a discrete facility in West Virginia, and—three months later—signed off on her adoption papers while she was still doped up from my birth. I was a cute baby. It didn't take long before I was bundled up, driven north, and handed off to an attorney and his pretty little wife.

Kirk and Bridget McKenna had wanted to round out their perfect life and had envisioned a dutiful daughter fitting nicely into it. I'd been the right race, the right gender, the right age. Everything else about me had been wrong. Had they known what they were getting, they would have probably sent me back, a neatly written note pinned to the front of my bib. *No, thank you. Please find us someone else.* Instead, they kept me. Showered me with love and pink dresses and private tutors. When I ran away at twelve, they found me and brought me back. At thirteen, I found better places to hide but got caught by an Iranian stealing candy bars and snacks from a 7-11. He pulled a shotgun from under the counter and I tried to run. He chambered a round and I stopped. The cops gave me back to the McKennas and they sent me off to a private school, the sort with nuns and plaid, the place where rich girls snort coke and bitch about politics and speak Latin like it is their second tongue. When I ran away from there, I didn't hear from the McKennas. I hitchhiked across two states and when I finally turned my phone on, my voicemail was empty and my phone never rang. My credit cards worked for a month, then stopped. I used my debit card, watched the balance dwindle and then empty, with no replenishments made. I started to check my phone weekly, then monthly. Finally, in one drunk moment on the edge of the Ambassador Bridge, I dumped all of it—my prep school license, my credit cards, my phone—over the side. Goodbye, old life. Goodbye, Kirk and Bridget.

I look from my young mother to the man beside her, examining his face, memorizing it for the hundredth time.

The light changes and I close the visor. Pressing on the gas, the powerful engine jumps to life. I flip on the radio and skip past a news story about fashion mogul Vince Horace, stopping on some music with a beat.

CHAPTER 3

MARCO

I'm five floors up, and I can hear the crowd. They chant, a rhythmic cheer that changes every ten minutes or so. At some point, you'd think their throats would grow tired, their lungs give out, their energy cease. But it doesn't. It's been hours since the announcement, and still, they chant. I walk to the window and push the curtains aside, looking down at the street, our block filled with bodies, banners and signs, a rainbow of colors and faces, hands lifting and waving at the sight of me. I stay in place, meeting their upturned faces. What does someone do in a moment like this? Smile? Wave? I know what Vince would have done. He'd have pulled me to him, thrown his arm around my shoulders, and kissed me. Over the last decade, we'd had plenty of moments like this, when our street closed, police controlled the crowd, and the celebration or protest turned into a party as the night grew later. A few years ago, Vince brought a dozen models in through the garage, had their entire bodies sprayed gold and sent them out into the crowd with platters of Cristal. We've set off confetti machines from the porches and sprayed the crowd with silly string. Last Pride

Week, we'd had Cirque Du Soleil acrobats swirling above the crowd, suspended on silk ropes.

A showman, that's what Vince had been, that's what his entire brand had been built on. Colorful yet refined excess. Expensive. Daring. Fun. I know what needs to be done—starting the funeral arrangements—but it's the last thing I feel up to doing. Turning away from the curtain, I look to the closest individual. "Call Mario. Tell him to have it on Thursday at four."

The man's small frame scurries quickly out of the room. He'd have Mario on the phone within a minute, the event planner prepared. One sad side effect of Vince's illness—we've had a clear countdown to death, with plenty of time to make the proper arrangements. And Mario had needed the time. This won't just be a funeral, it will be one of the biggest parties New York has ever seen.

"Do you need help dressing, sir?"

I turn at the butler's question, then glance in the direction of the master suite. "I'd like a shave in thirty minutes. Have them start the shower now."

I step forward and stop before the table, a selection of fruit and crepes in neat and perfect rows along gold plated platters. I take a slice of mango and a sip of coffee, closing my eyes at the familiar taste of Vince's favorite blend. Outside, the chants hit a new crescendo. "What time is it?"

"Ten oh-five, sir."

Ten in the morning. At least a dozen more hours until this day ends. I hold out a hand and Edward places a hot, scented, white towel in my palm. I use the small terrycloth to clean my fingers and pass it back. Moving to the door, I inhale deeply and think of Vince.

———

Eleven years ago, I met Vince Horace at a Dolce & Gabbana show in Milan. It was at an after-party, and we practically brushed dicks in a gilded gold men's room that was doubling as a coke dispensary. He waited until I finished pissing, allowed me to zip up and wash my hands, and then introduced himself. His handshake was firm, his eye contact professional, and I relaxed in his presence, despite the entourage that crowded behind him.

"What would it take to pull you away from Frank?" Frank Foster, the reigning Creative Director at Dolce.

"Not a great deal." I smile, and it is a look that I carry well, one that has opened countless doors in this industry where looks mattered more than talent.

"Let's have drinks tonight and talk."

Drinks that night are at a quiet wine bar, one packed with industry heads. I sip a red wine that costs more than my rent and discuss trends and rumors with a group of women who work in merchandising. I am interrupted by a kid in a red leather shirt and a mohawk.

"Mr. Horace is requesting you upstairs."

Every lipstick-covered mouth snaps shut, eyes widen, and I excuse myself and follow the pink-tipped hair up a flight of stairs and to a private balcony where Vince Horace sits.

It is like meeting a God. He is a maverick at a time when our industry is becoming stale and pushes the envelope continuously with his designs. He is controversial, not just in those designs, but also in his personal life. He's promiscuous in an unapologetic way, wildly gay in a manner that has advocate groups rallying and fanboys flocking. He has become an entire culture, one with a million members, their hopes, dreams, and expectations, all resting on one thin, dignified man. A man who sits, calm and collected, at a tiny table on a Milan balcony and gestures to the seat beside him.

I sit, and he sips from a glass of wine, silent for a long while. When he speaks, his voice is wistful, and that of a man older than forty-five. "Do you have any children, Marco?"

"No."

"Well. You're a little young still. What are you, thirty?"

"Twenty-six, sir." It is a common mistake. I don't look my age. Neither does my resume nor my position.

His eyes linger on my face. "Are you single?"

I don't shift in the seat, but the urge is present, various muscles in my body tensed for flight. "Yes."

"There seems to be varying opinions in regards to your sexuality."

"My sexuality isn't anyone's fucking business."

The corner of his mouth lifts, and he purses his lips together, the hint of a smile disappearing. "Including mine?"

I look away, off the balcony and out on the night, the city peeking out at us in between skinny buildings, the music from downstairs drifting up to us, paired with the scents and perfumes of a hundred strangers.

He uncrosses his legs, his thin frame extending, and he plucks a speck of something from the cuff of his sleeve. "I often find that those who don't discuss their sexuality are confused by it."

"I'm not confused about anything." I reach forward and take a piece of cheese from the tray that sits between us, popping it into my mouth and giving him enough eye contact to enunciate the point. "If you're looking to hire me, and a condition of that employment is to be one of your fuck toys, I won't. If a condition of my employment is that you know whether I'm straight or gay or some grey area in between, then tell me that now, and I'll clear up your curiosity."

He smiles. "I don't want your cock, Marco. Just your talent and intelligence. Forgive my nosy questions. I just want to know a little more about the man I am bringing into my brand."

"Potentially," I interject, reaching forward and picking a grape up from the tray, my fingers rolling the purple fruit between my fingertips. "Potentially bringing into your brand."

He laughs. "Don't be coy. If I want you, you'll be here. You may not become my fuck toy, as you so crudely pointed out, but you will work for me. It's the right place for you, Marco."

He was right. His company was the place for me. And I came, without hesitation or negotiation.

But he was also wrong. I did become his fuck toy, in name, if not in action. It took a year of friendship to build up to it, but it eventually happened, and when it did—everyone knew.

CHAPTER 4

AVERY

Hank Williams croons from the jukebox and I glance at my watch, the restaurant empty given that it's almost noon. I crack open a peanut and glare at the greaser who decides to settle into the stool next to me. He gets the hint and picks one a little further away.

"Here ya go." The bartender slides a cheeseburger toward me. "Want a refill?"

I nod and lift the burger, my nails biting into the soft bun, a drop of ketchup and mustard falling off the end of it. I bring it to my mouth and scoot closer, leaning over the plate in an attempt to keep my shirt clean.

"Nice watch," the girl remarks, her eyes lingering on the platinum timepiece.

"Thanks." I stuff a fry in my mouth.

"It's too bad," she sighs, her eyes still glued to the face of it. I hate when people do this. End a sentence in a way that requests a response.

I don't bite, focusing on my plate and the attempt to drown out the bluesy sound of a country legend.

"I mean he's *so* young." She leans forward and lowers her voice. "I mean, fifty-five? I'm almost that age myself."

I give up on the guessing game. "Who?"

Her eyes finally lift from my watch and meet my eyes. "Vince Horace. Didn't you hear? He *died* Sunday night." She says *died* in a hushed tone as if I'm unfamiliar with the concept. She gestures to the television behind her. "It's all they've been talking about for two days."

The television is on an entertainment talk show, and I watch as the screen shows a ridiculously handsome man stepping out of a Rolls Royce, one hand lifting to block the camera from seeing his face. I squint, trying to picture him in board shorts, on the front of a yacht. Yep. It's my fantasy boy from last night.

"That's him?" There's no way in hell he's fifty-five.

"No—that's his boyfriend. They say he's inheriting *everything*. Can you believe it?" She turns to face the television, her elbows resting against the bar top. "That slice of gorgeous is about to be a billionaire."

I watch the man stride toward a brick building, the afternoon sun catching on his features. Close-up, and in a suit, he looks different than on the boat. Older, more refined. He's attractive in an almost painful way, the kind that stabs you in the gut and reminds you that you are inferior, each angle only making him more appealing. It isn't fair for men like that to exist, much less for them to inherit a billion dollars.

The photo changes, showing a handsome older man who must be Vince Horace. He looks familiar, and I straighten on the stool, watching as a slideshow of photos flickers across the screen. Him and the hottie boyfriend on stage at the VMAs. Him, on a catwalk, beside a team of models. Him, a pen stuck behind one ear, beside a dress form. I half stand, leaning onto the bar, and blink, trying to improve my vision, trying to calm my thoughts and watch the content without jumping to conclusions.

But the older man is <u>him</u>. I'm almost certain of it. The eyes are the same, the dimple in his right cheek, the closed lip smile. Granted, there are some differences. His hair is short, his features more mature, and he's clean-shaven, his clothes clean and not rumpled. But if you take away some of the years, some of the composure, the refinement … I scramble for my bag, for the photo I keep there, the photocopy of the one in my truck. I barely get it out in time, the segment wrapping up, a final image of him filling the studio's screen as the camera pans out to include the two hosts who chatter back in forth in front of the man's face.

I flatten the photo on the bar top and look frantically from it to the TV, my finger pinned on his face, the other people in the photo unimportant. It matches, enough of a match for my heart to hammer against its cavity, my breaths shortening as I practically pant, my focus closing in on the image I've carried around for the last seven years.

It's a photo of three people, all clustered on a blanket, beer cans littering the plaid fabric, the glow of a fire hanging off the left end of the photo. The blonde sits cross-legged beside a cooler, her gaze off the camera and on the guy to her right. The guy smiles into the camera, his hair shaggy, his eyes warm, one of his hands gripping the arm of the man beside him. The blonde is too young to be there, and the guy looks too old for her, but I can see myself in both of them. My fingers tighten on the edge of the photo and I glance back at the television, but the story on screen has changed.

I push to my feet and dig a hand in my front pocket, pulling out a wad of cash and peeling off two twenties. I place them on the bar and reach for my drink, finishing off the soda as I stare down at the face I've spent seven years memorizing. My eyes move to my watch, the timepiece purchased on a whim during a New York shopping spree. I'd known the brand, known the stories of the man but had never bothered to look up his image.

Vince Horace. A household name, and one of the richest fashion designers in the world.

My father. A hippie from a concert, one who impregnated my teenage mother.

Vince Horace. A well-documented gay man. Now dead.

My father. Never found.

Could they really be the same person?

CHAPTER 5

MARCO

I don't feel any richer. Maybe it's because I've spent ten years in this house, with Billy ironing my fucking sheets, Edward carrying around the telephone on a silver platter, and a staff of twenty others catering to our every need. I miss the nights when everyone would leave, where we would finally have privacy, and if Vince or I needed anything, we would just get it for our damn selves.

Part of me wants to fire them all, to wipe my ass with a piece of toilet paper that hasn't been stamped on its end. To settle my head on a pillow that hasn't been fluffed. To peel my own boiled egg or answer my own calls. A larger part of me doesn't care enough to change anything. Since his death, I haven't cared enough about anything.

I run my hands through my hair, rinsing out the rosemary soap, the scent of it filling the space, the steam clearing my lungs. I think about that night in Vince's home, a year into our friendship and work relationship, when I'd been in the shower and he had stepped into the bathroom.

I shut off the water and look toward the door, spying him through the fogged glass, my muscles tensing when he flips the lock shut. He turns away, his hands settling on the marble countertop, and speaks quietly. "Marco, I have a proposition for you."

A proposition. I step from the shower, pulling a towel off the rack, and carefully consider the best words to use that won't offend the man. I know the standard—any other intern or house employee would be rock hard at the thought of a moment with the legend. The distinguished forty-five-year-old has a build perfectly set off by his designs, his appeal enhanced with his fame, talent, and money. But I'd been clear, in our initial interview and in the time since, about my sexual orientation. I had a talent and passion for men's fashion—not cock. And he hadn't seemed bothered by that fact, assuring me that any stays in his New York home would be absolutely professional.

I wrap a towel around my waist, and wait, unsure in my footing. When he begins to speak, I listen. And when he proposes an arrangement between us, I consider it.

Now, I turn off the water and wipe my face, reaching for the heated towel and stepping onto the warmed tile. My feet flex over the stone, my eyes catching in the large mirror that stretches the length of the room.

To say that Vince wanted me for my design skills was a lie. My body, my face ... that was why he had picked me. I rub the towel across my cock and watch it respond, thickening out of habit. He had liked *it* too, and liked showing it off. The parties we attended, the naked Sunday pool parties we hosted ... half the gay men in New York knew that Vince Horace's boyfriend rocked a cock that rivaled his perfect face.

I used to scowl at the thought, my public reputation almost not worth the high lifestyle, the front seat into Vince's design and thought process, his confidence, his respect. *Almost* not worth it. But as time passed, I learned not to give a fuck. I knew who I was, and so did Vince, our respect and bond growing stronger as the years passed, my access greater and opinion more valued with each new season.

Vince had given me the keys to a kingdom. I had given him my reputation. It had been an equitable trade in my eyes.

Tossing the towel to the side, I step into the dressing room. The tailor averts his eyes, hanging the first of three outfits on the display hooks.

"These are the options for the interview?" I stop, thumbing the collar of the first vintage suit.

"Yes, Mr. Lent." He pulls back the jacket to show me the shirt, and I move to the next.

"This one." It's powder blue, a color Vince used in countless campaigns, and is paired with a charcoal turtleneck. I pull the scarf off the hanger and toss it to the side. "It's ready?"

"Yes, sir. Of course."

I turn away, moving to open a nearby compartment and pulling a pair of pressed underwear off its hanger. I step into the boxer briefs and pull open the drawer to select a pair of socks. "Wait for me by the shoeshine station. And polish the Patek Phillippe."

"Certainly."

When he leaves, I return to the suit, carefully removing it from the hanger and dressing, each moment almost reverent, thoughts of Vince heavy on my mind. In the mornings, our dressing had been a ritual, ideas and inspirations pulled as often from this room as from the drawing room floor. I glance toward the front of the room, where the long mirror sits, the dressing counters empty, the lights off. As Vince's condition had worsened, his need for concealers, spray tans, and the makeup team, had grown. Now, there is no need for any of it.

I press a button and the belt rack moves, a smooth rotation of leathers, all sliding by. I remember us building this room, knocking down walls and laying out the design. Each cabinet had been custom-designed and constructed, the discrete lighting shining off the pieces as if they were jewels. Over five hundred pairs of pants. A thousand shirts. Coats and jackets from every designer known to man. More custom pieces than not. A separate room dedicated to shoes. A watch and cufflink collection insured for a hundred million dollars.

I stop the action and pull a caramel colored belt from the display, sliding it through the loops and fastening the clasp. Sliding into the jacket, I step up onto the platform and look into the mirror.

"God, you're pure sex." Vince's voice comes from behind me and I meet his eyes in the mirror, working at the neck of the jacket to get it flat. "Here." He steps up and lifts his arms, batting away my hands and taking over the action. "You know, if I ever fire you as a designer, you could work as a model."

"Tried that." I grimace. "Couldn't keep those frisky designers from trying to paw at me."

He chuckles, smoothing his hands over the fabric. "I can see the problem." He moves beside me, looking at his own reflection, next to mine, in the mirror. "It's not fair, how the clothes hang off you. It makes my job too easy."

"I won't tell anyone if you don't."

He grins, and I laugh and—in this moment—there doesn't seem to be anything wrong with our lifestyle or our lie.

This suit, like all the others, hangs perfectly. Part of that is due to the custom fit created by our tailor's needle. The other half of the equation is my build. Vince was right. You take a six-foot-two man, one with an athletic build and perfect proportions—and clothes behave. It never hurts that my pretty mug is stuck on top. I scowl at the mirror and the package only perfects. Every day, for the last decade, my looks have had a purpose, one that Vince and I exploited to benefit his reputation and brand. Now, I look in the mirror and don't know what to do with myself.

———

"The interview won't last long." Paulie wears a suede jacket with a pocket square that clashes with his belt. I stare at the belt and force myself not to mention it. "An hour tops." He stops in front of me, and I nod, distracted by the nervous clasp of his hands, the fidget of joints and fingers and twisting of wrists. Jesus. Has he always been so hyper?

"Who is this for?"

"*GQ.*"

"And this had to be *today?*" I watch the crew prep the area around the sitting couch with light screens and stands. A separate group stands by the window, looking out at the crowds, and discussing the noise. As if on cue, a new chant of Vince's name begins. "Are we doing the photos before or after?"

"Whichever you prefer." A bead of sweat makes it halfway down his temple before he captures it with a silk handkerchief.

"I'd prefer some lunch."

"Yes sir." He clears his throat, then nods. I watch him leave, whispering the order at the assistants as if my lunch request is top secret. I hear the feminine lilt of a voice and turn my head, watching a leggy redhead enter, her heels clicking across the floor. She spies me and I meet her halfway, extending my hand to meet hers.

"Peggy Nance, *GQ.*"

The interviewer. They didn't tell me it was a woman. I tighten my jaw and force a smile. "Marco Lent."

She blushes, and I don't miss the glance that sweeps over me. "It's a *pleasure.*"

A stupid thing to say, considering she is here to interview me about my dead boyfriend. I let my displeasure show and pull back my hand. "Terrible circumstances."

"Yes. Of course." Her hands grip the edges of her portfolio, and she manages to conjure up a frown.

I don't want to spend an hour with this woman. I don't want to answer her questions, to feel her eyes, and to watch that mouth.

"Mr. Lent?" An assistant gestures toward the dining room. "Lunch is ready."

I nod, pulling off my jacket and passing it to Edward.

———

Lunch is an elaborate clusterfuck of expense, as every meal in our lives is. I once asked Vince about it, his tongue loosened by wine and success, his guard down. He confessed that at his first design jobs, he used to sneak into the restroom and eat his lunch there. He was ashamed of his peanut butter and jelly sandwiches, his inability to afford eating out with the other designers. When he first made it big, he made a habit of eating out at the hottest restaurants, ordering the most expensive items and overtipping the waitstaff. As his wealth increased, so did his meal budget. In came the private chefs, the commercial kitchen, the five-course meals. In this house, we have over three dozen sets of china and hundreds of table settings. I sit down at the head of the table, in Vince's old place, and take the napkin from the attendee.

"Bring the interview in here," I look down at the tiny soft-boiled egg, brilliantly showcased in a silver Tiffany stand, set atop a Versace plate. "Set a second place."

"Certainly, sir." There is a quiet flurry of movement, silver, and china quickly set, fresh flowers brought in to frame the setting. I enjoy my egg, setting down the spoon as the woman settles in next to me, a recorder in hand.

"Do you mind?" She lifts the recorder.

"No." I sit back as my plate is cleared. "Go ahead."

"Great." She digs into her bag and pulls out a pen and notepad, placing them on the table next to her plate.

The next course arrives, a crisscross of dressings over thinly-sliced steak. I wave off the server and watch as she eyes the meat.

"It's carpaccio. Tenderloin carpaccio."

"None for me, thank you." She glances down at the pad, then at me. "Mr. Lent, we're very familiar with Vince Horace's life, but know little about your personal relationship with him."

I twist the fork through the meat, piling it high before I bring it to my mouth. I take my time chewing and wonder if there is a question coming. She falls silent, and I pat at my mouth with the napkin before speaking. "Privacy is something that was important to both of us."

"Privacy?" A small laugh coughs out of her. "Excuse me for saying this, but your lifestyle is anything but private."

"Our lifestyle. Not our personal relationship." I set down my fork and met her gaze squarely. "While Vince was fiercely loyal to the gay community and its causes, our story didn't need to play a publicity role in that."

"I wouldn't view it as publicity," she crosses her arm, resting her forearms on the table. The woman must have been raised in a kennel. "I'd view it as the documentation of a beautiful love story."

A beautiful love story. Ha. I pick up my fork and pay careful attention to my plate, delicately scooping up the next bite.

"Did you know that Vince Horace hired a historian?"

"Of course." That damn man had spent thousands of hours with Vince, moving painstakingly through every single day of his life, as if anyone cared about Vince's high school prom date or the time he spent a night in a Cincinnati hostel. "If you'd like to save me a great deal of time, you can just read his book." The book had cherry-picked from Vince's tales, each excerpt carefully selected to put Vince in the best possible light. The result—a glowing tale that made it seem as if Vince had single-handedly started the gay pride movement, along with every major fashion trend from the last three decades.

Her lips tighten, and I'm glad she's a bitch. It makes this experience much easier, any temptation much more manageable. Not that I have any temptation, that disappeared when she pulled out the recorder.

"I've read it." She smooths the front of her shirt, pulling it tight over her ample chest. "I want to talk to you about what *isn't* in the book."

"You'll have to be more specific." I reach forward, lifting my glass of wine and wonder if chugging it would show weakness.

"There's nothing in the book about the two of you."

I shake my head and bring the glass to my mouth. "That's not true." I'm all over the final chapters, minute mentions that paint me as a sexual Adonis and Vince as a well-taken-care-of stud. Think Hugh Hefner, finally settling down and getting married—that is us, in black and white text, in that damn book.

She reaches forward, gently touching my arm, and I recoil, the reaction obvious enough that she thinks better, and retracts. "There's nothing personal about the two of you. Was your love instant? What was your relationship like? Our readers want to know the details."

The *intimate* details. That's what she wants. I watch the signs from the crowd, bobbing by the window, and regret agreeing to this interview.

"Marco?"

My eyes snap to hers. "It's Mr. Lent."

"Okay." She adjusts the napkin in her lap. "When did you fall in love with Vince—Mr. Horace?"

Never. While I loved Vince like a brother, being "in love" was never part of that equation. I pick up the closest utensil, a dinner knife. "You know, Miss Crawford, when I met Vince, I was just a struggling designer, trying to get someone to listen to me." I watch the way the light glints off the blade. This is a Presidential set, from Kennedy's term. He probably handled this same knife. Cut his meat with it. Lifted the fork to his mouth.

"And Vince gave you a chance."

I carefully set the utensil back down, in its spot in the setting. Glancing toward the kitchen, I nod at the closest uniform, ready for the next course. "Yes. He gave me a chance."

My chance hadn't been on the design floor, it'd been in that bathroom, the opportunity brought on by my looks and not my talent. Vince had been a vain man, and I'd had to overcome my looks to get him to see my talent. In that first year of "dating," we'd fought more than we'd gotten along. And I'd been away from him more than I'd been at his side. I pick up the tiny fork that lies to the left of my setting and hold it up. "Do you know what this is?"

She focuses on the utensil and I can tell she doesn't. I set it down. "It's an oyster fork. Before I started working for Vince, I couldn't tell the difference between that and a salad fork." Six weeks of etiquette training, eight hours a day, had taught me that.

"Before Vince, I spoke English and a few rudimentary phrases of Spanish." Now, I'm fluent in Italian and French. Half our staff is Italian, and I can find my way around Rome and Paris drunk off my ass.

"So… what?" She rests her chin atop her fist. "Vince taught you things?"

I move my hands off the table, sitting back as the lamb tenderloin is delivered. "Vince taught me *everything*. About fashion and about life."

Her lips purse. "It doesn't sound very romantic."

It hadn't been. His proposition, first made in that opulent bathroom, later legalized in a stack of documents, had been simple. Vince had just had surgery for prostate cancer, the complications which had rendered him unable to perform sexually, and void of any desire to. His image and reputation—one carefully built through three decades of screwing half of New York's hottest men—he wasn't ready to give up.

"I don't understand." I run a hand over my face and avoid his eye contact. "Why don't you just find a boyfriend, someone who doesn't mind your..." My mind gives out, leaving me stranded and without the proper word.

He brushes off the idea with the toss of a well-manicured hand. "Most gay men don't know how to keep their mouths shut and their dicks to themselves. Especially not the sort of man I would need. One with your..." His eyes travel the full length of my body, and the meaning is as clear as a Times Square billboard.

He'd wanted a stud who wouldn't try to fuck him. A stud who wouldn't try to fuck anyone else. A stud who could stay loyal, and quiet, and give him the credibility and reputation he'd always had.

I pull the plate closer to me. "The two of us weren't interested in appearing to be romantic to columnists, Miss Nance."

Her cheeks flush and I look down, cutting my meat with the detached air I've perfected. "We were men. We enjoyed each other's company. We learned from each other, me more than him. Did we fall in love over candlelight and champagne? No. Did we read poetry to each other, or share heartfelt conversations in a manner that you would understand? No." I stab the tender piece and bring it to my lips, pausing and meeting her eyes. "I think we're done here."

Her gaze darts to her list of questions then comes back to me. "I'm not done."

I chew the piece slowly, focusing my attention back on the plate, dividing the remainder of the filet into four small pieces.

"What will you miss most about Mr. Horace?"

I ignore her, lifting my glass and taking a sip. I clear my throat and Paulie steps forward. "Miss Nance, thank you for your time. If you could, follow me."

"I'm NOT *done*." She raises her voice, sputtering when Paulie all but pulls her out of the chair, their journey out of the room loud and argumentative. I wait until they leave, silence returning, then spear the next piece of lamb with my fork.

Maybe it's too soon for press. Or maybe I'll never be ready for them. Vince always handled questions about us. I had always just shown up, looked pretty, and smiled for the cameras.

"Should I cancel the photo shoot?" Edward speaks softly, leaning over the table to refill my drink.

"Let the attendants do that," I snap. "And yes." The thought of posing, *more* posing, at this point, drives me mad. "Have the executive team assembled. I want a meeting in Vince's office in thirty minutes."

"Certainly." He glances down at my wine. "Should I bring you a stronger drink?"

"Hell no." I stuff the last bit of lamb into my mouth, manners be damned, and reach for my napkin. "And have them bring out the rest of the courses."

Three days. He'd been gone three days, and everything is already falling to shit.

CHAPTER 6

AVERY

I spend the evening researching Vince Horace. Fuzzy socks on, eighties music playing, I purchase an eBook called *Vince Horace: The Real Story*. It contains a detailed history of the man's life, and I intend to scroll through until the eighties, but get sucked in by chapter one, and lose four hours reading. I stop sometime around two in the morning, stretch my stiff neck, and head to bed.

I can't sleep, my mind filled with the stories, ones of an upper-class and conservative family. They hadn't understood or supported a young Vince who enjoyed dressing dolls more than crashing trucks and had spent hours planning his outfits. There had been photos at the end of each chapter, grainy images of a serious-faced child, one who often looked as if he was fresh off an admonishment. I had zoomed in on each photo, tried to pair his chubby cheeks with my own, and I'd almost picked up the phone and called the McKennas to ask for some childhood photos.

I hadn't. It had been too late, and an unexpected call, to ask a favor, after seventeen years of silence ... probably wouldn't be appreciated.

I roll on my side and turn my pillow, trying to calm the knot of emotions in my chest. It is exhilarating, the thought that I have finally found my father. Vince Horace is someone everyone knows, even me —a girl who shops without thinking, and dresses without concern. He is huge. Famous. Talented. Revered.

If Vince is my father, then I *am* someone special. I was born from someone great, I have special blood in my veins and fame in my history. Screw Kirk and Bridget McKenna and their country club and linen napkins. I am a motherfucking Horace, and my father dined with Presidents, and partied with rock stars, and created a billion-dollar empire from pure talent and grit.

And… if Vince is my father, then my father is dead. Just like my mother. And I am discovering all this, just days too late. Days to sepa-rate hugging my father versus visiting his grave. Two days to separate a memory versus mourning. Maybe, if he'd known about me, he might have lasted a little longer. Maybe, if I'd known about him, I would have lived my life differently.

I roll onto my back and stare at the ceiling, watching the slow turn of the fan. When I was a child, I used to go to bed as early as possible. Sleep, for most of my adolescence, was my escape. I once told that to a psychiatrist and immediately felt stupid for it. What did I have to escape from? I had a room filled with anything a girl my age would want. At twelve, I had a horse, kept at the best riding academy in town. I had everything except the feeling of a family.

It wasn't their fault. For one, I was a spoiled pain in the ass. For two, I don't think that Kirk and Bridget are the molds that families are built from. They loved each other in the narcissistic way that a man loves his first sports car. They were a status symbol for each other, a way to impress, a way to remind themselves that they have succeeded. They were each other's perfect embodiment of a spouse, and I was the loose thread in their seamless life.

When I was seven, I trained myself to fall asleep by reciting the list of

Presidents. If I made it from Washington to Clinton, then I started again, this time working backwards, counting them down and imagining each of their faces in my mind. If that didn't work, I started back with Washington and made myself recite an interesting fact about each of them as I went.

George Washington's "wooden teeth" were actually made of hippopotamus ivory, bone, animal and human teeth, lead, brass screws and gold wire.

John Adams blamed a day of fasting for his reelection defeat.

Thomas Jefferson was one of the first American farmers to employ crop rotation.

For the purposes of this exercise, I'd spent an entire summer, memorizing two interesting facts about each president. If that sounds like a bleak summer activity, it was. But, it was worth it, arming me with the ability to bore myself to sleep, an ability I've used ever since.

I start with Washington and only get to Grant before falling asleep.

———

"I'm not a taxi service, Kate." I rip open the pop tart package with my teeth. "This is why I have a shuttle. If you missed that, use one of the bikes in the lobby."

"Anna said girls on bikes get knifed." This wisdom is delivered in the halting English of a fresh Russian, and I break off a piece of the pastry and stick it in my mouth.

"Ignore Anna." I sit on a barstool and pull a sock on. "She lives in Herman Gardens. Everyone gets knifed there."

"Can't you just pick me up?"

"No." I glance at the clock, and yank the second sock on, pushing off the stool and working my feet into tennis shoes. "I'm late. Either hop on a bike or catch a bus, but I *need* you there."

I end the call, mutter out a string of curses, and grab my keys and wallet.

Money laundering is a simple enough game, assuming, of course, that the people—like Kate—keep their jobs. High turnover increases my risks, and disgruntled employees tend to talk, which isn't good for anyone in our business. So, while laundering is my primary business, I'm actually just a glorified babysitter. A well-paid, highly illegal, babysitter.

There are a dozen ways to wash cash, but mine is fairly simple. I own an employment company, one that provides legitimate short-term employment visas under the guise of American internships. I have partners in Russia and the Ukraine, and bring over four hundred girls each year. Four hundred girls who live in three different apartment complexes which I own, the mortgages paid for by my clients' dirty money. The girls work in a variety of jobs, mostly in retail centers, all owned by my clients. According to accounting and tax records, the girls work as unpaid interns, with a stipend of two dollars per hour to cover their rent. In actuality, and according to the cash included in my Chinese food deliveries, they earn ten dollars per hour. Four hundred girls, fifty hours per week, ten dollars an hour. Two hundred grand per week of off-the-books expense for my clients. Almost eleven million per year of additional income for their front businesses that they can claim, pay taxes on, and account for.

The two dollars per hour stipend - the one that's on the books? That's my cut, transferred legitimately into my bank accounts and covers the apartment complex costs, plus the shuttle bus and security, leaving me with a profit of about four hundred grand a year. It's not Vince Horace money, but in Detroit? I'm balling.

Stepping into the car and hitting the garage switch, I start the SUV and shift into gear.

CHAPTER 7

MARCO

I lay naked on the table, cucumbers and a scented towel over my eyes. In here, behind the stone walls and noise-deadening construction, the music outside is inaudible, and all I hear are the grinding of salts, and the soft patter of feet against the spa's stone floor. I inhale deeply, the stress from lunch already seeping away, even before the first drop of the scrub hits my skin.

"Who is that?" I ask, the hands beginning at my ankles, a second pair drizzling the scrub along my chest.

"It's Rocco and Andy, sir."

I say nothing, the names familiar, my favorites out of our spa team. There is the gentle massage of sugar and oil into my feet, talented digits working the pressure points of my soles, and I forget, for a moment, the GQ interview and the questions I had struggled with.

"Do you have a problem with a man touching you?" Vince stands next to me, watching critically as I flip the tie over itself, knotting it with perfect precision.

"You're going to have to clarify that," I say, reaching my arms out and letting him pull the jacket on.

"In public, I will rest my hand on your arm, hug you, hold your hand." He pulls the jacket tight, too close to me for comfort, and faces me squarely. "I won't kiss you, not right now, not until you are comfortable."

"I'm not sure that I'll ever be comfortable with that."

He smiles in a way that isn't a smile, but more of a threat. A reminder that this situation is one I am lucky to be in, and I need to remember that. "You'll learn to be comfortable." He squeezes my shoulders with both hands. "It's lips brushing. It's nothing. But I'll give you a few months to adjust to the idea."

My lips, brushing against another man's. My skin crawls at the thought.

Talented fingers run across my thighs, spreading the exfoliator across my muscles, working the oily mixture in. I don't flinch when they come near my cock, don't think twice about their journey, or the fact that I am bare to their eyes. There had been several factors that had contributed to my slow acceptance of Vince's lifestyle. He certainly hadn't been gentle in my immersion. Moving into his home had been a dunk into the deep end of a very gay pool. Working in the fashion industry had already exposed me to being around gay men, and getting hit on had become as commonplace as ripped seams. But the exposure I'd received in the workplace and fashion school … it had been a sunburn compared to the bonfire that existed in Vince Horace's world. A bonfire of hedonism, exhibitionism and boundary-crossing behavior. It would have been tempting if there had been women involved. But it was always men. Only men, everywhere you looked.

"We won't be long." Vince leans forward, pulling a pair of shot glasses out of a side compartment and setting them out on the Rolls' tray tables. "Fifteen minutes. Long enough to be seen, then we can escape into one of the bedrooms."

I watch him fill both glasses and grab the one closest to me, downing it in a hearty sip. I lift the glass. "Am I going to need this?"

"Probably." He sits back, crossing his legs at the ankle and glances out the window, the palatial Hamptons mansion lit in red, the yard already dotted by black suits. "Just prepare yourself for dicks."

I chuckle, pushing the shot glass forward. "As long as they aren't reaching for mine."

"Stick next to me and you won't have anything to worry about." He swallows the vodka with the leisurely air of a man with no taste buds. Swallowing the liquor, he passes me the glass. "Fill us back up."

I watch a couple kiss against one of the columns. "You miss this?"

He smiles. "A little. To be honest, I'm getting more attention with you. Turns out, it's rather attractive to be unattainable." He follows the rise of liquor in his glass and holds up his hand when it is half full. "That's enough."

I move the bottle to my own glass and am recapping the bottle when he speaks. "You ever been in love, Marco?"

"Can't say I have." I set the amber bottle down and regard him.

"That's good." He runs his hand along his thigh, smoothing the lay of the fabric. "It'll make it easier to keep you if you don't know what you're missing."

He'd been in love before. I knew the story of his three-year affair, one that had fizzled out unexpectedly, aided by Vince's pre-surgery desire to fuck anything that moved.

I grin against the edge of the shot glass. "Hard to fall in love when there aren't any women in sight."

He shrugs good-naturedly. "I always stack the deck in my favor." He picks up the shot and gestures to mine. "Let's take these and go inside. Get this over with."

He lifts his in a toasting fashion. "To my fake lover, and a true friend."

I touch my glass to his and pour the fire down my throat.

Hands, roaming across my shoulders, gently knead the area that they will, over the next few hours, work every kink out of. Another set, at my calf, work their way higher. That night in the Hamptons had been my first party, my first real exposure to what happens when zero inhibitions and alcohol meet. I'd stuck close to Vince, glared at any man who looked my way and let Vince paw me without complaint. We'd circled the room and I'd met some of the most influential men in the fashion world. We had retreated to an upstairs bedroom and conducted a boring, two-hour conference call with Vince's factory head in China. Afterward—my tie undone, my shirt's top button artistically ripped off, and my hair mussed—we left, a brick of the Vince Horace legend added to the stack.

It was sad, his dogged pursuit of a reputation.

It was pathetic, my agreement to participate.

But back then, it hadn't felt that way. It had felt reasonable. It had made sense. And with each performance, it had become easier.

Everything I knew eroded, my standards and normality dissolving. A year passed, and he kissed me, our first brush of lips in front of a crowd-full of gay pride protestors, and it felt almost natural. Another year passed, then two, and the first time a man knelt before me, I almost let it happen.

Candlelight. The sweep of a breeze, the sounds of Amsterdam following it inside the balcony door. Vince undoes my shirt, pulling it open, and I allow it, a shot brought to my lips by the man to my right. I've drunk too much, smoked too much. Everything blurs, and I snap my fingers at the model to our right, who tugs on Vince's belt. "Get the fuck away."

Even with the alcohol, I keep the slur away from the vowels, the order coming out strong, and he glares at me but obeys, moving away. The Dom. That's what they call me, that's the nickname all the queers have come up with. They think I'm a top, which I sure as fuck would be if I had their inclina-

tions. They know, from three decades of Vince's dick dancing through America, that he's also one. Two tops don't make a right, and I've heard the whispers of speculation and enjoyed their attempt to figure out our fuckery.

There's a woman here. A sister to one of these French boys, and she's eye-fucked me since the minute we walked in. I find her, watch her lean forward against the balcony rail, her ass sticking out, waiting for a pounding, and feel my cock harden. The musclehead to my left notices, his hand drifting along my thigh, and when his fingers brush over the bulge, it reacts.

He says something, moves closer, and I watch her breasts sway, heavy against that tight sweater. I want to fuck her. God, I want to get behind her, grip those breasts in my hand, and shove myself inside of her. I'd come in a minute from her moans, from the sweet feminine sounds of her orgasm. Her body clenching me, hot and wet and perfect.

My cock is rigid, pushing against my slacks, and I don't notice the hand, the grip of it on the outside of the fabric, until it is too late. I yank my eyes off the bubble of her ass, snap them to my cock, and see the man in between my legs, his hand on my zipper.

I kick his chest, a hard shove of Italian leather against cheap cotton, and he falls. I stand, my hands pushing my sleeves up, my open shirt gaping, and will my cock to soften. Will the room to stop spinning. Will that woman to get the fuck out of here before I screw up everything.

"Vince." I speak loud enough to get the attention of everyone in the room.

"Yep?" He drawls the words but I hear the hint of the warning in them. Don't fuck this up. Don't blow your cover. Don't lose your cool.

"I want you naked, right now." The words are for her and they fall as convincing as a silk sheath under cashmere.

Vince brushes off his suit and stands, his hand clamping on my shoulder with a possessive grip. "Sounds good to me. Let's get the fuck out of here."

That night, I'd stood in the shower and jacked my cock until it was sore, thinking of her. That day, I crossed a line I never came back from. That day, after that party, the rumors started, stories of our sex grew, and the legend of Vince Horace and Marco Lent took flight.

That day, I lost my old life and turned myself over to him.

I roll over on the table and wonder if I'll ever get it back.

———

Two hours after my massage, the will is read. The event takes place in our attorney's office, a large room with a view meant to impress, the long walnut table filled with black suits and somber faces. I nod to the lot and take the chair at the head of the table, settling into it with a sigh.

The contents aren't a surprise. As with every other action in Horace's life, I had been beside him when he'd created the will, been present in meetings where assets had been cataloged, documents signed, and trusts established. I am already aware of the estate taxes I will be responsible for, and the full bulk of the empire I am inheriting.

It takes hours for the attorneys to move through the document. Hours to explain that I will receive eighty-eight percent of the Horace Mann estate. Ten percent will go to various LGBT organizations, fashion programs, and libraries. Two percent is headed to faithful staff and houseboys. The rest, to me. For a man who touched so many, he loved so few. No children. No family. Only me.

When we finish, I push away from the table and stand, my back stiff as I shake hands with strangers and take copies of the documentation.

Three and a half hours. Eight hundred and fifty million dollars richer. I loosen the top button on my shirt and walk out of the room, flanked by a sea of suits.

CHAPTER 8

AVERY

There's no mention of the LiveAid concert in 1985. In fact, from 1984 to 1986, Vince Horace was in Miami. If he went to Philadelphia during those years, there's no notation of it. The book skims over his time in Miami with few details, and I open the photos at the end of the chapter with a reluctant fear. Maybe I'm wrong, so anxious to find my father that I'm chasing blind leads. Vince Horace *looks* like a photo from the eighties, and suddenly I think he's my dad? I've been stupid. The first photo loads, a worthless shot of a Miami apartment building, and I scroll to the next, zooming in on a blurry side profile.

"These are four-hundred-dollar seats, and you're reading."

I grab a handful of peanuts without looking up from my phone. "What's to see? No one's on base. Two outs. Kinsler is up."

Andrei sighs, slouching back in his seat, and lifts his beer. "Screw you."

I give up, locking the phone and pushing it into my jacket pocket. *"There.* Happy?"

"Yes." Kinsler swings and we watch a foul ball skid past us. "What were you reading?"

"Something dumb."

The book *is* dumb. The fawning way it describes Vince Horace is all fanboy. And Horace is *clearly* gay. Every interaction, from his first kiss in sixth grade, to the high school fling with the football player, to his relationship in the early eighties with his Creative Director ... they all had one thing in common. Gay. Homosexual, penis-loving, gayness. I haven't read a word that has hinted at a flirtation, a confusion, or a tryst with a woman.

And again, no mention of Philadelphia. No LiveAid. No concerts at all.

The book sucks. My hopes were stupid. All of this, a giant waste of time and energy.

I reach for my beer, slump in my seat, and watch Kinsler strikeout.

"Got plans tomorrow? I have a building to show you."

I flick a peanut shell off my thigh. "I don't need another building."

"It's not for you." He leans forward, tenting his hands together. "I'm thinking of moving our office."

"Really?" I watch his profile, the way the stadium lights reflect off the wire rim of his glasses. "What's wrong with the green palace?"

Andrei's company sucks up the front corner of an old strip mall, the lime-green building squatting on one of the more desirable corners of downtown. The sign out front advertises legal services, but immigration and visas take up the bulk of his billing. He handles all my girls, and cuts me enough of a break to continue our friendship, a Tigers' season ticket included. We've sat through five years' worth of games, and mourned and celebrated over hundreds of beers. He likes to bitch about his wife, I like to check out the players. In the entire city, there's no one I trust more.

"The green palace is starting to smell."

I smile. "Thank God. I thought that was Marcia. I didn't want to say anything but…"

"Oh no, she smells too. This is something else, like a moldy wet scent. I think it's making me sick."

I groan and shove his shoulder. "You're terrible."

"Hey, you're the one who said she smells. I just agreed with you."

Chase Stern steps out of the dugout and I lean forward, admiring the perfect fit of his pants, his confident stride to the sideline.

"So, the building is a few blocks down, where that shoe repair shop used to be."

I nod, half listening as I watch Chase grip a bat, taking a few practice swings. I eye the scoreboard. Not a good time for him to bat, not with the score tied and a Ranger runner already on base.

"I'm seeing it tomorrow at two."

"Two?" I chew on the inside of my cheek. "I don't know."

"You don't have shit to do. Come on."

I stretch my legs forward and think about Vince Horace, about the stupidity of my hope, a hope I can't seem to dash. "What do you know about inheritance law?"

"Inheritance law?" His voice sharpens, the building forgotten, his interest piqued. "What about it?"

"Hypothetically speaking…" I pick at my bottom lip, pulling at a tag of dry skin. "If I found out I was related to someone, someone who has passed away, then what are my rights?"

"Rights to what? Their estate?"

"Or a blood test. Or … yeah, I guess. Their estate."

I hadn't thought as much about the estate, about the fashion line, or whatever assets Vince Horace had left behind. I suddenly remember the bartender, the news clip of the young boyfriend, stepping out of the Rolls Royce. Billion? Is that what she'd said? *That slice of gorgeous is about to be a billionaire.* Yeah. I feel a moment of despair. There are probably dozens of "children" coming out of the woodwork, gunning for that fortune. I'll be seen as crazy, and maybe I am.

"Can we *not* speak hypothetically for a moment?" He turns in his seat to face me. "This is about your father? Your real father?"

I nod. "Yeah." He already knows that history, the story shared over nachos in the Tigers club level a handful of years ago.

"You think you found him?"

"I don't know." I see the beer guy and raise my hand, digging in my pocket for a ten and passing it to Andrei. He stands, half-crawls over the aisle behind us, and gets my Bud Light. "I thought I did, but now I'm doing some research, and…" I make a face and take the beer from him. "Thanks."

"You're doing some research and you think you're wrong?"

"Probably."

"So, do more research. You said the guy died?"

I nod.

"Have you reached out to his family? Introduced yourself?"

"No family." I tip back the bottle and allow myself a healthy sip. "No kids."

"Unless you fit the bill."

"Right."

"How much do you know about him?"

I should just tell him. Just blurt it out, no matter how stupid or immature I'll look. My lips open, my tongue moves, but I can't. I might as well tell him that the Queen of England is my mum, and I'm going to skip off to my castle now, with a quick stop at a psych ward along the way.

"He's leaving everything to a friend of his." It is all Andrei should need to give me advice.

"You need to find out who his executor is. Contact them—or better yet, *I'll* contact them. Let them know that you are contesting the will and that you're a potential heir. First thing they'll do is have you take a paternity test. But it'll tie up any assets until the results of that test come back." He meets my eyes. "You think there are any assets?"

"Yeah." I take another sip of beer to keep my mouth busy, and muse over the idea of Andrei sending the letter on my behalf. He's right, it'd be better off coming from an attorney than from me. And it sounds simple, the way he explains it. We send a letter, they order tests, and then I'll know. No Sherlock Holmes assembly of clues needed. No more wondering.

"It's Vince Horace." I don't look at him when I drop the bombshell, and he misses its blast altogether.

"What's Vince Horace?" Chase Stern hits a line drive that our infield can't touch, and Andrei groans.

"I think he's my dad."

He cocks his head to the side and studies me. "The fashion guy?"

"Yep."

"But he's gay."

"Yep."

"So... are you sure?"

53

I shrug. "Nope."

He runs both hands over his short-trimmed beard. "Avery."

"I know." I kick one foot up on the concrete wall in front of us. "It's ridiculous."

"It's not ridiculous."

I pick at the corner of my beer's label. "It is."

"What makes you think it's him? The photo?"

"Yeah." I get off half the label before it tears.

"Let me see it." He holds out his hand, and I sigh, leaning forward and reaching into my jacket pocket, pulling out my wallet.

"It's not a great photo." I work the laminated photo out and pass it to him. He rests it on his lap and opens a web browser on his phone, googling Vince's name and clicking on an image of him.

"Not that one." I reach over, scrolling through the image results until I see the one that most closely matches the campfire photo.

"Who's the pretty boy with him?" Andrei mutters, zooming in on the image and then holding up the photo next to it.

"His boyfriend." I lean in, baseball forgotten, and watch Andrei, his eyes flicking between the two images.

He sighs and holds the photo out to me. "Boyfriend? How long have they lived together?"

"I don't know," I snap, carefully returning the photo to its spot behind my drivers' license. "Does it look like him?"

"It does."

I am so prepped to hear a denial, and my head jerks up when he delivers the opposite. "It does?"

"Yeah." He grimaces. "But Avery, this is a mess if all you have is a photo. To be honest, I'm not even sure a judge would order a paternity test over a photo. Do you have any proof that he was at the concert that that photo was taken at?"

"No." I slump back in the seat. "Not that I've found." *Yet*. Not that I've found *yet*.

"Either way," his voice softens. "We should try."

"Yeah?" I look at him.

"Hell yeah." He grins. "Do you know how *badly* I need work? Milking this disaster could cover the first year of rent on that building."

For the first time all night, a laugh breaks out of me and I lift my hands in surrender. "Fine. Take advantage of an orphan. If it gets you and Marcia out of that turtle shell of a complex, I'm in. And if I inherit a billion dollars, I'll buy you that damn building."

"Deal." He holds out his fist and I bump it, our camaraderie inter-rupted by the crowd, who explodes in a cheer. Forgetting the fist bump, we jostle to our feet, our eyes on the field, our world back to normal for at least three more innings.

———

Marcia was my first girl. When I saw her, she was a pretty brunette, walking on a bad street, just before dusk. I passed her, saw two guys duck out of a gas station a block away, and pulled a U-turn. When I pulled up next to her, she flinched. When I offered her a ride, she hesi-tated but chose my warm car over the darkening Detroit street. Smart girl.

I drove her over to Brightmoor and asked her a lot of questions, her answers delivered in halting Russian I barely understood. But I got enough of the gist. Eleven months left on her visa. Sweatshop hours. A boss who seemed to double as a pimp. She was two weeks in, somehow owed her employee two hundred and twenty dollars, and seemed a hairs breath away from being sold into the sex trade. I drove past Brightmoor and took her to my house. Fed her a TV dinner, and made some calls. Found an immigration attorney downtown who said he'd meet with us pro bono and give us some advice.

That guy was Andrei. Marcia was his sexual kryptonite and my new dependent. I found her a short-term sublease, paid off her boss and got her a legitimate job at the hamburger place down the street. Brushed my hands off, patted myself on the back, and considered it my good deed for the year.

A week later, she showed up with a friend, this one marred by a swollen lip and black eyes, her hip branded with a tattoo from one of Detroit's nastier gangs. I was just a bartender, one who knew how to use a gun and had been in the city long enough to learn the players. I didn't know what to do with her. I didn't know what to do with *any* of them. But still, they came to me. Needed me. Told me stories of cramped living conditions, slave labor, and sexual assault. They drained me of cash and favors, of emotions and fear.

Then, one died. I had met her two days earlier. Shared pizza and a beer with her. Learned a few words of Russian while attempting to discuss movie stars. Two days, and then she was dead in the street, mugged and killed for money she didn't have.

Someone had to do something. Someone had to protect them, manage them, set them up with better jobs and better bad guys, the sort who needed employees and not prostitutes, the sort who would pay them fairly and wouldn't make them suck a dick in order to get paid.

I didn't want to be that someone. I wanted Andrei to be that someone. I stood there, while Marcia cuddled up to him on the couch, and gave him a fucking *perfect* PowerPoint presentation on an easy way for him to handle it all. "Why not?" I had accused him. "Why not earn all this money and help people? What are you, selfish?"

I should have toned down my highfaluting guilt trip. Because when he turned the tables around, dumping the project in my lap, I didn't have shit to say in terms of a rebuttal. When he said he'd do the first two years of visas pro bono, I felt the noose tighten.

I turn down the television's volume. On screen, the Entertainment Tonight special shows a close-up of Marco Lent, his head tilting back, champagne flowing down his lips. I look down at the eBook and study the image, one of Vince Horace and Marco Lent, leaning over a building's railing and looking down on a crowd. They are both smiling, their bodies relaxed, the photo a festive one. I turn to the next image, one of a fashion show, Vince on the catwalk, waving to the crowd. Closing the reading app, I set my phone to the side and unlock my computer.

I print out payroll spreadsheets and check deposits, pay a handful of bills and then turn to the counting machines. Washing eleven million in cash a year is laborious, especially when dealing with four hundred girls, four hundred bundles of cash, twice a month. It'd be easy if the girls each worked exactly fifty hours, but that never happens. People get sick, lazy, and some work overtime. Which means I have four hundred headaches, twice a month. I used to have a crew of two that handled it, but fingers get sticky when they do nothing but count out cash. Now, I do it all myself, aided by fifteen electronic cash counters. Four hundred envelopes, each with a name on it, stuck in a bin for their apartment building. I make the deliveries myself, accompanied by Bruce and Eddie—two guys who pack enough heat and muscle to bring down a small army.

Flipping on the radio, I pull my long hair into a ponytail, grab the first spreadsheet off the printer, and move to the line of counters, entering payroll amounts on each screen in the line.

When my mother died, my *real* mother, nobody bothered to contact me, the funeral passing by without my presence. It wasn't until I called her cell, some months later, that I found out the news. A car accident, head-on collision. It was pouring rain, and she was alone in the car, my brother and sister unharmed and safe at home. Her husband was fairly cold on the phone and gave no explanation for not contacting me. Maybe he thought I didn't deserve to be told. I certainly hadn't been a communicative daughter, once I found her. There had been that initial visit, the gingerbread cookies, photo book session, and then just one other meeting—an awkward half hour at a Starbucks ten minutes from her house. I'd left from that encounter and decided I wouldn't pursue the relationship any further. I just couldn't see any of myself in her and each interaction seemed to make the feeling of lonely detachment worse.

Working on latex gloves, I pull thin bundles of cash out of the machines and insert them in envelopes, sealing them and writing the girls' names on the outside. I didn't use to be all-female. In the beginning, when I was young and dumb, I employed men too. That first year was a disaster. Men didn't like reporting to a woman, and they couldn't seem to take an envelope of cash without offering a sly remark, or undressing me with their eyes. Between the sexual harassment, the blatant disrespect for my rules, and the inaccurate time cards, I almost quit the business. It took a stiff drink and a bitch session with Andrei to find the root of the cause—the penises. I removed them from the equation and my sanity and profitability soared. Now I just deal with hormones and girl drama. I can handle that.

I sing along with Eddie Money and work quickly, the activity calming my nerves. Crossing off names as I move down the list, I studiously avoid the letter from Andrei, printed out and sitting in the middle of my desk, waiting for my approval. He had worked fast, locating the attorney in charge of the Horace estate. The letter requests medical records, recent financials, and a paternity test. Just reading it, I felt invasive and demanding, and way out of my league. Andrei's accompanying email had been short and sweet. *Please review and approve.* I've reviewed it, I just can't seem to pull the trigger on approving it.

Cyndi Lauper comes on, and I hum along with the bouncy beat as I knock out another dozen envelopes, tossing them in the bin as I work. I make it through the first hundred, then take a break, jogging down the stairwell and to the first-floor vending machine. I grab a bag of Doritos and a grape soda, taking my time on my return climb, locking the deadbolt with my elbow when I walk back in. Sitting in my chair and crunching on a chip, I eye the letter and spin, using my foot to turn in a slow circle, surveying the stacks of cash, ready for distribution. Funny how scant half a million dollars can be, how little space it occupies.

I should have Andrei send the letter. Why not? It's not as if I have to *do* anything. He'll handle it all. If they laugh at me, make fun of my request, I'll never know. I'll be sheltered and oblivious, all the way over here in Detroit.

I complete the spin, the letter coming back into sight. I know the problem. It's fear. Fear that I'm wrong and my euphoria at having a famous and talented father is misplaced. It's fear that I'm ordinary, and will discover it through the most embarrassing method possible. What if the press finds out? What if my name gets leaked? What if I am wrong, and everyone finds out?

The poor little orphan girl. So desperate for love and attention, she tried to claim a dead gay guy's fortune.

I crunch a chip in half and study the computer, my email minimized to just a small icon on the bottom of my screen. Leaning forward, I click the mouse, and it expands to fill my screen. I open his email and reread it.

Please review and approve.

I glance at the clock. Barely one o'clock. Plenty of time for him to get the letter into an overnight envelope and headed to New York. It could arrive by tomorrow morning, step one of the process completed.

CHAPTER 8

Step one of my redemption or embarrassment, completed.

Reaching forward, I place both hands on the keyboard and type.

Send it.

CHAPTER 9

MARCO

It never takes much for us to throw a party —we own both sides of this block, and with lights hung between the buildings, a permit obtained, the street closed, and a stage set up on one end? Done.

At least, that's how it always appeared to Vince and I. Everything goes smoothly when you have a staff, one well-schooled in our lifestyle and with unlimited budgets. Every house employee has been trained to the Ritz Carlton service standards, a program which preaches ownership of tasks and issues, along with perfect manners and an unwavering commitment to service. Partygoers always enjoyed the benefits of our entertainment and lifestyle—and got a peek into the world that Vince Horace reigned over.

It had taken me years to get used to the opulence of his world, the constant buffet of nudity and drugs and excess. Now, I don't even notice it. Maybe that's a testament to my tolerance, or maybe it's a sad side effect of my digression. I look back, at the man I'd been when Vince met me, and I can barely find that individual anymore.

"Sir?"

I look up to find Mario in the doorway, a gold clipboard in hand. "Yes?"

"The Celebration of Life is about to begin."

Ah, yes. Not a funeral, since that is something that stiff old men have. Instead, a Celebration of Life. Vince's will have a star-studded lineup of speakers, then the party will begin. There will be no viewing, his remains already cremated, the ashes to be shipped back to Connecticut and buried alongside his brother.

"Everything has progressed as expected, and the speakers are almost done."

I nod. "Okay."

"We need you on stage, whenever you are ready."

I glance down at my watch and note the time, the second hand creeping past the half-hour. Already, four days have passed without him. I feel his absence in the house, in the hushed silence of the staff, the lack of life in the air. I stand and smooth the front of my jacket. "I'll come now."

―――――

The street is full, brightly colored ropes of cafe lights and flowers stretched between the buildings, the sea of people packed beneath them. Later tonight, there will be a catwalk that stretches halfway down the street, through the thousands of bodies currently packed in the space. I look to the end of the street, where the crowd continues. "The main road is closed?" I ask Mario sharply, spotting the police lines, the horseback officers moving through the crowd.

"Yes. They've filled the next block over too. We are speaking to the police now about crowd control and moving further east to try and keep the crowd off the avenue."

It's the biggest crowd we've ever had, and there is a sharp flare of pain at the fact that Vince can't see this, the outpouring of love, the visual proof that he lived, he affected, he inspired. I step onto the stage and nod at The Who, shaking each of the band members' hands. They will kick off the party, playing their hits from the 60's, before turning over the stage to the Kinks. The Celebration of Life will last over ten hours and will evolve in both its music and decor, spanning the five decades of Vince's life, the theme changing every two hours.

I glance at my watch, then back at the crowd, their chants subsiding as I approach the microphone.

"We love you, Marco!" From the middle of the street, a woman screams and there is a general chuckle that moves through the crowd.

I smile and work the microphone loose from its stand. Lifting it to my mouth, I speak.

"Four days ago, I lost a man I've loved for a decade, a man who many of you also loved. We lost a man who cared for this community in ways that I struggle to explain. You supported his lifestyle. You supported his brand. You supported his passion, and most of all, you supported his fashion."

A cheer starts at the end of the street and swells, thousands of hands clapping and voices lifted in support. Someone turns on their cell phone's flashlight and the trend catches on, thousands of lights suddenly lifted and waved in the air, illuminating the dusk with a sea of white specks.

"Tonight is the first annual Vince Horace Memorial event," I continue, swallowing a bit of emotion that comes at the physical wave of support. "We will spend the next two hours celebrating the 1960's, and all that it brought to our world and to the fashion industry." Against the backdrop of the north building, an image flickers to life, a thirty-two story photograph of a baby Vince. "This is the decade that Vince Horace was brought into our world. It was the beginning of the Gay Liberation movement." At the mention of the movement, the cheers increase, the energy rising. Beside me, a butler extends a glass of champagne, which I take. "Now, we will toast and celebrate the birth of gay liberation and the greatest man I, or fashion, have ever known." I lift my glass and wait a moment, watching as a sea of tuxedoes move into the crowd. "Vince, we love and miss you dearly."

There is the synchronized pop of hundreds of champagne bottles, and the band dives into song, the cheers reaching a new crescendo as I tilt back the glass and down a thousand dollars' worth of champagne.

Funny how, in a crowd of so many, a man can feel so alone.

CHAPTER 10

AVERY

The closest spot is two blocks away and I shove the SUV into park and fly out of it. Slamming the door shut, I sprint forward, the curb hidden in the dusk and catching my toe. I right myself, take a deep breath and keep running, Andrei's building bobbing into view as I manage two cross streets without being hit.

The door to his office sticks, and I slam my shoulder into it, my entrance inside more of an uncoordinated tumble, rather than a step.

Marcia looks up at the sound, her greeting cut short when she sees me. "He's on the phone."

I straighten, wheezing a little as I move forward and almost collapse on her desk. "Please tell me that my letter didn't go out."

"The overnight to New York?" She raises one fuzzy, untamed brow, her Russian accent still thick despite the years. "It picked up. A delicious mailman."

"Noooooo." I groan, sliding down the front of her particle board desk and onto the cheap carpet. "Tell me you're joking."

"Nope. Dee-licious. Tight juicy ass. A new one."

"Not the mailman." I glare at her, and I liked her better before she mastered the English language. "The package. Tell me you're joking about the package."

"It's gone, *apyr.*" She pokes at my hand, pushing it off her desk with one sharp jab of her pen. "Now go. I have work to do."

Gone. Poof. Stuck in the back of some juicy-assed mailman's truck. Tonight, it'll be on a plane, flying to New York delivery. "Can you have it redirected?" I call out.

"With the post office?" She snorts in a manner that inspires little confidence in our nation's mail service. This is my fault—using Andrei's cheap ass. Any other attorney would use FedEx, my package instantly found, stopped, and returned to where it belongs—the trash can.

I moan, kicking my feet out and crossing my arms over my chest. I hear footsteps and slide right, peering around the edge of Marcia's desk and seeing Andrei's thin build move down the hall. "Andreeeei…." I groan.

"Oh God." He stops beside me, hands on his hips, and looks down. "Tell me you've got some sort of protective layer between yourself and this carpet."

"Tell *me* you didn't mail that letter."

"We mailed the letter." He turns to Marcia. "Did it get picked up?"

"I *told* her. It got picked up."

He looks down at me. "It got picked up."

"Thanks," I snap tartly.

"Having second thoughts?" He crouches down, cupping his hands under my armpits and pulling me off the floor.

I refuse to support myself, keeping my legs limp, my weight heavy on him. "You shouldn't have sent it. You knew I would regret it."

"You guys want to move this conversation somewhere else?" Marcia calls loudly. "I got work to do."

I glare in her direction, then look back to Andrei. "I don't like her," I whisper loudly.

"Yes, I know." He smiles. "You've mentioned it several times."

"She was checking out the mail guy," I say loudly. "She called his ass juicy."

"Bitch," Marcia mutters.

Andrei struggles a little under my dead weight, and I don't assist him, intentionally lolling to one side, my arms hanging like pendulums. He stumbles to the side and attempts to prop me against the wall. "You know I'm billing you for this."

"What if I'm wrong?" I lift my head, looking up into his face.

He smiles. "Then we'll get through it."

Getting through it isn't an acceptable plan. I push off his chest and stick my tongue out at his wife.

———

I buy the ticket without thinking, the airline app making the process too easy, a thousand dollars gone with a few easy swipes of my index finger. Bam. Done. I'll beat USPS to New York, snag my envelope before it has a chance to be opened, and retain my sanity—and my reputation.

"You're crazy," Marcia remarks, settling into my office chair, the plastic creaking under her weight.

"Probably." I watch the counters work and glance at the clock, working through my timeline. I am cutting it close. It's already six. I need to finish packing envelopes, drop them off at all three buildings, head home to pack and be at the airport in time for the ten o'clock flight. "Grab that stack. You stuff, I'll label."

She groans, pushing to her feet and moving with absolutely *no* sense of urgency. "They not going to give you the envelope. You know that?"

I don't respond. They'll give me the envelope. If I have to tackle the delivery driver and wrestle it out of his hands myself, I'll do it. What's he going to do, call the cops?

"God, this is boring." She pushes a stack of twenties into the letter envelope with all the care of a drunk hippo.

"You're getting fifty dollars an hour to be bored. Think of all the fake Vuitton purses you can buy."

"Hey." She points one lacquer covered finger at me. "My shit real."

"Hey." I point back at her. "Stuff that shit faster."

This is why I don't use her—she talks more than she works. But she's trustworthy, was available last-minute, and I am officially desperate. I run my hand down the spreadsheet and turn the page. "Come on. We've got about fifty left. Hustle."

I turn away from her and call my heavies, telling them to be here in a half hour. Crossing to the computer, I pull up my email and print out my boarding passes. I glance at the clock. Four hours. If Detroit behaves, we can do it.

———

I make the flight, thanks to a brisk jog through the Detroit airport with my backpack. My last-minute ticket puts me in the middle seat, squashed between a chubby man and a kid barely old enough to be out of diapers. I crawl into place, kick my bag underneath the seat in front of me, and pull out my phone. There are a few minutes before takeoff, and I ignore the safety presentation and scroll through recent news stories on Vince Horace. No surprise children popping up. Maybe I'm the only one stupid enough to take that leap.

There is a recent video of his boyfriend, and I click on the image and plug in my earbuds.

"Vince, we love and miss you dearly."

I watch as Vince's boyfriend lifts his glass of champagne, the gorgeous movements of that mouth. When he tilts back his head, the glass meeting those lips, my body involuntarily twitches in a pang of need. I shift in my seat. I shouldn't be looking at his lips. Talk about being weird and creepy. I switch tabs and find another article, one that shows Vince's house, a huge structure in Manhattan. I glance down at the caption, the address plain as day, available for any tourist or stalker to jot down and visit. I take a screenshot.

The stewardess walks by, pins me with a look of warning, and I stuff my phone in my jacket pocket and pull my seatbelt across my lap. My watch catches my attention and I look down at it. His name shines out from the oyster dial, and I remember the store I bought it in, the haughty salesman and the high price tag. I had liked its funky attitude, the luxurious mix of tiny spikes and fine accents.

It's funny how life works. It's a watch I don't wear often, my absent-minded selection a tipped domino that had started this entire disaster. What if the bartender hadn't noticed it and pointed out the news story? I probably should have given her a bigger tip. I drop my hand into my lap and think of the man from the video, Vince Horace's boyfriend. Those lips. That throat.

The guy next to starts to sneeze and I slide lower in the seat and rest my head back.

He probably isn't my dad, just a guy who looks like him. In all of America, there has to be a thousand guys who resemble thirty-year-old faded photos.

The plane rolls forward, picking up speed, I think about the letter, and everything it asks for. Financials. Medical records. A Paternity test. Andrei was right. We could find out the truth, know the answer for sure.

I tighten my hands on the seat belt and tug at it, checking its secureness as the plane begins to tilt, the engines loud, our takeoff in progress.

It's too late now. Whether I should be or not, I'm heading to New York. In the morning, sometime before the delivery, I can figure out what I'm doing there.

———

Midnight and the taxi line at JFK is as crowded as a theme park in July. It takes twenty minutes and a painfully dull conversation with a German couple about goats to get to the front of the line. I wave goodbye to them, slide into the back of a filthy yellow cab, and read off Vince Horace's address. Sometime between takeoff and landing, I'd caught blog posts and news articles about his Celebration of Life— a party that seems to be still going on. Assuming I'm not too late, I'm hoping to catch some of it.

A grunt sounds from the driver and is accompanied by a violent shake of the head.

"What's the problem?"

"Too crazy." The man waves his hand.

"Too crazy? What do you mean?"

"Too many people. I can't get there." He pushes the piece of paper back toward me.

"Just get me as close as you can." I shut the door and move to the middle of the seat, unwilling to accept a scenario where I get back in that line. After a moment, with an overly loud and annoyed sigh, he pulls forward.

Fifty minutes later, we inch forward in traffic. I look out the window and looking for a cross street, try to see *anything* through the crowds of people on the curb, sidewalk and street. "Are we close?"

"Too many people." He slams on his brakes and leans forward, cursing at the crowd and waving at them to get out of his way. They ignore us, a scrawny man in a tutu blowing me a kiss, and the driver reaches forward, flipping the switch on the meter. "Get out here."

Soooo friendly. Bet this guy has Employee of the Month certificates wallpapering his house.

"This is it?" I look out through the front window and pull out my wallet.

"That way." He points forward, gesturing in the general direction, with no indication of whether I need to go a half block or six. "You'll have to walk."

I pull out eighty bucks and pass it forward, cracking the door open and pushing at it with my foot, grabbing my backpack. I step out of the car and stand, the night cool, the sounds of the city dominated by a song, the music coming from ahead, where the crowd gets even worse. Hitching the bag higher on my back, I jog forward, moving down a broken sidewalk and around people, the area lively, the energy high. It's a refreshing change from Detroit and I smile at a passing group, veering around two men kissing and lift up on my toes, trying to see what is past the crowd.

CHAPTER 11

MARCO

There is love in the air. I watch as Madonna waves her arms on stage, and watch two men kiss, my gaze moving over a body-painted couple, writhing together near the stage. By the edge of the party, a Chinese tourist with a selfie stick gets kissed on the cheek by a topless girl with silver hair, wearing angel wings. I look up to the sky, the stars hidden by the city lights, and try to feel Vince's presence in the crowd.

"Enjoy the show," I say quietly. "Wish you were here." He had loved the energy of a crowd. Loved music. Loved anything that made a person feel. It was what he tried to evoke with his fashion and what he'd never found in love.

The song ends and the lights change, the spotlights swinging across the crowd and focusing on the catwalk. A bass beat starts, something strong enough to shake the ground, the soles of my feet vibrating against the balcony. I straighten, crossing my arms, and watch the first woman sweep down the wide stage, dressed in an early 2000s design, the first of a series of outfits selected by Vince.

The model is a pro, one we've used before. I watch her spin on five-inch heels and delicately stomp her way to the end of the catwalk, which begins to rise, smoke expelled as the platform spins upward. She stays in place, her hand on her hips, and peers down at the crowd. She spies me on the balcony and blows me a kiss. I nod in return, allowing my eyes to move over her body. She's too skinny for me. All of the models are—our industry prefers a gazelle-like structure that never did anything for me. Personally, I always liked a woman with curves. A body that didn't break when I fucked it like I wanted to.

I force my eyes away from the model before my thoughts go too far. But God, I need to fuck. The last time was eighteen months ago in Bermuda. Vince fell asleep in a private cabana overlooking the ocean, and I went down to the bar. I bought a drink for a forty-year-old divorcee and was in her suite fifteen minutes later. She rode my cock like a champ, sucked my dick like a whore, and never asked my name. It was forty-five minutes of perfection, and I wanted it again less than an hour later.

Except that an hour later, Vince was awake, and we were dressing for dinner and then on the jet and heading back to New York.

Now he's gone, and I'm fighting to stay in this life, in this role that no longer has a purpose.

The crowd starts to chant, Vince's name a heartbeat, one that beats, faster and faster, in my chest.

My sentence isn't over yet.

I push off the railing and turn, stepping inside the house and meet the eyes of Edward, who waits, as always, to assist. "Get the car ready."

CHAPTER 12

AVERY

I have vastly underestimated my possible father.

I realize this the moment I duck under the barricade and enter the Celebration of Life, which is not only still going on, but in full force. It is a street party of outlandish proportions, and it takes forty-five minutes to claw through the crowd, a chant starting, a "Vince, Vince, Vince, Vince," mantra that doesn't seem to have an ending point. I'd lived thirty-one years without knowing his face, and these people, all these people seem to *worship* him. Maybe it's a gay thing, much of this crowd male, rainbow flags and clothing everywhere I look. I lift my chin, my gaze moving over the opposite building, balcony doors open, strangers visible and chanting along with the crowd, everyone oblivious to the late hour. How is this *allowed*? Aren't there sound ordinances and rules to follow? Don't these people have jobs and kids and obligations? I push through the crowd, needing some space, some freedom from the noise, and find my way to the other side of the street. I stop in the first empty square of sidewalk and take a moment to catch my breath and recover.

Total madness. I say a silent prayer of thanks that the letter from Andrei hadn't been sent here. I lean against a light pole and look at the crowd, my gaze moving up and traveling over the house, half of it illuminated by the party. The back half is dark, the pitch of the building too high to see into. I let my eyes drift over the windows and wonder where his bedroom was. I wonder if he used to sit on any of these balconies, reading the paper or watching the street. I straighten and walk further down the side of the house, free of the crowd, the street quieter down here, and stop at a large iron and wood gate, one framed in ivy and impossible to see around.

Huh. I move further and glance back, trying to orient the gate to the house, the curb cut my biggest clue of the alley that must stretch behind the house.

A new song begins and the crowd grows louder, everyone's attention pulling to the show. I glance right, then left, then grip the railings and begin to climb.

I am at the top in less than thirty seconds, and I push off the pointed spikes and land with both feet on the cobblestone path. Brushing off my hands, I straighten and wait, my body tense, ready to run.

Silence. Well, not silence. There's Madonna and Lady GaGa, and ten thousand people, and horns and chants and enough noise to wake a baby … but nothing from the alley. No blare of an alarm, no security guard sprinting out, no cock of a gun or stern warning shout.

I step quietly forward, moving past a commercial grade dumpster and a dozen scooters. There is a row of garage doors, and I am moving past the largest one when it clicks, hums, and begins to move.

Oh shit. I sprint backward and duck into the closest shadow, crouching down and peeking a glance at my watch.

It's almost two in the morning. Someone is either arriving or leaving, and considering that the gate behind me is still closed, I'm assuming the latter. It could be a hundred different individuals. An employee, or security, or maybe one of the performers. I narrow the list further, this garage the largest of the row. Employees wouldn't park here, not in this exclusive spot. This is someone important. The rear end of a Rolls Royce glides backward, the silver behemoth unveiled in the glow of the alley's streetlight, and I tense, crouch-stepping backward until I am deeper in the dumpster's shadows. I only have a moment to come to a decision—remain hidden and allow the vehicle to pass, or step forward and make my presence known.

I tense, swallow, and war over a dozen conflicts in my mind. The gate behind me rumbles to life and I watch the headlights flick on, the engine revving as the Rolls shifts into drive.

It is almost beside me when I make my move.

CHAPTER 13

MARCO

I need out—away from this party, from their chants, from the weight of Vince that hangs in every hall, the stitch of every garment, the scent of every room. Everywhere I look, there are memories. Everything I feel is a weight of obligation and expectation, this party a brief distraction before the real work begins—running one of the world's largest fashion brands. I've prepared for it for years, but still—in this moment of insecurity—it's daunting.

I jerk my fingers through my hair, aggressively digging them into my scalp and loosening the product. The Rolls pulls forward, down the alley, and when it skids to a stop, it is in the gracefully soft way of a bowling ball landing on nine stacks of pillows. I look forward just in time to hear Edward curse and to see a silent combination of arms and fabric roll onto the hood of the car.

Fuck. For the first time in years, I open my own door and step into the cool night. The house barely insulates the sound of the crowd and the music, and in the air is the scent of sweat and colognes, perfumes and engine exhaust. My boots click on the cobblestones as I jog to the front of the car. There, in a heap of combat boots, skinny jeans and a knockoff jacket from Burberry's 2014 line—is a woman. Arms splayed, back awkwardly bent across a bag of some sort, blood already bright red and brilliant on what might be a beautiful face.

Edward pales at the sight of me. "Sir. *Please*. If you return to the car, I can—"

Behind us, I hear the faint sound of the Rolls attendant asking, through the car's speakers, if we need assistance.

"Edward, talk to them." I point to the car, and crouch beside her, carefully moving the dark hair away from her face, her eyes opening, her pupils moving wildly, then focusing on my face.

Contact. She smiles, and I place a hand on the ground to keep from pedaling backward in response.

I can't be around a smile like that. Even covered in blood, it's dangerous. Tempting. Mischievous.

"Are you okay?" I force my eyes off her face, and I survey the rest of her, my hands carefully patting her down and accounting for each limb and joint, all which seem, miraculously enough, to be in proper working order.

"Can a great horned owl smell?"

I stare at her blankly, and she scrunches up her face and laughs. The action produces a fresh current of blood, and she immediately stops, her hand lifting to her face in the same moment that I reach for it.

"Shit." She blinks rapidly, looking up to the sky, her weight heavy in my arms. "That hurts."

"*Can* a great horned owl smell?" I ask her, and if not the most idiotic conversation I've had all day, it is certainly the most interesting. She's soft. *Feminine.* Underneath the disastrous combination of punk fashion and plaid, she has curves. Warmth. I lean forward in the guise of peering at her nose and smell, through the car exhaust and the scents of the alley—a light scent. I force myself to pull away. I should get in the car and let the staff deal with this. I need to put as much distance as possible between me and her.

"No." She closes her eyes, then reopens them. "They can't."

"Most birds can't." The addition comes from Edward, who has reappeared beside us. "Should I call an ambulance, sir?"

"No." I hold my hand toward him. "Give me a handkerchief."

"Talk about a battering ram." She smiles, and despite the blood, she's beautiful. Large eyes. Full lips. A delicate nose and cheekbones I could design an entire line around.

"Excuse me?" I lean forward, and she reaches forward, her hand swaying in the night air before closing on my jacket, crushing the fine fabric as if it is a dime store napkin.

"Help me up." She pulls on the jacket and Edward is suddenly beside me, apologizing as he tries to work her hand free.

"Ma'am, *please*. Let me help you."

"I'm good," she snaps at him, and looks at me. "Can you tell this idiot to leave me alone?"

"Edward," I sigh, and he steps away, worry showing on his face.

"I should call the attorneys."

The woman flays her hands in a frustrated attempt at attention. "God, do you understand the concept of chivalry? Help me *up*."

"I'm not certain you should move," I say the words even as I cup her under the arms and lift her to her feet. "You did just get hit by a car."

"A tank." She corrects me, wincing as she glances down. I follow her eyes and notice the blood-soaked rip in her jeans, mid-thigh and most likely caused by the Rolls' diamond-tipped grill. "A tank with teeth."

A slogan Rolls Royce should certainly consider. She hobbles left and reaches up, gingerly touching her nose. She swears.

"It looks broken," Edward states the obvious, the bad news delivered in the haughty, British-laced accent that perfectly accompanies his vehicle, his stance, and his excess salary.

"Yeah," she snipes, taking the handkerchief from me. "I can tell."

My attention is caught by a small crowd, one that has gathered at the end of the alley, in front of the still-open gate. They are watching us, peering in, and I can see the verbal discussion about whether or not to enter.

"Was the gate left open?" I turn to Edward, who sputters in response.

"Certainly not, sir."

My eyes flick to the girl, who presses the handkerchief to her nose, then pulls it away, examining the result—a smear of blood on the white embroidered cloth. "How'd you get back here?" She shouldn't have been in a position to be hit by our car. She—

"I was…" The word falters as she stares at the blood, one knee buckling, and I watch as her eyes roll back, her body wobbling forward. There is a moment of suspension before she faints, and I reach out, catching her fall, my chest colliding with hers as I fight to keep us both upright.

She smells like pears, and I curse at the elements of this situation.

CHAPTER 14

AVERY

"Fuck."

I hear the curse through closed eyes, my limbs as heavy and limp as I can make them. I picked a great time to faint. The action has his body flush against mine and if he wasn't gay *sohelpmeGod*—the things I'd do to this man. A hard body underneath that suit. An expensive cologne that flares my arousal and dulls any reasonable thought process. His strong hands lift me easily, despite the dead weight of my limbs.

I want to peek, to see where he is carrying me, but that would destroy any illusion, so I only sag, my head lolling forward, against the front of his shirt, and I sneak in a sniff. Yep. If orgasm had a scent, it'd be this one. Masculine. Virile. Expensive, yet subdued. To fully explore it, you'd need to rip open his shirt, crawl up that chest, and nibble your way along that neck.

Which, of course, an unconscious woman would never do. He lifts my torso, someone grabs my ankles, and I float forward.

"Should we take her inside?"

"No. Put her in the back."

The back? Maybe fainting wasn't a good idea. I'd had visions of entering the house, being offered a bedroom, an excellent opportunity for snooping before I decided to reveal, or not reveal, my true purpose. Putting me in the car introduces an entirely new set of scenarios, none that excite me.

Still. I am with Marco Lent, the man who knew Vince Horace better than anyone. I'll take that in any form or fashion I can get it. I swallow the instinct to speak and try to understand what is happening. A car door opens and there is a jostle of movement as I am slid across the seat, my hair pinned uncomfortably underneath my shoulder blades. The door closes, silence falls, and I cheat a wee bit, pulling my head up and freeing my hair. Another door opens and my feet are lifted, hands wrapping around my ankles, and the door is shut. Something shifts underneath my feet and I feel the loosening of leather as my boots are undone.

"You can stop faking." That strong voice, the deep growl in the tones... it is the sort of voice you could drizzle over ice cream and binge on for hours.

I keep my face slack and force the illusion by allowing a bit of drool to escape, the evidence making a long and irritatingly slow journey down the side of my face. There is the thud of my shoe as it comes completely off and hits the floor.

"For fuck's sake." There is the rustle of fabric, and then something soft crudely brushes across my face, the saliva captured, part of it smeared across my lips. "Stop that. I'm not sitting on your spit every time I get in this car just so you can continue this charade. Now sit up, before you bleed all over the interior."

I don't move. He's bluffing. Guessing. There's no way my dramatic act reeked of anything more than a blood-sighting-induced faint. The napkin thing was covered in blood. A hundred women, or men, or anyone with a weak stomach, would have done the same.

A car door somewhere in front of us—the chauffeur's—opens, shuts, and there is a quiet chime as he shifts into gear. The car moves forward, and it's almost eerie how silent it is. No engine noise or city sounds. I guess that's what a half a million buys you. The best sound engineering in the world.

He falls silent, pulling my sock off and I relax, my ruse bought. I probably could have done without it all together. But I needed to distract him from the gate and my unauthorized presence in the alley. Fainting was the first thing that came to mind. And thankfully, it seemed to have worked. If I wasn't fake-passed-out, I would smile.

Then he moves his finger, and I quickly see the potential issue.

CHAPTER 15

MARCO

She has nice feet. In another life, the one where I went down on Stephanie Nelson in the bathroom at prom, one where I smiled and girls, not guys, swooned—in that life, I liked feet. I liked narrow ankles and wrapping my hands around them. I liked cute toes and seeing what color they were painted. I liked soft soles and running my palms along them and the difference between their feminine arches and my big hands. I liked the soft sigh of a woman as I worked my fingers along her calf and her eyes would hood, her body relaxing, her legs opening up for me.

It wasn't a fetish, but it was one of those things I loved about a woman's body. One of the things I've missed, like the soft weight of a breast, the smell of their shampoo, the smooth feel of their skin.

This odd trainwreck of a woman has nice feet. Dark blue polish. A high arch, symmetrical toes. I smile and trail my finger across her heel and down her arch to the ticklish point of her sole. I watch her face, see it tighten in concentration, her body following suit, and I softly drum the pads of my fingers before curling them against her skin.

She shrieks, kicking forward, my hand arresting the appendage in the moment before it smacks me in the face.

"Ah…" I drag out the word with satisfaction. "So, the fainting beauty awakes."

She props up on her elbows, and my humor dampens at the blood caking around the split on her nose. "Tickling isn't fair." She spits out the phrase with the self-important air of a lunatic.

"Isn't fair?" I question. "I wasn't aware that we were playing a game, Miss …"

She pauses, her eyes darting to the side, and if this *is* a game, she's sorely outmatched.

"Hartsfield….?" There is almost a question mark on the end of the word, and I raise my eyebrows in response.

"Hartsfield?" I repeat.

"That's my last name."

"Are you sure?" I smile despite myself.

"Yes." She nods as if cementing the decision in her mind. "My name is Avery Hartsfield."

"Marco." I stretch out my hand, and she shakes it with brisk efficiency. I nod to the front of the car. "That ancient stick of British severity is Edward."

"Charmed to make your acquaintance," Edward mutters. "May I ask where we are headed, sir?"

"Not yet."

He sniffs in return and the corner of her mouth twitches into a smile.

"I pay him extra for the haughtiness." I feel myself leaning forward, into her smile, and I force my spine to straighten, moving her feet off my lap and onto the floor. I hold out my hand. "Sit up. Let me look at your nose."

She hesitates, then warily leans toward me. I reach forward and gently touch the skin just above and around the split. "The bleeding has stopped, which is good. It should be elevated, though. Tilt your head back for me."

"I suppose you're a doctor?" She says tartly, her chin obediently lifting.

I pull the ice bucket toward me and grab a handful of ice and drop them into the towel, folding the napkin around the cubes. "I boxed in high school. Broken noses were the norm more than the exception." I reach forward and press the linen pack against the break. "Gentle pressure. Hold it there."

She obeys, wincing at the cold contact and settling back against the seat.

I replace the bucket, then turn back to her. "May I ask why you felt the need to falsify a faint, Ms. Hartsfield?"

"Ah." She pauses, her voice slightly muffled by the napkin. "I don't think we determined that I fake fainted."

"You certainly did fake faint."

"I feel like we are over-using this verb." She glances at me, the corner of her mouth lifting in a suppressed smile.

"Fake fainting?" I frown in mock thought, and she laughs. The sound is thick and unapologetic, and she surprises me further by dropping the cold compress and looking around the car.

"Where's my bag?"

"I placed your knapsack in the trunk," Edward interjects.

"Thank you, Edward." I reach forward, pressing the button to raise the privacy glass.

"It must be exhausting," she remarks. "Always calling each other by name."

Everything is exhausting. It shouldn't be, not in this life where everything is done for me. Most of the irritation comes from the waiting, the answering of questions and the explaining of everything. It is one of the reasons why we've had the same house staff for so long. Once they learn all the idiosyncrasies of our lives, it's too arduous to start all over.

I stretch my legs out and glance over at her. "Where do you live? We'll drop you off."

"Detroit." She smiles. "Long way to drive."

Detroit. I shouldn't be disappointed that she is a visitor. I shouldn't give a damn where she is from. Still, the answer doesn't agree with me. "Where are you staying in New York?"

She shrugs, and gently presses the ice to her cut. "I just got in. Haven't gotten a room yet." She turns her head and glances out the window. "Where were you headed?"

I was headed to Vince's house in New Jersey, wanting to be away from the partiers, the noise, the memories. I wanted to sleep in peace, to run on the beach, and to walk into town and fuck a tourist who didn't know my name. A tourist like her.

"I'm heading home."

"Home?" She raises her eyebrows. "I just assumed you lived… I mean —" Her words falter and she looks down at her lap as if the answer is there.

"I was just attending a party." I reach forward and pull a bottle of Perrier out of the ice, holding it out to her. She shakes her head in response and I take off the cap. I don't know why I lied, except that if she knows who Vince was and that I live there, it won't take too much brain power to figure out who I am. And tonight, with this woman, I don't have the energy for that charade.

"I saw all of the people." She twists the top of the napkin holding her ice and reaches forward, putting it in the bucket. "Looked like a good party."

"I was ready to leave." I take a long sip of the bubbly water and skip to the point. "You need a place to stay tonight?"

It catches her off guard. I can see the stiffening of her spine, the way she carefully glances in my direction without meeting my eyes, her gaze moving over the car in a slow, calculated movement. I'm not blind. I haven't been with a woman in a year, but I can tell when a woman is attracted to me, have caught the appreciative linger of her stare, the flush of her skin when I lean close. If I wanted, I could have her. Not that that is why I am extending the offer. It's a ninety-minute drive to Spring Lake, and it'd be nice to have some company.

"You don't have to offer that." She eyes her boots and picks up the first sock. "But yes, I would appreciate a place to stay."

"It's a bit of a hike. Just in case you need to be in the city tomorrow."

She pauses, then nods. "I'm fine with wherever."

Something is off, her willing acceptance to go home with me. Maybe it's my staggering looks and the chemistry that's sparked between us since we met. But still, we are strangers. She's a single woman in a dangerous town. *"I'm fine with wherever."* A great way to be hauled off by a psychopath and chopped into bits.

I press a button on the door and tell Edward to go to the Spring Lake house, a directive met with quiet acceptance and no questions. Maybe I *will* keep him around.

"What do you do in Spring Lake?" She works the sock back on her bare foot, and I watch the process.

"I'm an architect." I have no idea where that comes from, but it breaks out of my lips before I can bring it back, and once there, I leave it alone. Hopefully, she won't ask me anything else. I know next to nothing about architecture.

She pauses, the sock halfway on, then continues the action. "You don't *look* like an architect."

"Really," I say dryly. "And what do most architects look like?"

She shrugs. "Why'd you take my shoes off?"

"I couldn't exactly tickle you through them." Another lie. I took her shoes off because I wanted, *needed*, to touch her in some way, to get my hands on her skin. Eighteen months has been too long. I am a junkie, and women are my fix. A fix I'm practically trembling for. I take a pull of the water and force my eyes off her and to the window, missing the bare arch of her left foot as she pulls on the second sock. "What do you do in Detroit?"

"Fund management."

"I wasn't aware anyone in Detroit still had funds."

She laughs. "Yeah, well. People still do." She runs a hand over the seat's supple leather. "Not this kind of money, though."

I don't respond. *Fund management?* What the fuck is that? "Like, trust funds? Or REITs?"

"Not exactly." She plays with the buttons set into the door. "What do these—" She stops talking as the seat begins to move. "Oh, that's nice."

"Spectacular," I deadpan and watch her face, the blood still on it. "Come here." I move closer, undoing Edward's handkerchief and dipping it into the ice bucket.

She obeys, and I sneak peeks at her as I carefully swab the area around her split skin. Her skinny jeans are ripped, additional distress manufactured into the fabric in a cheap attempt to add character. The blouse is delicate cotton, with a lace neckline that reveals a peek of cleavage.

"You're staring at me."

"It's not you," I say, snapping my gaze back to her face, irritated by the amusement in her eyes. "I was looking at your clothes. Let me guess— Forever 21? H&M? A Walmart special?"

"God, you're a snob." She snorts, and the action causes tears to well. She hisses, and I catch the scent of peppermint on her breath.

"Only in the face of terrible fashion choices." I dab the cloth against her cheek, catching the tears, and her eyes meet mine.

"You're wearing a SCARF," she says, and the scorn in her tone doesn't match the look in her eyes. She wets her lips and all I can think about is kissing them.

CHAPTER 16

AVERY

He retreats to his side of the car and I settle into my seat, enjoying the feel of the seat massager against my back and ass. It isn't my first experience with one, I had a Nissan a few years back that had a switch that shook the entire seat and made your butt numb within ten minutes. This is nothing like that. This is a smooth roll of machinery that seems to seek out any tight muscle in my ass and thighs, and gently kneads it into submission. I swear, the thing is responsive, and a moan slips out of me. He glances over, and I catch the hint of a smile.

"Enjoying yourself?"

"I am, thank you very much." I stretch out my legs and arms and spy a hinge in the ceiling liner. I press it, and a mirror pops down. I examine my nose, which has certainly seen worse. "Think I need stitches?"

"Probably."

I flip the mirror shut and sneak a peek in his direction. He's sprawled out on his side of the car, his long legs stretched out, his arm taking up the entire center console, his hand in reach of my leg. If I move my knee a little to the right, his fingers will brush it.

I've done this all wrong. From the beginning, as soon as I saw him, I should have introduced myself and told him why I was here and who I thought Vince was. Now, we're starting off on a lie. A lie that he seems to also be a part of, though I don't know why. Why lie about being an architect? Even if I hadn't researched him on the flight, I would have seen through that. I'd have known it from the way his eyes had cut away from mine—a tell as glaring as I've ever seen. A tell I've tucked away in my back pocket for later.

It's dangerous, giving a girl like me that sort of knowledge.

Almost as dangerous as it is for me to be so close to a man like this, close enough to touch. It's been a long time since I was touched. Cared for. Kissed.

The last time was two years ago—a one-night stand in Philadelphia. We'd met on the plane, enjoyed drinks at dinner, then walked through the park. He'd told me stories of Europe, and his softball team, and his dog. We'd gone back to his room, got room service, drank wine and made love. It was quick but good, he'd been apologetic but sweet. In the middle of the night, I'd woken to find the bathroom door shut, his voice hushed as he spoke to his wife. I'd laid there in bed and felt stupid. In the morning, I'd smiled when he'd talked about seeing each other again and acted as if there was a chance of a future between us.

I should have told him off. I should have interrupted his chat with his wife and called him a dirty, cheating asshole. I should have yanked the phone from his ear and told his wife everything we'd done. I should have done anything but slinked back to my hotel, packed my bags, canceled my meeting, and flown home.

It shouldn't be so hard to find someone. I shouldn't have to borrow another woman's husband while he's on a business trip.

I look out the window as the car moves over a bridge, the traffic thin, the lights of New York a colorful backdrop across the water.

"Why do you live in Spring Lake?"

He shifts, and he seems out of practice with lying. It's a good thing, and I warm to him because of it. I don't want him to be a prick. If Vince Horace is really my father, I want him to have chosen a likable man, for him to have spent the last decade with something more than a pretty face.

"Spring Lake isn't my full-time home," he finally says. "I just needed to get out of the city tonight. I needed some space."

I can understand that. I was in that crowd for less than an hour and had already needed the space, the escape.

"So, the party you were at was about that fashion guy?" It is the safest way I can broach the topic, and he turns to look at me, surprised. I'd intentionally picked a clueless choice of words in my reference to Vince, and his eyes drop to my boots. He nods as if reminded by the fact that I am not a part of his fashion-conscious world.

"Yes," he rolls the response out with the care you'd treat a bomb. "I knew him. We were old friends."

"Old friends?" I raise a brow. "You don't seem old enough to have an *old* friend." He doesn't respond and I widen my eyes and use my best innocent voice, amused at this ridiculous game, one he isn't even aware we are playing. "Did you design one of his houses?"

"No."

I wait for some further explanation, a compound of the lie. Nothing.

"So...how did you know him?"

"You never told me why you were behind the house." He switches the conversation unexpectedly and pins me with a stern look that almost melts my panties. Gay or not, this man has some serious sex appeal rocking.

"I had to use the bathroom." The fib rolls smoothly out, and I add a blush to the mix to increase credence.

"The party had private restrooms," he says, watching me more closely than I like.

I shrug, "Well, I wasn't at the party. I was walking by and saw it. Stopped in to see what the fuss was all about."

"So, you weren't there long?" he asks, and he's probably wondering if I was there for his speech, which I had watched on the plane, courtesy of YouTube. If I had, I would know that he isn't an architect from Spring Lake and—to be honest—I don't know why he's keeping his true identity a secret. Why does it matter if I know who he is? Is he worried I will ask personal questions about Vince? Is he worried I will sue him for his money, his impending inheritance? None of it makes sense, and the mystery of his evasion raises my suspicions.

"You seem like you're hiding something." I confront the beast head on and am rewarded with a laugh.

"You seem like *you're* hiding something," he counters.

I say nothing, and he says nothing, and the fact that neither of us denies the accusation, hangs in the car.

I throw out a red herring. "Maybe I should find my own place to stay tonight."

He snorts. "In Spring Lake at three in the morning? Good luck with that."

He's got a point. I feel like we're going a ridiculously far distance, every mile an additional deterrent to me getting back to Manhattan in the morning. I haven't thought this through, haven't figured out a plan, a way to be present and waiting, when the mailman arrives. But I couldn't not go with him, couldn't pass up this opportunity to see behind the curtain of Vince's life.

"What brings you to New York?" There is a quiet detachment in his voice, as if he doesn't care much about the answer, but is instead seeking a change in topic.

I weigh my options and decide to go with a modified version of the truth. "I'm here to meet someone, who I think might be my father." *A dead someone.* It is as close to a confession as I can get without sharing everything.

His interest is piqued, and he turns his head, meeting my gaze, his eyes pulling away to move back over me. I don't know what his obsession is with my clothes. Maybe it's a fashion thing, but it seems as though, with every pass of his eyes, he pulls new details from the mix. "You don't *know* if he's your father?"

I pull at the sleeves of my shirt. "I was adopted." I straighten in my seat, a defensive habit born from years of pity and condescending remarks. "I found my mother a few years ago, but she didn't have a lot of information on my father."

When I was young, I used my adoptive status proudly. It was proof I didn't belong to the staunch conservativeness of the McKennas. I quickly learned that most people are uncomfortable with the idea of adoptees. They don't know the questions to ask, how to get the answers they want without the sense that they are prying.

At some point, I stopped telling people and stopped having the sort of close relationships where people asked about my parents. It wasn't intentional, my slow departure from society. It's just that in an industry like mine, there isn't room for a lot of friends. My circles are mostly men and not the sort that I want to hang out with. They are nothing like this man. He's a smooth glass of chardonnay versus my buffet of Pabst beer and cheap tequila. And... if I have to guess, I bet he doesn't have many friends either.

"When were you given up for adoption?" *Given up.* An interesting and demeaning choice of words.

"At birth." I reach into the ice bucket and pull out a bottle of water, then eye the cabinet to his right. "You got anything stronger than this?"

"Sure." He slides open the compartment and reveals a row of crystal decanters. "What's your poison?"

"Vodka, if you have it."

"It'll have to be a shot," he says. "They didn't stock the car."

"You aren't a drinker?"

"Not much of one." He presses on another side compartment and unveils two shot glasses, a monogram of initials etched into their side. He pulls out a tray table and I raise my eyebrows, impressed at what the car offers. He sets two shot glasses on the platform and fills both, pushing one in my direction. Ignoring a toast, he tilts his head back and takes the shot. It is sexy, watching the stretch of his neck, the cut of his jaw, the flex of his cheek as he swallows the liquor without a shudder. For a man who doesn't drink much, he takes it like a champ.

He wipes his lips with a napkin, then glances at me, his eyes dropping to my still-waiting shot. I bring it to my lips and toss it back. It is a smooth burn, an expensive slide of fire down my throat, and I barely grimace as I set it back down.

"My mother was a teenage pregnancy." I lick my lips. "Her family wasn't interested in adding another child to the mix."

"But you've met her?"

"Yes." I nudge the empty shot glass toward him. "About seven years ago, I got curious and tracked down the adoption center. My mother had filled out a form, requesting to be contacted if I ever inquired about my paternity." It had taken all of twenty minutes to get her name and number, and I remember being pissed at how simple it was, and thinking about how many years I'd wasted.

I reach forward and grab a bottle of water from the ice, twisting off the lid and washing down the liquor. "The center didn't have any information on my father and neither did my mom."

He refills his glass and doesn't ask about my mom, probably didn't think about the weight of a daughter's first meeting with her mother. I've thought about it too much. On the way to meet her, I'd had to pull over on the side of the highway. There, I'd retched into an empty Subway bag, the taste of vomited ham sandwich still thick on my tongue when I'd finally met her. I shouldn't have been nervous. She'd been nice. Very nervous and quiet. She'd brought me into her home and introduced me to her kids—two grubby-faced toddlers who'd blinked at me with disinterest. They were my half-siblings—and I'd stared at them and tried to will myself to feel *something* for them. We sat in that tiny brick home in upstate New York, listened to a story about her and a concert, and I'd wanted to get out of there. I'd run away from the McKennas because I felt like I hadn't belonged in their world. I'd spent my adolescence blaming that itch, that uncomfortable fit to the fact that they weren't my blood, they weren't my real parents, they were so different from me. But then I sat in that cozy little house and looked into the eyes of the woman who'd birthed me, and I'd seen nothing of myself. I'd seen a slightly frazzled, ordinary woman. One with a ketchup stain on her shirt and half-cut coupons on the dining room table. When I went to the bathroom, I'd snooped through her cabinets and found a giant box of tampons, a worn copy of a women's workout magazine and toilet bowl cleaner. I'd sat on her toilet, run my hands over my arms and felt that same uncomfortable itch, that same disappointment, that same feeling of not belonging.

"So, how did you find your dad?" Marco brings the shot glass to his lips, pauses, and then slowly, almost tenderly, tilts back the glass. I watch him and try not to picture those lips between my legs, his tongue palming out, his eyes meeting mine.

"I had a photo of him," I manage. "Someone recognized him in the photo, told me where I could find him." Not a lie, but almost. I think of my mom, producing the photo with a reluctance that suggested she didn't want to part with it. *I never got his name,* she'd said. *Or if I did, I forgot it.* She'd blushed, and I'd been reminded of her description of the drugs. I'm surprised she even remembered the sex.

"Does he know you're coming?" He pushes the empty shot glass forward, lining it up next to mine, a twin pair of demons.

"No." I swallow. "I had planned on spending a few days in the city, working up the nerve to approach him."

"Big city to find a man in," he remarks.

I look out the window of Vince Horace's car. "It won't be too hard."

"Does he live in Greenwich?" The question catches me off guard, and I turn my head to find him watching me. "I was wondering how you discovered the party."

"Oh." My fingers find the split on my nose, and I run the pads of them carefully over the cut, blood still damp and staining my skin. I pull my fingers away and, without thinking, suck the blot of blood off the end of them.

He pulls at my hand, sliding the fingers gently out of my mouth.

I've only been around a handful of gay men in my life. It's not that I've got anything against homosexuals. It's just that life as a money launderer in Detroit ... I'm not exactly bumping asses with them on a regular basis.

I flick my eyes from his hand to his eyes, which hold mine in a stare that rocks some serious heat. As I said, gay people and I aren't well acquainted. But unless I'm confused—and that's a very likely possibility—I'm pretty damn sure this guy is coming on to me.

I wet my lips and his eyes drop to them.

Yeah.

I swallow and speak to fill the gap. "I used to have a friend who lived in Greenwich. I was wandering around, trying to find her place, when I saw the crowd. I came close to get a look at what was going on. See what the fuss was about. Plus," I add, "I love Lady GaGa." I smile. "Only in New York can you score a free concert like that."

He smiles, but it is an automatic response, his eyes still on my lips. When he pours us another shot, I don't object.

CHAPTER 17

MARCO

The atmosphere in the car is changing. Maybe it's the alcohol, maybe it's the fact that I'm exhausted and delusional, but whatever it is, she's now resting her weight on the armrest between us. Her legs are crossed, and when she occasionally bounces her foot, it brushes against my leg. We're three shots down, and I can feel the edges of my control diluting.

Is it a mistake to bring her to Spring Lake? Absolutely. Probably. I don't even know. I don't like how convenient it was, literally running into her as we left. A younger, more optimistic man, might have thought it was fate. But I don't need fate. And I don't need a soulmate. I'm looking for a woman to bang the fuck out of. And right now, with her next to me, I'm finding it hard to figure out why she's not the perfect candidate.

She doesn't know who I am. She doesn't seem the type to gossip, to jump on social media and brag on, or research, me. She hasn't pulled out a phone once since we met. There will be no Instagramming photos of the Rolls Royce, no tweets about the Vince Horace party.

She's perfect. So…why am I hesitating?

I look in Edward's direction, the partition between us still closed. He won't be able to stay at Spring Lake, I'll have to send him home, and he'll wonder why. Maybe he'll even suspect the truth. He's not stupid, and he's spent a decade with us. If he hasn't figured out the truth by now? I could lay this woman across the hood of the car, fuck her senseless, and he'd still be clueless.

Still, regardless of what Edward might suspect or know, I'll have to send him home. I won't be able to think straight with him there, I won't be able to enjoy myself, knowing he is somewhere in the house, in potential earshot of the absolutely filthy behavior I plan on participating in. I need this. I need this so badly that my fingers itch, my blood pumps, heart pounds. I can't stop looking at her, at the way her shirt clings to her curves, and the peek of bare skin I can see through the rip in her jeans. I can't stop thinking about how soft her skin felt when I touched her face, the warm hitch of her breath when I leaned in close, the faint smell of fruit and honey that drifts off of her.

I need it.

She shifts in the seat and I allow the tips of my fingers to graze her knee. Her eyes drop to the contact, then snap to mine. I can see something heavy on her lips, the start of a sentence welling in her throat, but she swallows it down and says nothing.

The car turns, climbing the hill to Spring Lake, and I should make my move now or back away.

She tilts her leg toward me, a clear signal for more, and I want to slide my hand upward, along her inner thigh, until I get to the cheap button of her jeans. I clamp my mind down on the next fantasies, ones that involve her on her knees, my cock in my mouth. Her on my lap, naked. Bouncing. My hands on her bare breasts, my mouth on her flushed skin.

I let go of her knee and run my hand over my mouth, forcing my gaze to the window. I point to the dim lights of the town. "That's Spring Lake. We're almost there."

I need to get ahold of myself.

CHAPTER 18

AVERY

I hooked up with a girl once. I was in a hotel bar in Atlanta, doing peppermint shots with a gorgeous blonde from Amsterdam. Our bodies grew closer with each shot, our elbows brushing, her hair tangling in the sequins of my top. She scored a barstool and we shared it, one of her legs flung over mine, and we discussed ex-boyfriends and the city as her hands roamed over me. First, it was just the tickle of fingers along the top of my jeans. Then, the slide of her hand across my breast. I let my hand rest on her bare thigh, and leaned in closer than was necessary when I whispered things into her ear. Between us, the air heated, and when we went to the bathroom to freshen up, I let her pull me into the biggest stall, her hand flipping the lock, her giggle filling the air.

She had tasted like alcohol and bubble gum. She had kissed in the tentative way of a high-schooler. I had pulled down the top of her dress and marveled at the look of her breasts, the soft and squishy feel of them. I'd flicked a tongue over her nipple and felt the grip of her hand on my hair.

The anticipation and buildup had been like a drug. A foreign, forbidden, drug. But the act itself?

It had done absolutely nothing for me.

Fun. Different. But unimpressive just the same.

I watch Marco Lent pull away and wonder how far this gay boy thinks he's going to take this. Maybe it's the alcohol. Maybe it's his grief. Maybe it's the upheaval in his life, and my unexpected arrival in the midst of a personal crisis. But there's no way he's sexually confused enough to fuck me.

I think.

I fight the urge to dig in my bag for my phone, Google his name, and reconfirm every detail I've read about him. Because in every article I've read, he's definitely gay. Not a bi-sexual confused individual who waved a rainbow flag once. He's like... super gay. Speaks at annual conventions. He and Vince hosted and orchestrated almost every gay pride event that's occurred in the last decade. I've seen photos of them kissing, photos of Vince's arm around him on the deck of their yacht, read articles that describe orgies in their pool and sex-filled parties in the Hamptons.

There is no way, according to everything I've read about Marco Lent, that he is anything other than 100% gay.

And there is no way, according to everything I've felt in this car, that he isn't planning on ripping off my clothes with his teeth once we arrive at his home.

The car slows, the dark ocean coming into view, and I find the button on the door, lowering the window. The whip of ocean air fills the car, and there is a sound from Marco that sounds suspiciously like a growl. I ignore him, my eyes on the gate, which shudders to life, parting before the car.

They like their gates. I think of the one in New York, and this one is almost laughable in comparison, a low-slung frame that would keep out vehicles, and not much else. A fountain comes into view, the car curving around a circular drive until my side is right up next to it. My vision adjusts to the dark, and I laugh when I see the fountain's centerpiece, a naked man, in a pose similar to that of David, if David's package had been five times bigger.

"Interesting." I open the door and step out, looking up at it, surprised to see that the statue's face is Marco. I let my eyes fall back to the marble manhood and raise my eyebrows. "Really?" I drawl and look over my shoulder at him.

Marco steps out and rests his wrist on the open car door, looking over the top of the Rolls at me. "Ignore that."

"It's hard to ignore." I laugh. "I mean, *seriously*." I turn to face it. "You know this is really weird, right?"

It must have been something Vince commissioned. And if it was, I like my potential father more for it. I can't exactly blame him. If I was dating a guy who looked like *this* naked, I'd put statues of him in every single room. But Marco doesn't know that I know about Vince, and I use that to my advantage, moving closer to the statue and crossing my arms, giving it a detailed exam.

"God your ego is…" I let my eyes fall to the massive organ that hangs between muscular marble thighs. "Huge," I finish, turning to him, and he makes a face in response.

"Did you pose for this thing? Or…" I wince. "Is this a small penis thing? Like, you don't want people to know what you really look like, so you overkill it with this giant … presentation?"

He ignores me, climbing the front steps of the house, and I am hit with a withering look from his driver, who lifts my bag with a distinguished scowl. "Madam, your knapsack."

I grab the bag, hurrying around the back of the car and jogging up the stairs to catch up with Marco. "Or… is this your signature architectural flair? Like, buy a house plan and get a free giant penis statue of the architect?" I ask the question as innocently as possible and am awarded a black look. Entering a code into the lock's keypad, he grips my arm and opens the door, practically shoving me inside.

"Stay," he commands, holding up a hand as if I'm a dog. I snort, a response he probably doesn't catch in the moment before he closes the door and leaves me inside. He jogs back to the car, and I watch him speak to Winston Churchill, a discussion that probably involves me. I take advantage of the moment and turn to see the house.

It is, in every seam, corner, and pillow stitching, gorgeous. I had expected a Versace-like display of color, everything gaudy and over the top. This was the opposite. White granite floors with veins of gold and dark chocolate swirling across the massive expanse. Giant leather couches dotted by white fur throws and fluffy pillows. A stone fireplace stretches three stories high and is framed by a floor-to-ceiling view of the water that dominates the room. I think of my watch and glance from it to the room, the mix of edge and class present in both. I move closer and notice the smaller details that give the room bite. The giant polar bear head mounted on the fireplace that is in a teeth-baring snarl. The lamps, suspended from the ceiling, that are more gothic than beachy. The glass globes on the coffee table that hold shark teeth and tiger eye eggs.

I step into the dining room, looking at everything. It is a visual orgy and I wish I had time to go through every room and examine every piece. The dining room table is set, glass crystal set off by red china, a fresh flower arrangement stretching down its middle. On either end of the room, the ocean view between them, giant oil paintings display more nudity. I stop before the first one, a close-up of two male torsos, side by side, one hand over each other's cock, the organs still visible between their splayed fingers.

The front door shuts and I turn as Marco strides into the room, his features calm, hair mussed. He sheds his jacket, then shirt, tossing them onto the couch in a fluid motion that could have been on a Milan catwalk. He yanks the scarf from his neck, baring his chest, and God, he's beautiful. No wonder, out of all of New York, out of the entire fashion industry, Vince chose him. I can't imagine a more beautiful specimen, can't look at him and find any flaws. And if what's under his pants matches the outside … Good God. My knees almost buckle at just the thought.

"You seem to be a little obsessed with penises," I joke, watching him round the end of the table and approach me. I nod toward the painting and am caught off guard when he doesn't slow. His hands grip my waist and lift. My boots leave the floor and I grab at his shoulders for balance. "What are you—"

I barely get the words out before my ass hits the table. Table settings fly as he sweeps his forearm over its surface, and I watch as a pile of expensive china hits the floor and explodes into pieces.

"Do you want this?" He pants out the question, his hands sliding down the back of my jeans, gripping my ass, and he pulls me to the edge of the table, his body fitting between my open knees.

I don't know what he's asking, but I know I want it. Even if *it* is a drunk gay man's attempt at a one-night stand. I nod, and his lips crash down on mine.

CHAPTER 19

MARCO

There is fire in her kiss, an electrical impulse that shoots through my mouth, burns my chest and hits straight to my dick. I'm hard before she even reaches for me, before her hands collide with my chest, run down my stomach, and her nails scrape across my abs. Her legs move, wrapping around me, and I plant my hands on the table behind her, leaning forward until the table digs into my thighs, and I deepen the kiss, pushing her back, a futile attempt she fights with the energy of a stallion.

Fuck, I love her kiss. It's wild and untamed, unapologetic as it captures my tongue, samples what I have, and gives it all back. Have I ever been kissed like this? Have I ever met a mouth so addictive? I think of it wrapped around my cock, that tongue wild against my tip, and I almost nut from just the thought of it.

I straighten a little, leaning back, and grip her hair, pulling her tighter, and dive back into her mouth.

I used to hate kissing. I used to hate it and now, with her, I never want anything else.

Her hands slide lower, blindly finding the top of my pants. Outside, headlights sweep along the surf and catch my eye, a reminder that we are in a million-dollar fishbowl, on display for anyone who walks on the beach. I reach down, stop her hand, and pull away from her mouth. "Wait." I lift her off the table and flush against my body. "I don't want to do this here."

She glances over the mess of china and glass, then smirks up at me. "Maybe you should have decided that before destroying three place settings."

"Fuck the place settings," I growl out the words, and that smirk, that light in her eyes, it does something to me.

"I'd rather fuck something else."

Five simple dirty words that destroy any thought of stepping away and being a gentleman. I let out a hard breath and nod toward the front of the house. "Up the stairs. Any bedroom on the right. Now."

She almost runs up the stairs. In the bedroom, her shoes fall to the floor with a few quick yanks of laces. Her socks skim off easily. She lays back on the bed, undoes her pants, and I hook my fingers under the denim and work the material over her hips, my mouth finding the exposed skin and kissing it, sucking it, biting it. She squirms beneath me, working her pelvis and helping me shed the jeans. When I get them off, she crosses her legs, and all I can see is a V of red cotton, half-hidden by the tee she wears. I wrap a hand around each ankle, pull her to the edge of the bed, and when I reach for her shirt, she stops me. "No."

No. The most painful syllable I've ever heard. "Please." I've lost all composure and the word is practically a beg. I undo my pants, push them down and step out of them. I run my palm along the outside of my underwear, gripping my dick through the thin cotton, and watch her eyes drop, her cheeks heating. I move closer and pull down on the boxer briefs, letting them fall to the floor, and stand fully naked before her.

"Please." I work my hand over my cock, squeezing the shaft with one hand as I gently tug on my balls with the other. "You have no idea how badly I want to see you."

Her eyes are huge, and I can't wait to see them when I push inside of her, when she feels every inch of me, and all that this cock is capable of. She scoots back on the bed, reaches out, and pulls on the cord of the bedside lamp. The room goes dark, a hushed silence falls, and all I can hear is her breathing, soft huffs of air, ones that lead me closer until my knees bump against the mattress.

"Come here," she whispers from the dark, and I crawl onto the bed and toward her.

———

It's so dark. The blackout curtains do their job, the Tiffany clock unlit, no source of illumination anywhere. If I'd had them properly prep the house, there'd be a fire in the hearth, candles glowing along the mantle, and the curtains would be open, bed turned down, fresh flowers on the sill.

There is none of that and I curse, then reign in my frustration, because there's also perfection in the darkness. I can't see anything, and am forced to go completely by feel, by scent, by sound. Her hands are hesitant, softly patting over me, and when her hand brushes against me, I can hide the break of my face, the dissolve of control. I almost, but don't quite, suppress the grunt. A second hand joins her first, and she grips my shaft with both hands, one on top of the other, my head coming out of the top. When she tightens her grip, I almost come, the delicate touch of her hands, coupled with the absolute darkness in the room … I pinch my face in concentration and reach forward, moving closer, my knees sinking into the bed, brushing against smooth skin, and when my hands find her in the dark, the blouse is gone, no bra to be found, and I slide my palms over her stomach and across the curve of a bare, perfect breast.

117

"You're so big," she whispers the words, and I'm lost to them, lost to everything but the feel of her body beneath my hands. I'm a fucking teenager again, a teenager with wood so hard it's painful, one whose orgasm is barely contained, and who is fascinated, fucking mesmerized, by the feel of this woman. It wasn't like this, the last time, or the last ten times I've been with a woman. This is a fucking holy experience, and I don't know if it's because Vince is gone, or if it's just been too long, or if this woman's body is some sort of a drug, but I kneel over her, her fingers exploring my cock, and worship her body with my touch.

I slide my hands down, run my fingers over the soft thin cotton of her underwear, and tug gently on the fabric. "I need these off."

Her hands leave my dick, and the absence is almost painful. She shifts beneath me, and I move higher on her body, dragging the weight of my cock along her stomach. I find her breasts in the dark, cushion them around either side of my shaft, and squeeze them together, sliding my cock higher, hovering it over the place where I imagine her mouth to be, and wait.

She's a fucking mind reader, and when she pulls it to her mouth, there is no hesitation. She closes her lips around the head, sucks hard, and slides it down into her throat, her wet muscles flexing around it, her tongue yielding, the sensation perfection.

"Jesus," I swear, my hips pulling back, then thrusting forward, her hand keeping me where she wants it, the soft sound of her gag pushing me even closer to release. I can't control myself around this woman, can barely keep my orgasm in check. How will I handle it when I'm between her legs, my hands on her hips, her thighs, her breasts? How will I be able to push inside of her and not immediately come apart?

I feel the swell of an impending orgasm and pull back, out of her mouth, and move down her body, my chest over hers, my mouth finding her lips. They are wet and messy and I kiss her like I wished

I'd fucked her. This new position has my cock wet and heavy between her legs, her soft pubic hair brushing against the shaft of my dick, and I'm so close to being inside of her I almost come. I reach down, finding her, and I curl my fingers against the soft patch of hair between her legs. I memorize the feel of her pussy, the tight folds of her body, the hard bud of her clit, and I torture myself with every detail of her except the part I need the most. She widens her thighs, curves upward with her hips, and begs me, my name a pant on her lips, her nails raking along my back, her teeth nipping at my neck. "Please…" She groans the word and I yield, spreading her legs apart and pushing a finger inside.

One finger. One finger that gets to sample the sweetest fucking pussy in this world.

Hot, tight muscles bunch around the digit, her body slick and yielding, flexing around my finger as if sucking it inside of her.

I push another finger inside, and the fit is perfection, her body tightening beneath me, and her breath stalls on my skin.

"You like that?" The words come out harsher than I intend, my mind barely in control of itself, and the need to turn on the light, to see her face… it's enormous and only second to every feral desire I have to position my cock at her entrance and go to fucking town on her pussy. I work my fingers, groan at the feeling, and when she responds, I barely hear her through the pounding in my head.

"I need more," she whispers out the plea and one of her hands find my cock, her fingers wrapping around me, her grip starting to move, to squeeze and rotate and jerk. I pinch my eyes close, say the Latin alphabet backwards, and lose every single battle I attempt.

I kiss her because I need it, it grounds me, focuses me, and when I come back to life, my fingers find the velvet swell of her g-spot and I press on it, an action that has her hips rising off the bed, her hand dropping off my cock, her body jerking in pleasure.

"That spot—Marco—"

"I know," I lower my mouth, bumping along her skin until my lips find her breast and I close my mouth onto the skin, my tongue flicking across the nipple, my fingers starting to work across the bundle of nerves, everything inside of her heating up around the action. "Don't worry. I won't stop."

It takes less than a minute, and when she comes, it is with a series of soft sobs, over and over again, her body thrashing beneath me, her skin hot around me. I stretch it out as long as she can take it, and when she is done, I spread her legs, move in between them, and, in the moment before I push inside of her, realize the problem.

CHAPTER 20

AVERY

"Fuck."

I hear his swear in the dark, and it doesn't sound like his others, the worshipful sounds of a man barely in control. This swear sounds pissed, and I lift myself out of my orgasm-induced haze long enough to find his location in the dark. "What?"

"I don't have a condom." There is the unexpected brush of fingertips, hitting my stomach and dragging down to the wet patch of hair, and he gently rolls them over my clit before he slides, what feels like a thumb, inside of me. "Fuck, fuck, fuck, fuck, FUCK."

I almost tell him to just do it. To grip my thighs, push that thick cock inside, and let me experience heaven. I almost tell him that it doesn't matter, that I trust him, that it will be okay.

But then I remember. I remember every story I've read, the sort of life he leads. Drugs. Sex Parties. Ten years with Vince Horace, who was apparently the biggest slut in New York City before he settled down with Marco. I can't have unprotected sex with him. I don't know what

I was thinking, scrambling up his staircase and yanking off my clothes, without a single thought of condoms.

"There's not one in the house?"

"No." One of his hands closes over mine and he brings it to his cock. "Jack me off."

I don't want to jack him off. I want him. My body *needs* him—on top of me, behind me, dominating me. I wrap my hand around his thick shaft and my good sense wars with my raw need. I pump my hand to his tip and back down, and he lets out a hard breath of approval. "Faster."

His hand slides up my stomach and cups my breast, his second hand mirroring the action. I arch into his touch, immediately addicted to the tender way he caresses my skin, the rough pads of his fingers moving over my nipples, the almost reverent way he touches them. I squeeze his shaft as I move my hand up and down, his cock stiffening under the stimulation, hardening to a point that must be painful.

"Hold your hands still." He releases my breasts, and I feel his hands atop mine, positioning one on top of the other, covering the majority of his dick. "Hold tight." He squeezes them, then I feel him shift, the bed adjusting with additional weight, the brush of muscular thighs against mine. He thrusts with his hips and his cock slides through my hands. Forward and back. Forward and back. He fucks my grip and I jump slightly when his mouth lands on my shoulder, then my breast, a line of soft kisses moving across my chest. He finds my mouth, deepens the kiss, then pulls away, his hips moving faster, my grip tightening.

"I'm gonna come. Fuck, Avery. I want to see you."

In that moment, his breath quickening, body shuddering, hips working … I wish I hadn't turned off the light. I'd been so worried that he'd be turned off by my feminine curves … I'd feared he would chicken out, or come to his gay senses, or see my breasts, screech at the top of his lungs, and sprint away. I hadn't wanted anything to disrupt the contact I'd so desperately needed. And now, one of his hands finding my waist, holding it for balance, his breath hard in the darkness, I only want to give him everything. Me, in the light. My body, condom or not. His orgasm, and mine, and anything else he ever wants.

In the darkness, with just sound and touch between us, he is so beautiful.

"Avery. Holy fuck." I squeeze him tighter and he grips my waist, grunting as his release hits my stomach, a shot on my breasts, my cheek, my ear. It is long and plentiful, and I am laughing by the time he finishes, his come everywhere, covering my hands, my body, my hair. He groans, falling beside me on the bed, and I scoot higher, finding the lamp's switch and flicking it on.

"Oh my God," I manage the words through a laugh as I survey the damage, four or five long streaks of him splattered across my breasts. I turn to him, his eyes closed, his naked body sprawled across the bed and there is a moment when my heart stops, when my breath catches, and I wonder what in the hell made me turn off the light.

There are no words for a man like him, no explanation for how perfectly he is created, the lines of his body, the cut of his jaw, the thick line of his lashes, the rough pout of his lips. He should be too pretty, but he's not. He's rough on the edges, muscular where other men are soft, and … my eyes drift down to his cock, still thick and hard against his stomach. Adding *that* to the mix makes him impossible. Maybe it *was* a good thing I turned off the lights. If I'd seen all of this, above me, looking down at me, hard against me … my mind would have come apart.

I reach out a finger and poke him, half to test if he is real, and the other half because I want someone else, other than me, to see the mess he has created. "Hey."

His eyes open, his mouth curving, and he props himself up on one elbow, his eyes dropping to my bare breasts. "Hey."

I fight the urge to cover up. "Did you see how much you came?" I gesture to my body. "You shot it all the way into my hair."

His mouth curves and he inches closer, sliding a hand across my stomach and pulling me closer until I'm flush against the side of his body. I let myself fall and land on my back, looking up at him.

"I'm sorry." He runs his hand up, smearing the white traces of him across my skin, and slides his hand over my closest breast, cupping it. His mouth drops and he gently sucks my nipple into his mouth, the gesture so unexpected that I gasp in surprise, my eyes closing slightly, the flick of his tongue across my tender flesh, the soft motions of his mouth ... I whimper despite my best attempts to stay cool.

The sound catches his attention and he lifts his eyes, moving his mouth to my other breast, his hand sliding down the planes of my stomach and in between my legs. My thighs part without instruction, my pelvis tilting up to him, and I reach out, grabbing his neck, pulling his mouth to mine, and stiffening in the moment his fingers push back inside of me.

"Last time I missed this." He speaks softly, pulling off my mouth and running his eyes over my body, my skin sticky from his juices, my hips moving uncontrollably to the tune of his fingers. "I missed the way your body looks naked." He lets his eyes move over me, my nipples stiff and red from his mouth, my thighs beginning to tremble from his touch. His eyes find the tremor and he stares, his voice thickening. "Touch your clit. Rub it."

I don't hesitate. My forefingers find their way through the damp curls, my hand brushing his, my touch soft as I roll the pads of my fingers across my clit, short quick strokes that have my eyes closing, the pleasure—when combined with his touch—almost too much.

Almost.

"Fuck, you're beautiful."

I believe him when he says it. He rasps out the words, his voice catching on the syllables, and I open my eyes, catching the heat in his, his gaze sharpening when I gasp, his fingers quickening when I begin to pant. My body curves into his touch and I try to warn him and can't, try to speak but only freeze, a low cry coming, over and over, over and over, as the orgasm explodes, a brilliant flash of pleasure that streaks through me, blinding my thought, my vision, my everything.

I come down from it, everything hazy and loose, his taste on my lips, my scent in the air, his hands unapologetically roaming my body, a junkie getting his fix, his mouth rough on my own, his need still evident in his cock, now rock hard and jutting forward.

I don't think, I just move. Out from under him, my hand digging into his shoulders, pushing him down on the bed. My leg, swinging over his hips, my hand gripping his cock, positioning it where I need it, my body lowering onto him, the stiff bulge of his cock so wide, so large that I yelp. My body is unaccustomed to his size, and my teeth grit as I fully settle atop him. He groans out my name, and I reach forward, digging my nails into his chest, lifting my body slightly from his pelvis, and then do what I've dreamed about for the last few hours.

I ride the fuck out of that cock.

CHAPTER 21

MARCO

For ten years, I lived on Vince's schedule. We ate when he was hungry. Traveled when he was bored. Showed up when he was booked and left as soon as it was appropriate. Now, on his wide deck, overlooking the water, a beautiful woman next to me, I'm lost—half drunk on the freedom, half terrified by the risks.

She stretches on the chaise lounge, a bare foot escaping from the blanket, and despite itself, my cock gives a half-hearted attempt to move. I smile, reach for my glass, and hide the expression behind a gulp of whiskey.

I like that she isn't a talker. She laughs too much, asks too many questions, but at times, like right now, she shuts up. Which is good, since right now, I need some space to think. I need to figure out what a life without Vince looks like, and how I can enjoy it without destroying his image.

"It's beautiful here."

I nod, looking out on the water, the white caps reflecting off the moon's light. This high up, you can't see the road between us and the water, the sound of cars diminished by the waves. "Yes, it is."

"If I were you, I'd be out here every night."

I don't say anything. Vince and I had rarely stepped out on the balcony. Our visits to Spring Lake were mostly spent catching up on sleep and discussing business, away from the noises and distractions of the city. Still, there were a few memories—cigars on this deck, conversations about lost loves and childhood stories. Lots of whiskey and discussions over the brand, the industry, and our future.

"You ever been in love?" I rest my forearms on the railing and look down, watching the top of a car as it rounds the curve below us, its headlights sweeping over and illuminating the rocks.

She shakes her head. "Not really. There was a guy once..." her voice trails off and she lifts her wine glass and takes a sip. I wait for her to continue. "He wasn't a nice guy. It took me too long to figure it out."

Wasn't a nice guy. My stomach tightens at the words. "He hit you?"

"No." She speaks quickly. "No. He just..." she shrugs. "He thought he was a gangster, or wanted to be one. And when I met him, I was lost, and didn't really have a place to stay or a solid job." She pulls her foot back underneath the blanket. "It was nice, at the beginning, to have someone take care of me. To not have to worry about anything."

I think of my first month in Vince's house, the way my life had, in a period of days, changed so drastically. Goodbye, studio apartment that I could barely afford. Hello, giant mansion and a personal butler dedicated to me. Goodbye, fast food and takeout. Hello, private chef and impromptu dinners in Spain. I'd traded taxis for a Rolls Royce, and Banana Republic for Brioni.

My student loans were paid off by one check from Vince. My monthly expenses, suddenly gone. My annual salary, tripled. I had settled nicely into the life of the uber-rich, and within a few months, I'd grown accustomed to the lifestyle, my appreciation waning into something much more dangerous—expectation.

She sets her glass down on the side table. "I overlooked a lot with him. Stuff he was doing, women he was fucking…" she yawns. "And I finally realized I didn't love him enough to make up for all of it. I probably didn't love him at all." She turns her head and rests it on the back of the chair, looking at me. "What about you?"

I glance down, tilting my wrist to see the watch, and step away from the railing. "God, it's late. I'm gonna head to bed."

She gets up also, and I follow her up the stairs, wondering what etiquette dictates at this point. Are we supposed to sleep together? I haven't slept next to a woman in over a decade. Vince and I slept together, a situation that took me weeks to get accustomed to. The first nights I spent stick straight in his bed, worried, with every toss or shift, that he was reaching for me, or trying to make a move. Finally, as our relationship grew closer, and my comfort level expanded, I started to relax and sleep through the night. After a few months, I didn't think twice about getting into bed at night, or talking with him in the moments before I fell asleep.

Anyone can grow accustomed to anything. I didn't believe that at one time, but I am proof that it can happen. Proof that a straight man can be kissed and not shudder. Proof that, after seeing so many things, a mind can become numb.

Our Manhattan bed had been custom made, large enough to hold four grown men. He and I had slept on separate sides, and could toss and turn without bumping limbs. And when we came to Spring Lake—a house without fear of morning interruptions—we'd slept separately. Him in the master, me in one of the smaller suites.

Now, we reach the landing and she steps into the guest room, glancing back at me expectantly.

"Everything you need will be in the bathroom or the dresser drawers."

I step toward the master, glance back, and see her watching me. "Goodnight."

"Goodnight." There is an amused lilt to her tone, one that irritates me, and I ignore it, stepping into the bedroom and flipping the latch on the back of the door, locking her out.

What did she expect? Us to spoon? My body curled around hers? More pillow talk?

I step toward Vince's bed and pause, taking a moment to think of him before I pull back the covers.

Live well, Marco.

It's probably just this room, the ghosts of memories and all his things, but I swear that somewhere in the dark, I hear him chuckle.

CHAPTER 22

AVERY

He shuts the door and I hear the subtle sound of a lock turning. I head back into the bedroom, the smell of sex still in the air, and eye the bed. Sheets rumpled. My jeans in a pile on the floor. Shirt tossed on the bed.

I came to New York to stop Andrei's letter from reaching its destination. At what point had that mission gotten lost? With the shots? With the kiss?

I fall onto the bed and think about the way Marco had gripped me, his eyes dark, his mouth desperate. He had acted like a starved man, the heat in his stare enough to ignite my skin, flame my desire, and wipe my mind clean of everything but pleasure.

I roll over and stare at the ceiling. If I am Vince Horace's daughter, this situation is beyond creepy. If I'm not Vince Horace's daughter, then it's confusing. Either way, I need to get out of this house and back to the city. I reach out and find my bag. Groping through it, I pull out my cell phone and set an alarm for five o'clock. That'll give me an hour of sleep, and plenty of time to sneak out of here and find a taxi back to New York.

I close my eyes. God, he was so good. The way my body came to life under his touch—I've never come so hard before. Everything tonight —the raw way he fucked me, the reckless chemistry that sparked between us, the stretch of my body around his cock. He had panted out my name, roared when he came, and been ready to go again.

It was a mistake, one that didn't make any sense, an act that occurred between the two worst people possible.

But I don't regret it. More than that, I want it again.

———

I open my eyes, and it's still dark. Which can't be right, since I feel awake. I sit up, trying to find a bit of light in the room. Patting the top of the covers, I find my phone, waking up the display and cursing when I see the time. *9:42 am.*

"No, no, no, no, no." I unlock it and open my alarm clock app, cursing when I see the alarm. My drunk fingers had set it for five o'clock PM, not AM.

"Shit!" I roll off the bed and fumble for the curtains, the room too big, and I have to move across half a football field just to find the velvet curtains. I pull them open and groan when I see the bright sun illumi-nating a beach already full of families and bikinis, a volleyball floating from one group to another, everyone oblivious to the fact that it's got to be fifty degrees outside.

I should be sitting on the steps of his attorney's office right now, a muffin and coffee in hand, my flirtation skills prepped and ready for the mailman. I drop the curtains and rush back, snagging my jeans off the floor and hopping into them, one leg in, then the other, my shirt yanked on inside out. It doesn't matter. God, what if he walks in? Knocks on the door? What if he is downstairs, waiting for me to wake up? I rapidly think of excuses. A sick grandmother. Urgent doctor's appointment. Forgotten... ugh. My brain twists sideways, sticks its tongue out at me, and gives me nothing. I throw my jacket on, work my arms through the straps of my backpack, and shove my feet into my boots. I yank the laces into a knot and quietly turn the handle and pull open the bedroom door.

The hall is quiet and empty, the door closed on the other end of the hall. I leave the door ajar and quietly move down the hall to the top of the staircase, my boots squeaking a little as I take the stairs. I hear a voice coming from the direction of the dining room and I crouch down, half-crawling down the final few stairs. Reaching the bottom, I stay ducked over and run, my thighs cramping as I make it across the great room. *Almost there.* My back aches and I don't look toward the living room, my eyes on the giant double front doors. *Fifteen feet. Ten.*

"Going somewhere?" The bored drawl has me freezing, one foot in front of the other, my hands gripping my backpack straps in an attempt to keep it from bouncing. I am still hunched over and have to choose between falling over or straightening. I decide to straighten, and brush the hair out of my eyes in as casual a manner as I can manage.

"Oh. Hello. Good morning." I smile, and manage to look everywhere in the room but at him. From just the peripheral, I can see a bare chest. White pants of some sort. He lifts one hand and I dart my eyes to him, prepared for battle.

It's not a weapon, or phone, or Priority envelope. Instead, I see a coffee cup. A large ceramic mug, not delicate or gold-leafed, a logo of some sort on its side. He's getting more butch by the minute. Next thing I know, he'll be wearing trucker hats and spitting tobacco. "Nice mug," I smirk, despite my best attempt to behave.

"You didn't answer my question." He steps closer, the mug lifting to his lips, and I watch as he studies me, his eyes sharp and intelligent as they peer over the top of the mug. Such beautiful eyes. Perfect brows. A messy claw of hair that—even now—looks photoshoot-ready. I flush and look at the door. "Going somewhere?"

"I forgot." I tug at the straps of my backpack and pull them tight. "My grandmother's sick. I have an appointment to take her to, ah, the podiatrist." My lies run together in a spectacular fail.

His mouth curves from behind the mug and he lowers the cup. I try not to look at his chest, the defined cuts of muscle that flex with each movement. "That sounds serious. Is this sick podiatrist appointment here or in Detroit?"

He doesn't believe me. I can hear it in the sarcastic lilt of the question. I don't blame him. If he didn't sniff out that lie, he's an idiot. A painfully beautiful, sexual freak of nature, idiot. I shift my weight from one foot to the other and ignore the question. "Thank you for giving me a place to stay." I extend my hand in the most businesslike way possible. It is a carefully calculated move, designed to entertain and distract him.

It works. He glances down at the hand and his lips tighten, an attempt to contain his amusement. I leave it dangling, and he finally transfers his coffee to his free hand and reaches forward, his palm meeting mine, a stiff shake occurring. When I try to pull back, he holds the contact, lifting my hand to his mouth and placing a kiss on the knuckles.

A smooth move from a gay guy. As smooth as the way his eyes hold mine, the heat in them a reminder of last night. I let my hand drop and edge closer to the door. "Thanks again," I call out, waving at him in the animated way of the mentally unhinged.

"Do you need a ride?" He is barefoot, his feet tan against the white floor.

I step forward and wrap my hand around the door handle. "No, thank you. I'm fine."

He shrugs. "So ... this is goodbye."

He must think me a huge slut. One who hopped into his Rolls Royce, drank all his vodka, and then stripped naked and bounced around his cock. He's probably surprised I'm not asking him for payment. "Yes." The grip of my shoe catches on the lip of the door stop and I half-trip, catching myself on the frame. "Okay. Bye."

"Bye." He crosses his hands over his chest and his biceps pop in a way that probably makes all the gay boys drool. But not me. Nope. I'm leaving, and quickly, so I can get to Manhattan, rescue my stupid letter and then scamper back to Detroit, this entire ridiculous trip, and this tongue-twistingly sexy man, all forgotten. Back to normal life. Back to my search for a normal, non-famous, non-gay, father.

I step onto the front porch and pull the door closed.

CHAPTER 23

MARCO

This woman is a walking disaster. I watch her duck out of the gate and stop at the curb, glancing left and right along the busy road. She got hit by my car, less than twelve hours ago, and now she's playing Frogger for no good reason than to get away from me. I smile at the thought.

Maybe I've lost my touch. The prior woman I fucked was singing my name in tongues before I pulled my cock out of her. This one… this one is odd. Crawling down the staircase and sprinting for the door like she had a Faberge egg hidden in her bra. Hell, maybe she had.

I move to the kitchen, and look out the window, watching as she practically runs down the sidewalk, her attention on her phone, her backpack bouncing. Bouncing.

Her ass bent over before me, the jostle of curves as I drive myself into her, her back rigid, head lifting, my hand fisting in her hair. I lean forward and feel the swing and bounce of her breasts.

I slide my hand down my stomach, under the loose drawstring of my pants, and grip my cock. She'd been incredible. So sexy and confident. She'd laughed in the midst of it, grinned up at me when she'd rolled over. I'd worked my hips, used my fingers and flashed her my own smile when I'd fucked her laughter into a groan, and then a cry of pleasure.

That same woman is now cutting across four lanes of traffic and hopping a ditch. Literally sprinting through the roadside gutters of Spring Lake to avoid accepting a ride from me. Maybe she's mental. That would be my luck.

Actually... I remind myself, that *would* be my luck. I'd wanted a no-strings-attached night of fun. I should be thanking God that she was sprinting out of my life without so much as asking for my number. I take a long sip of coffee, watch her backpack disappear into a crowd of beachgoers, and wonder if I'll ever see her again.

Setting the cup down, I pick up the house phone and press the button for the staff.

"Good morning, sir." A voice I don't recognize speaks crisply into the phone. "How may I serve you?"

"I'd like breakfast in twenty minutes. Vanilla creme French toast and a green juice. I'll eat on the porch."

"Certainly. Is there anything else we may do to assist you?"

"No." I hang up the phone and grab an apple from a bowl on the counter, taking a bite from it as I walk into the great room. The dining room is still a mess, shards of china and glass scattered across the floor. I think of the look in her eyes when I'd walked toward her. The playful lilt in her voice that had turned husky.

I like seeing the mess. It's rare to see things out of order and imperfect. I also know that any of our staff would die before leaving a room in this manner. The mess is proof positive that they obeyed me and stayed out of the house.

"Sir," Edward speaks from behind me. "Will you be dining alone?"

I turn, and his eyes widen as he takes in the mess. "I'm so sorry, sir. We didn't realize—"

I cut him off with a wave of my hand. "It's fine. I lost my temper last night. Just... thinking about everything."

He buys the excuse, his features softening. "Certainly, sir. I myself am struggling without Mr. Horace."

I feel a moment of guilt, a stab of emotion that reminds me that my best friend has died. How quickly I forgot that. She'd fainted in my arms and my sensibilities, my responsibilities, my grief ... it had all dissolved.

"Yes," I answer his earlier question, my eyes moving back over the wreckage, struggling to replace the image of her, her chest heaving, eyes on fire. "I'm eating alone."

———

My lie, from the very beginning, never extended to my parents. It didn't need to. They have a strict aversion to the internet, gossip magazines, and anything invented after the 1960s. They live in a community in the middle of Nevada, drink filtered rainwater, and weave fucking baskets in their spare time. Literally. Fucking baskets. They sell them on the side of the road, out of the back of an El Camino. Their community is all about rediscovering nature, letting go of physical possessions, and talking to the stars. They speak to me every other week or so from a payphone that squats in the middle of their commune. Any day now, some phone company will come to their senses, yank that payphone out of the ground, and I'll have to track them down and force a cell phone down their throats.

I scroll down to the number, execute the call, and put it on speakerphone. It rings, and I cut a neat wedge of French toast and whipped cream, lifting the bite to my mouth. It rings, and I sip my juice, take a wedge of strawberry, and enjoy the view. It rings, and I settle back in the chair, kicking my feet up onto the opposite chair, and push the sunglasses back on my head, getting some sun on my face.

"Yallo." A man speaks, his voice languid and smooth, as if he has taken his sweet time in getting to the phone.

"May I speak to Marilyn or Keith please?" There is movement beside me, and I watch as a chaise lounge is carried onto the deck, an ice bucket set beside it, a towel draped and pillow fluffed. It's almost annoying, the constant attention to my movements, the continual effort at anticipating my slightest needs. *Almost* annoying. I consider moving but don't. I wait, listen to the man sigh, and force myself to remain patient.

Phone calls to my parents are a continual effort in patience. The first hurdle, the one I am slowly crawling over now, is the simple act of getting them to the phone. Chances are that they are in the midst of meditation. Or cooking. Or gathering basket materials. Or doing a celebration of the sun or some other ridiculous act.

"I'm not quite sure where they're at right now." Each word was an unintelligent drawl, the vowels dragging along and bumping into each other, like crowds moving through a turnstile.

"Could you look for them?" I clamp my teeth down in an effort to not scream the words. "It's important."

"You must be their son." A sloth would speak the words quicker than he does.

"Yes. And it's important. Please." God, the next time my parents go off the deep end, I hope they choose a cult that's a little more efficient.

"Okay, okay. Keep your tits on." There is the bump of something against the receiver, and I imagine it being set on top of the booth, the mouthpiece black from use and covered in the germs of a hundred hippie wannabes.

I reach forward and grab my drink. Swirling the juice enough for the contents to mix, I lift the glass to my mouth and finish the contents, wincing at the bite of the ginger.

"Hot towel?" I jump at the voice and turn. Edward extends silver tongs, a rolled white towel gripped in its clutches.

I curse and hold out my hand. "I'm going to put a bell on you."

"Brilliant idea, sir." His features remain slack, and I smile despite myself, dropping the towel back on his tray.

"Marco?" My mother's voice comes through the line and I lift a finger to my mouth, gesturing Edward to be quiet. I point to the house and he retreats, his feet quick across the deck, the glide of the sliding door following his exit.

"Good morning, Mother." I stretch, placing my hands behind my head and linking my fingers.

"What's wrong? Kermit said that it was important."

"That's a joke, right? His name isn't Kermit. Please tell me you aren't sharing space with a man named Kermit."

"Our names don't define us, Marco. They're just labels, placed on us for societal recognition."

I snort in response. She used to work at a bank. She wore pantyhose, and hairspray, and snuck me lollipops from the drive-thru. She ate TV dinners at lunch and read trashy novels before bed. Now, she sleeps in a hammock slung between two trees and has a pet rat. A pet *RAT*.

I hear my father in the background and wait for her to speak to him, her attention diverted for longer than necessary. "Mom."

She ignores me, speaking to him, and I hear the words 'cactus' and 'cleanse.' I glance at the beach and wonder if I should stay another night. It's peaceful here. Private. I close my eyes and I can almost hear the chant of Vince's name from Manhattan. "MOM."

"Yes?"

"Vince passed away."

"Oh dear." She repeats the news to my father, and I hear his voice, suddenly close to the receiver.

"We are energy, Marco. Vince is with you right now. He's in the air, he's on the breeze. Inhale, and he will be inside of you."

"Jesus Christ, Dad." I grimace. "You're not helping."

"He was such a dear friend of yours," Mom chimes in, and her words have that ethereal, spacey tone she's adopted in the last few years. *A dear friend of mine.* She doesn't know it, but she is right. "When is the funeral? We'll come."

"No." My father speaks before I do. "We can't fly with the new moon."

Thank God for the new moon.

"Well, maybe it won't be during the new moon." She hushes him. "Marco, when's the funeral?"

"It was yesterday."

"Oh drat." She sighs. "But your father is right. We wouldn't have been able to fly during the new moon. And tonight, we've got a celebration planned."

There is a beep, and I glance at my phone, my attorney's name displayed on the screen.

"I've got another call coming in. I was just calling to tell you about Vince."

There is a chorus of rushed goodbyes, and I switch lines and answer the other call.

———

"You're kidding me." I pinch the bridge of my nose and listen to the deep tones of John Montreal, Vince's private attorney for the last two decades. "A daughter?"

"That's what this letter says. This isn't a huge surprise. People come out of the woodwork when there is an estate of this size."

"But she's not legitimate, right?"

"Come on, Marco." The man chuckles. "You know Vince better than anyone. Ever seen him with a woman?"

No. Vince had a wandering eye that lingered over every man he saw. But women—unless they were being fitted for one of his designs, they were invisible to him. The idea that he would have sex, an encounter that had the ill fortune to produce a child—impossible. "Who's the girl?"

"We're running a background check on her now. She says her mother and him met at a LiveAid concert in 1985."

A LiveAid concert in 1985? That produces a bit of concern. Vince went to LiveAid in 1985. I've heard his stories. Drugs everywhere. Sex everywhere. In that environment, the thought that his dick could have gotten generous and slipped itself into a woman … I feel a pain in my chest and find my way to the lounge chair, settling in and leaning back. I shield my eyes from the glare and gesture for one of the attendants to pull the umbrella forward.

"So … she's sat on this information until now? 1985 … she's what? Thirty-one? She waited thirty-one years, until five days after his death, and now she wants to be paid?"

"According to this letter, she was adopted. Didn't find her birth mother until six or seven years ago. Never knew the name of her father, just had a photo of him. With Vince being in the press so much in the last few days, she recognized him. It's flimsy at best. As far as any of us know, Vince wasn't even at LiveAid in 1985, and him resembling a thirty-two-year-old photo… doesn't really matter."

143

But he *was* at LiveAid, a fact I decide to, for now, sit on. God, I would kill for a look at that photo. *Adopted.* Something niggles at my brain and I look out on the water, trying to chase down the thought.

Avery, her back straightening, features stiffening. Her admission of being adopted, of being in New York to find her father. She had mentioned something about her mother … finding her. I close my eyes and try to remember the conversation, one I had only been half tuned into. Not that it matters. New York is a city with a billion people, a million adoptees, missing fathers, and discovered mothers. I think of her sprint out the front door, tripping over the stoop, desperate to get away. The tension in me builds.

"Anyway, I just wanted to let you know. We'll handle it on our end, but it will tie up the distribution of the estate for a little while, until we can disprove paternity."

"What's her name?" The question juts out of me, and I can hear the fear in it. I shouldn't be afraid. I'm about to be king of this city, lord of one of the biggest names in fashion. There is no place for fear on the throne.

"Uh…" I grow a year older in the time it takes him to place the name. "Avery McKenna," he finally announces. "From Detroit."

Avery McKenna. From Detroit.

Holy fuck.

I pinch my eyes shut and, if there is a worse woman I could have chosen to fuck last night, I can't imagine her.

———

I drive. I haven't driven in ages, but I get behind the wheel of the Rolls, wave off Edward's protests, and head for the city. On the way, I scan the streets, looking among groups of tourists and kids for a giant backpack and scuffed up combat boots. I think I see her a half-dozen times, but don't. She's been swallowed up by this beach town. Maybe she caught a taxi, is already back in Manhattan, and screwing up my life from there.

I flick my eyes away from the crowds and focus on the road. Finding her, right now, might not be the best course of action. What would I say to her? I can't think of anything; my thoughts taken by the giant vacuum my stupidity has created.

I've been played. She seduced me with those fucking doe eyes and her feminine scent, that nervous vulnerability and those shots of vodka. Did *she* suggest those? Maybe I had. I can't remember, can't remember much from last night other than the taste of her mouth, the way she had melted against my kiss, her hands tugging on my hair, scraping across my skin. God, I'd spent hours on her body.

A body that had been behind our house. Hit by our car. The number of coincidences in this situation are suspiciously high. I think of her pretending to faint, the cagey way she had avoided my questions, the hesitation before giving her name. I'd known Avery Hartsfield hadn't been right, had smelled the lie in that cautious announcement. But I'd still kept her in my car. I'd still taken her to my house, stripped her naked, and let her fucking *see* me. The real me. The man I've hidden from *everyone* for a decade.

And she might be Vince's daughter. Talk about fucking things up in a hundred different ways.

I see the exit for the bridge, cut across four lanes of traffic and almost clip the front bumper of a truck.

I have no one. No one to talk to, no one to ask for help, no one to confide in. Millions of dollars in my bank account, and I can't fucking *buy* advice right now. Maybe I should tell John. He knows about Vince, prepared our contract, knows I'm not really gay. He could give me, at least on the legal front, some sort of awareness of my actions and their consequences.

CHAPTER 23

I watch the flow of traffic ahead of me, roads splitting off and converging, and realize I have no fucking idea how to get around in this town.

CHAPTER 24

AVERY

"I have giant salami in my hand, so make this quick." Marcia's voice rolls through the receiver with all of the dignity of a junkyard squirrel.

"I need the tracking number of the package." I hop out of the taxi and huff across the Manhattan street, narrowly missing death by a Volvo semi. The driver blares the horn, and I show him my middle finger.

"Good morning, Avery." She intones the words, and this is not the time nor place for an etiquette class. "I'm finnnne. Thank you for asking. How are you?"

"I'm in need of a fucking tracking number."

She lets out a long groan. "Good God. I'm cooking right now."

Oh good. I was worried the salami reference was a sexual one, and that's a visual of Andrei that I may never, ever, get out of my head. "Please," I beg. "I'll take you to that shirtless guy restaurant for lunch. Just text me the number."

There is silence, the clatter of a pan, then the agonized grunt of Marcia doing a favor. I stand at the curb, watching traffic blow by, and eye the skyscraper a half block down. I look around for a USPS truck, but don't see one. Maybe I'm not too late. Maybe it'll arrive this afternoon, and I'll be bored and stiff by the time it arrives.

"Okay, I got it." She rattles off the number, then pauses. "But…"

I hate the sound of that word, the regret that coats the syllables. "But what?"

"But… it's been delivered. Was signed for at 9:14 by someone named Waters."

"Shit." I step back from the street and bump into someone.

"It's okay," she offers up. "This is good. Now you will know for sure."

"Yeah." But she doesn't know that seven hours ago, Marco Lent was deep inside of me, his mouth on mine, his hands on my breasts, hips thrusting against mine.

"So, you coming back home?" She speaks through a mouthful of food, and I turn away from the street, squeezing through the crowd and fighting for a clear spot of the sidewalk.

"I don't know." I get through and move north, trying to think through the situation.

"Oh, Andrei wants to talk to you." She says something to him, then he's on the line.

"Avery."

"Hey." I stop and lean back against the wall. "Give me some good news."

"They're running a background check on you."

I curse. "Why?"

"They don't know anything about you. They're wary. Worried about lawsuits and frauds. It's not ridiculous, especially if they grant you access to a paternity test."

Do I even want him to be my father? I think of Marco, his eyes skating along my body, his hips thrusting... he was Vince's lover. For ten years they were practically married. And Vince may be my father? The possibility sours on my tongue.

Maybe I should tell Andrei. It wouldn't take much. He knows who Marco is, understands his role in all of this. I could get it out in one quick sentence. *I slept with Marco last night.* He'll sputter. Ask me to repeat myself. Won't believe me. Probably laugh. And then he can give me advice, let me know how this affects everything, in terms of my possible heredity and stake in Horace's estate.

"You there?" Andrei speaks, and I think again of Marco, of him finding out about the letter. Guilt settles like a weight in my stomach.

I bite my lip, watching a girl with blue hair and a nose ring pass, and swallow the events of last night. "I'm here."

"If they authorize it, you'll need to provide a DNA sample. Mouth swab, or hair, something like that. The head guy..." I hear papers rustle and picture Andrei, his head resting on the tips of his fingers. "Mr. Montreal. He wants to meet with you. I told him you were already in New York."

"What?" I twist a loose piece of hair around my finger. "Why did you tell him that?" Not that it matters. I and my overly friendly vagina haven't exactly been discreet since stepping out of LaGuardia.

"I assumed you would want to knock this out quickly. We don't have a lot of time before steps are taken in the distribution of the estate. If you want a piece of it, we have to move quickly."

If you want a piece of it. It sounds so cold, as if *that* is the reason for all of this. As if my search for my father is secondary to determining who gets to have all of his money.

I push off the wall and look to the left and right, trying to find my bearings. When my eyes move over the skyline, I see a giant image of Vince Horace, one that takes up the entire side of a building, the man on a catwalk, flanked by models. Across the front of the image, two words that take up six floors of space. BE BOLD.

It's a sign. I mean, obviously. It's literally a giant sign. But it's also a sign. *BE BOLD*. I can hear the man speak it from the grave.

I don't know what *Be Bold* means, but I'm pretty sure it doesn't involve me running back to Detroit with my tail between my legs.

I interrupt Andrei, who's babbling about guardians and due diligence. "I'll meet with the attorney. What was his name?"

"Montreal. John Montreal."

"Great. Is it the same address we sent the package to?"

"It is. But Avery, I should come there. I don't like you meeting them without—"

"Just text me a time. I'm not waiting for you to get here, Dre." He starts to say something, and I hold up a hand he can't see. "Just do it."

I end the call, head right, and spot a hotel's sign, sticking out from the next block.

Be Bold.

I was going to *boldly* take a shower and a nap. Buy myself something decent to wear, and give myself one hell of a pep talk.

CHAPTER 25

MARCO

I don't need to be here. I have people for this. Six of them, each billing me hundreds per hour, perched around this table. The suit to my left is my asshole. John Montreal. Previously Vince's and my asshole, in the strictly heterosexual way. He can handle this. Interview the girl, strip her down to nothing and send her off feeling like an idiotic fraud.

The other suits are estate specialists. They've looked over Vince's will, analyzed Avery's letter to the T, and have all but told me that I'm fucked if she is his daughter. Not middle-class-in-Gap-jeans-fucked, but fucked all the same. Goodbye, eight hundred and fifty million dollars. Goodbye full control over the Vince Horace line. If she's his daughter, I'm going to be practically married to the bitch for the rest of my life. Listening to her. Working with her. Pretending that her opinion matters and yielding to it.

If she's his daughter. Talk about a giant IF in a sea of Not Fucking Possible.

"I told him this." John leans forward and growls out the words, stabbing his finger on the desk. "Were you there? I think you were there. I told him this was a risk, and that we needed to put applicable language in it."

Except that Vince *had* put applicable language in. That was the kicker that lubed up my ass and shoved a Budweiser-sized cock inside. Two stupid sentences, buried on page 42.

If an heir, proven by paternity, ever comes forward, any distribution of my assets will be determined and handled by Marco Lent. At minimum, the heir should have a permanent seat on the Board of Directors of Vince Horace, Inc.

He reads my mind. "That paragraph is a legal minefield. Don't worry. I'll protect you."

Of course, he will. At eight hundred dollars an hour, he'll do whatever it takes. "She's not his daughter."

"Of course, she isn't." The door at the end of the room opens, and he stands, fastening the button on his suit jacket. "From Vince? Please."

A secretary steps in, holding the door open, and one by one, all of the men around the table stand. I don't. I stay in the heavy leather chair, in my place at the head of the table. My foot jiggles against the floor, a tap-tap-tap of weakness, and I still it. I shouldn't be nervous. I should be in control. I have nothing to be ashamed of. *Touch your clit. Rub it.* I clamp out the memory and watch as the door swings wider, and the bane of my existence steps into view.

She's changed. Her mess of hair, dark and full, gripped in my fist, is now flat against her head, contained in a low bun. Her combat boots and ripped jeans are gone. She is in low heels, a pencil skirt, and a button-up that screams department store Calvin Klein. It's a costume, one that shouts a little more *good girl* and a lot less *crazy slut*. Or maybe I'm wrong. Maybe last night's outfit was the costume, and this is the original. A dreary conservative with my balls in her pocket. She steps forward, and the introductions begin, hands stuck out, names exchanged.

She makes it around the table, and if she's seen me, she hasn't reacted yet. The bald guy to my right moves and she is there, smiling at him, shaking his hand. I want to reach over and break their connection. Grab her shoulders and ask her what the *fuck* her game is.

"And ... this is Marco Lent." John gestures to me, his voice strained, the introductions of each suit taking entirely too long. I don't rise, don't offer my hand, and when her gaze swings to me, there is a long moment where we only look at each other.

"Mr. Lent." Her eyes drift over me, and when she glances down, I know she is thinking of my cock. "It's a pleasure to meet you."

I'm sure it was. I'd made damn sure of that.

"Miss... McKenna?" I raise my eyebrows. "Funny. Last name doesn't quite suit you." It's a stab at her earlier lie, the fake name she had supplied in the backseat of my car. The stab falls short, and I don't even see the opening I'm giving her until she smiles.

"Maybe that's because it should have been Horace." It is a clean point, one that I inadvertently set up, and I glower in response, watching as the bald guy pulls back his chair for her as if she's the fucking queen of England. She sits, crosses her legs at the ankle, and meets my glare head-on.

"It shouldn't." A weak response from me, and I should be better than this. Prior to her walking in that door, I was certain I *would* be better than this.

I don't like this. I don't like the fact that she doesn't seem afraid. I don't like that, at this angle, her profile reminds me a little bit of Vince's. I don't like *any* of this. Just days ago, I sat in this same room, bored out of my skull, and listened to a long and lengthy recitation of all that I was inheriting. Now, thanks to a *fucking* LiveAid concert and Vince's wandering dick ... the last decade could have been for nothing.

All of it. Ten years of watching a parade of naked men move through our house. Ten years of being practically celibate, focusing on the Vince Horace brand, and being a beard for him. Ten years, and she … this smirking *bitch* of a woman … she might destroy it all. Ruin his legacy. Expose my secret.

She leans forward, her elbows resting on the polished wood surface, and clasps her hands. "Soooo," she says slowly, as if we have all of the time in the world. "You wanted to meet with me?"

"We received your letter, Miss McKenna." John pushes forward her letter, which I've read a dozen times in the last fifteen minutes. It's short and sweet. She thinks Vince is her father and has nothing but a flimsy story and photo as proof.

"I'd like to see the photo," I speak right as she begins to. The interruption irritates her, and I watch as her hands make small fists under the table. That's what I want. I want to see the tiger beneath that conservative costume. I know she's there. A few sharp pokes, and she'll snarl.

She ignores me. Wets her lips and … I lose the first sentence out of her mouth. I'm too distracted by the thought of my dick between those soft lips, the slide of them against my shaft, the way her throat had flexed around my cock—she turns her head and I try to refocus.

"… as interested as you are in the truth." She spreads her hands, and whatever she just said was bullshit. She's here for the money.

"I'd like to see the photo," I speak louder, my voice booming in the room, and when she undoes the top of her bag and reaches inside—her shirt gapes and I can see her bra. Red lace. I know that bra. It is from our current line, the hidden seams holding the piece together, those seams hugging her breasts, pushing them up and in easy access to my mouth. She lifts her head and catches me looking.

She doesn't say anything, but I feel the loss of a small battle, the shift of pawns as my position weakens and hers grows. She's wearing my design, the bra part of my lingerie line, though no outsider would know that. My lines are against her skin, holding up those beautiful breasts, and I can't wipe that image from my mind. Is she wearing the panties too? I think of the lace and satin, and wonder if the cotton lining is damp between her legs.

She straightens, pulling a photo from the bag, and holds it out toward me. It's well worn, the edges weak, the color faded, and I take it, grateful for something to look at, something that isn't flesh and blood, sexuality and lust, temptation packed on cheap two-inch heels. I look down, and lose another battle in just the first glance at it.

It's Vince. He's sitting on a blanket, an elbow resting on one knee. He's smiling, his beard a few days too long, and wearing fucking *jeans*. Everything about the image isn't him. Dirt on his clothes. Product-free hair. A casual smile. I would have told you that he'd die before wearing pants with that cheap cut. I'd have bet my left nut that Vince Horace never had this level of grime on his hands, or a canteen hanging off a loop on his belt.

And I'd have lost that nut because it's him. I know it the moment I look at his hand, the one dead center in the photo. On that dirty hand, one that grips a cowboy hat as if he plans on wearing it, is a ring. A ring I've seen a hundred times. A ring I *know*.

I set down the photo and slide it back to her. "Nice picture. Could be anyone."

"I don't think so." She doesn't glance down at it, her eyes tight to mine. "I think it's him."

I snort, leaning back in the chair and smoothing down the front of my suit, reassured by the weight of the expensive fabric, the fall of perfectly cut and tailored lines. "You've got a grimy old photo and you expect us to just… what?" I raise my hands and lock them behind my head. "What are you wanting? Money? I can stroke you a check right now, and you can be on your way. You aren't worth the time in my day that you're wasting."

"Marco," John cautions, and I ignore him, pinning her with an expectant stare. "What do you want from *me*?" I clearly enunciated each vowel and watch as her hands uncoil beneath the table, her eyes flashing. Her chair jerks a little as she stiffens.

There. Tiger unveiled. Ready for battle.

"I don't want anything from *you*," she seethes. "I want to know who my father is."

I laugh. "So, that's it? Just a girl looking for her daddy. And you think your daddy was Vince Fucking Horace. Of all people in the world." I wave my hand in the air and she glares at me with a look that could cut wool.

"Not to state the obvious," John interrupts. "But you do realize that Mr. Horace was a homosexual man, a lifestyle he carried on for his entire life. The likelihood of him having a sexual relationship with a woman…" He parts his hands in the air. "It's very unlikely."

"Is it?" She spins her chair to face me, her eyebrows raising. "What do you think, Mr. Lent?"

I say nothing, but I don't like where this is going.

"Do you think it's 'very unlikely' for a gay man to have sex with a woman?" God, I want to stuff my cock past those lips. I want to grip the back of her head and go slowly, her nails digging into the cheeks of my ass, her eyes on mine as her tongue presses against my shaft.

"I think alcohol can make a lot of people do unlikely things," I speak evenly, but feel the scratch of the tally as she gains another point.

"I mean—" she shrugs, her hands raising in an innocent gesture. "You're a gay man, right?" She glances at the other men around the table. "I'm new to this situation, but I believe that you and Mr. Horace were—"

"Partners." I clear my throat and pick up the gold pen that sits on the portfolio before me. "Yes. We were."

"So, you're gay. Right?" She leans forward, perching her elbow on the table and resting her chin on her fist, looking at me with mock interest.

"I'm not sure what the relevance is, Miss McKenna." John clears his throat. "Mr. Lent is not the subject of today's meeting. You are."

I hold up a hand to stop him. "If you don't mind, I'd like to speak to her alone."

John looks at me as if I've lost my damn mind. "Marco," he lowers his voice and leans forward. "I strongly suggest—"

"Wait outside." I nod to the other men. "I'll let you know when you can come back in."

I don't look at her. I stare down the table and watch as the men, one by one, rise to their feet and leave the conference room. John is the last to go, and he takes his dear sweet time, buttoning his jacket and fixing me with a long look of warning. I don't know what damage he thinks I could do. This situation, unbeknownst to him, is already fucked up beyond belief. When he shuts the door, the heavy oak clicking into place with a finality that echoes, I swivel my chair until I face her fully.

"Drop the act. What do you want?"

"I told you. I want to know—"

"Bullshit." My hands tighten on the arm of the chair, and I fight the urge to stand. "You're a blackmailer."

"What?!" She seems bewildered, and I don't buy it. "I'm not here to blackmail you."

"So, you *genuinely* think that you are Vince Horace's daughter?"

"Yes." Her eyes dart to the side, and I can smell the lie. She doesn't think she's his daughter. Or, she's not convinced of it.

"And you wanted to fuck Daddy's boyfriend? Is that what last night was?"

"Gross!" She pushes away from the table and stands. "No." She crosses her arms in front of her. "Last night was ... I just wanted to know more about him."

"Funny, I don't remember you asking many questions about him."

"Yeah, well." She turns her head away, as if the far end of the conference room was interesting.

"Yeah, well... what?" I move closer, and despite the clothes, the hair, she smells the same. If I strip her naked, pull out her bun, and kiss the lipstick off that mouth, she'll look the same as yesterday. Gasp the same. Come the same.

"Nothing." She tightens the cross of her arms over her chest. "You're very ... distracting. I'm sure you know that."

Distracting. Vince had called me that more than a few times. From him, it'd been a playful compliment. From her, it's an excuse, one designed to elude.

"Besides, I thought you were gay." She turns to me, and the bump of her elbows brushes against my chest.

"I am gay."

"Are you sure?" She lifts her chin and the desire to kiss her is overwhelming.

"What were you doing in that alley behind the house?"

"Trying to get inside."

I blink at the quick honesty, then stab out while she is telling the truth.

"Did you get hit by the Rolls on purpose?"

"Yes."

"Did you like it when I fucked you?"

She inhales, a quick intake before she answers. "Very much."

Two words that destroy my world. I step back and slide my hands into the pockets of my pants. Turn away from her and fight to find my bearings.

CHAPTER 26

AVERY

I don't understand this man. He turns away, and I can't tell if he wants to kiss or throttle me. I've been off kilter since I walked in and saw him sitting at the end of the table, as if on a throne. I look down at the photo I've memorized every inch of. Before walking in, I'd been sure that the man had favored Vince Horace. But now, seeing the way that Marco had scoffed at it, I see it in another light. A faded photo, three decades old. A flimsy thing to build a paternity case on.

"I came to New York to stop the letter." I turn and he stills, his hands in his pocket, his head lifting to listen. "My attorney sent the letter, and I panicked. I thought I was being stupid, and…" I search for the right word. "Naive. So, I came here to try and get the package before it was delivered this morning."

He stays in place, and I hate his silence. I hate the stupid look of that suit, the way it hugs his build, the slick sheen of the fabric, the way it falls perfectly without a flaw.

"Go on."

I swallow. "I wasn't expecting you to be in the alley. When your car pulled out of the garage, I didn't think. I just…"

"You just jumped in front of a moving vehicle." He turns, but keeps his distance, stepping closer to the window.

I grimace. When put like that, it sounds stupid. "Kind of."

"That's exactly what you did."

"Okay, yes," I amend. "I jumped in front of the car."

"You lied to me."

"You told me you were an architect!" I sputter out the words. "And you failed to mention that you were GAY!"

"Which you already knew," he counters.

"But *you* didn't know I knew."

He looks up at the ceiling and blows out a frustrated breath. "If you came to New York to stop the letter, then … what? You overslept?"

"Yes."

He shrugs. "So, then I kill the letter. Shred it. You can take our jet home. Problem solved."

He's right. My panic from earlier, my mad rush across Spring Lake to get the package—we could just pretend it all never happened. I could be back home in a few hours, pulling on a pair of fuzzy socks, releasing my hair from this hell of a bun, and life could be back to normal.

Except I still wouldn't know who my father was.

Except I'd still always wonder.

Except that BE BOLD doesn't mean a free ride home on the Horace jet.

"What? You don't like that idea?"

I shake my head and don't trust my voice. What can I even say? That I promised a brick poster that I'd try harder?

"God, you're infuriating." He stops in front of a bank of windows and rests his hands on the ledge of the sill. Looks out the window and says nothing.

I *am* infuriating. God, I'm infuriating *myself*. I don't know what I want, other than I want to know something. I want to know, without a doubt, that Vince Horace is, or isn't, my father. And I thought that could be easy, thought that one letter from Andrei could start some process in motion and I could just wait a few weeks and then get a letter in the mail. Task done. Question answered.

But now, with the stack of attorneys in this meeting, with him glaring at me as if I've killed his puppy, it doesn't seem simple.

"Are you wearing the panties that match that bra?"

He is still facing away from me when he asks the question.

I shift and swallow, thinking of the small Vince Horace VH boutique I'd found, their lingerie department dominated by a life-size poster of Marco, one where he grinned at the camera, a bra hanging from his mouth. Emboldened, I'd skipped their cotton conservative options and gone straight for the sinful section.

I'd considered the selections and thought that the red and gold number would bring me courage. I hadn't planned for his eyes to find the bra. I hadn't expected my skin to heat, our eyes to hold, my mind to go haywire.

I'd thought we were past that, and back on solid footing that moves toward a common goal. He asks that question and we are right back at his house, in the crazy mindset where hands yank at clothing, lips find each other, and sensibilities fly out the window.

"I'm just curious." He straightens and steps away from the window, swiveling on the soles of his dress boots. Wandering around the conference table, the space between us widening.

"Curious?" I follow him with my eyes.

"I'm curious how far you plan to take this ridiculous seduction attempt."

My jaw literally drops. I can feel the gape of my mouth and I snap it shut. "You think I wore this to *seduce* you? I didn't even know you would be here."

"Plenty of other men in the room." He smiles in the most condescending manner possible, and it'd be a waste to break that beautiful nose, but I'd do it. A quick upward jab would do wonders for that smirk.

I'm not going to take his bait. I know that's what this is. He's goading me and a reaction other than cool dismissal would be wrong.

"Fuck you." Okay, so cool dismissal didn't win out that time. That's okay. I smooth down the front of my dress shirt and take a deep breath, irritated with his easy ability to get under my skin and fuck everything up. I shouldn't be the one flustered. He's the one who has acted inappropriately. He's the one who—well, maybe last night had been a joint event.

"Fuck you..." he repeats slowly. "An interesting notion, but I've done that. The experience wasn't good enough for a repeat performance. I think I'll just go back to men."

The comment, deliberately meant to provoke, still stings like a hot knife. I turn away, walking to the same window he had looked out of, and release a breath. "Are you always such an ass?"

"Yes." I hear the squeak of a chair. "And it is in the interest of continuity that I must insist that you go back to your shithole of a city and let the big boys handle it from here."

I turn and stare at him, wondering if he is intentionally goading me into digging my heels into the New York City ground and stay, or if he genuinely expects that directive to get him somewhere. "The big boys?" I repeat.

"Yes." He smiles. "You know what big means, right?" He tilts his head to the side as if he's thinking. "I *think* that's the word you used last night. Big? Or was it huge?"

"Your dick has nothing to do with this conversation."

"It doesn't?" He frowns. "That's interesting. So, what exactly *was* the purpose of getting me drunk and forcing yourself on me last night?"

"Whaaat? I-I-I-" My words jumble into a knot, unable to string together a coherent response. "That's a joke, right? You're joking."

"Oh, I'm not joking." His smile drops and he looks at me as if he is actually serious. "I don't know whether to blame it on the alcohol or on pity, but whatever you pulled on me last night was bullshit, and I don't appreciate it."

"You don't *appreciate* it? You seemed to *appreciate* it just fine when you were breaking me in half with your cock!" The response explodes out of me, louder than I had intended, and we both glance toward the closed conference room door. When our eyes meet again, his jaw is tight, his lips thin, and any humor is gone from his features.

"Vince is—*was*—gay. Not gay like me, where I can manage to fuck a girl and come. *Gay.* I spent ten years in his bed. Ten. *Years.* I ate breakfast with him every morning. Traveled the world with him. Listened to every story and chimed in on every decision. We went to orgies together, for fuck's sake. All male fuckfests. He was GAY. He wanted me, not…" He reaches forward and jabs a finger onto the photo, onto my mother's face. "Not this corn-fed hick."

Not gay like me, where I can manage to fuck a girl and come.

I think of his fingers between my legs, the hungry way his mouth had

165

met mine, the pant of his breath in the dark, the rigid bob of that cock, the hiss he had made when he pushed inside of me.

I'm not crazy. He can say whatever he wants, but I'm still sore from him, I can still remember every detail of last night, and he didn't *manage to fuck me and come.* He'd been desperate for it.

"I think…" He closes his eyes and collects himself. When he opens them, his voice is calm and measured, with almost an eerie level of control. "I think that you are taking this as some sort of a game. This is *not* a game. This is my life and your intrusion in it has seriously fucked things up for me. If all that you care about is whether Vince is your father, then you need to step away from the situation now. Let the estate settle and then come back to me in a few months and we can determine paternity."

I don't know how to respond. I don't really even know what I want anymore. Is my paternity the only thing that I am here for? Will I be fine with getting the news that Vince is my father and walking away? He may not be, and that will end everything. But if he is… if he *is* my father, then what?

"I can't do that," I say. "I can't walk away right now. I've spent the last couple of days with this hope—" My voice cracks on the word and I hate showing him that bit of weakness. "You don't know what it's like to spend years searching every stranger's face to see if they are your father, to see if they bear any resemblance to him. I realize that I look crazy. I realize that this is a long shot. You probably think that last night was some attempt to coerce you in some way, but even if this is a slim chance, it's the only one I have. This is—he is—the only man, in the years since I got this photo, that actually looks like him. All I'm asking is for you to help me cross him off as a possibility."

He studies my face and I watch a muscle in his jaw twitch. He looks down at the photo, my finger still pinned to the man's face, and then back up at me. "We can't just give DNA samples to every person who shows up. Not when all that you have is a photo, and some story that we can't validate. And what if we knew, with absolute certainty, that this was Vince?" He shrugs. "So, what? He's sitting on a log with three other people. And your mother, who supposedly told you this story, is dead. *Right?* Didn't even know his name, *right?*"

He spits out the words as if they are arrows, and they land where he points them, deflating my hope, piercing my heart, and wounding my pride.

"He was *gay*. Your mother probably fucked five guys that weekend and came home with one photo. Pointed out a guy and told you he's your father. You've got one story and I've got ten years, plus forty more of a well-documented lifestyle, one that never mentions LiveAid, or a random fling with a woman. So, no. I'm not giving you his blood. And I'm not letting you ruin his legacy."

He steps closer, and where I felt sexual tension before, I only feel threatened now. "You chase this down, Avery, and tomorrow I'll have a team in Detroit. They'll pull apart every piece of your life, and dig out every secret you've got buried. They'll find your mother and your adoptive parents, and do the same thing there. I've got eight hundred and fifty million reasons to bury you and your photo in a scandal. Give your mother, and *whoever* your real father is, some respect. Give up this stupid theory and *go home.*"

He pushes the photo against my chest, the force of it almost pushing me back. Turning away, he strides to the door and leaves.

CHAPTER 27

MARCO

Friday nights used to be reserved for orgies. It always started in the basement grotto, around and in the pool, the blue stretch of sexual perversion, the cool depths filled with Manhattan's most beautiful bodies—men and women alike, their naked figures glowing in the pale lighting, their playful shrieks growing more carnal as the night progressed and more champagne popped. Vince loved it all, the beauty of a woman's body, the strength of a man's—and he would drink and flirt and swim until the moment when we would move upstairs and leave them all to their debauchery.

I hated Fridays, grew bored with the constant buffet of naked bodies and men, the offers, the pressures, the *harassment* that comes with having a body and cock that no one is allowed to play with. Tell a woman or gay man they can't touch something? Might as well dip it in gold and dust cocaine over it.

And I was always untouchable, that rule established from that first moment in that bathroom. I was Vince's, no one else's. And he was mine. We were not a couple that swapped or shared. And it was, as he so often told me, none of their fucking business what we did with each other when we were alone.

Now, I step into the pool area and try to remember the last Friday party we had. It was before that France trip, the one where Vince got dizzy, and I got worried, and we visited that clinic in Paris. That was the trip where a cautionary MRI delivered bad news, and we came back home with a ticking timeline. A timeline that had been wrong, overly optimistic, his expiration date one that all the money in the world couldn't extend.

Ten months ago? Was that all that it had been? The door behind me opens and I see Paul, one of the house butlers, pause in the opening. "Will you be taking a swim?" He hesitates. "I can heat towels and prepare the sauna."

"No." I shake my head. "I'm going to head to bed."

"Certainly. Shall I close the kitchen for the evening?"

I nod, turning back to the pool and watching the water lazily spin. Vince had loved this pool, used to swim laps each evening in it. We'd often settled painful decisions with a race, our talent closely matched despite the differences in our age. He had called it his 'fountain of youth', a phrase always delivered with a wry smile, the joke as much about the parties as the health benefits.

Now, the joke falls flat. I look up and think of the six floors above me, the staff on every level, plumping pillows, dusting surfaces, and waiting for their next service opportunity.

Live well, he had said.

I think of Avery, and wonder what she is doing.

———

I didn't have to be such a dick. I knew that, even as I was slinging out insults and threats. I could have been nicer to her. But over the last decade, being a dick has become my armor. It's kept any staff from becoming my friends, anyone from getting too close. Building a wall between myself and the outside world has been the easiest way to keep my secret safe. And Vince actually liked my prickly persona. He liked being the nice one, out of the two of us. He liked being the only one who could make me smile. He liked the air of unattainability that I portrayed. And he liked when I was his watchdog, his protector of privacy, his spiked fence that kept the commoners at bay.

He was always the good cop and I was always the bad, and it's hard to turn off that switch just because he is dead.

I step into the elevator, select the button for the top floor, and lean against the wall. As it climbs, I think of her face, the way her pupils had grown, her face had paled. She is probably on the plane to Detroit now, squished between fat businessmen, a half-eaten bag of cashews on her lap, one of those stupid pillows cradling her neck. Or maybe she has landed, her combat boots weaving through a crowded terminal, on the way to her car.

It's good for both of us that she leave. I meant everything I said. I'll rip apart the privacy of her life, and her family, and her friends. I have, as I mentioned to her, eight hundred and fifty million reasons to do so.

All she has is a photo.

The elevator quietly dings, coming to a stop on our floor, and I step out. The doors to the master suite are open, but I ignore them and head for the dressing room. Stepping in, dim lights illuminate the rows of clothing, half of them protected by glass cabinets.

"What's with the ring?" I grip my arms tightly and look out on the water, my breath fogging the air, the tips of my ears smarting from the wind.

Vince glances down at his hand and pulls the cigar closer, holding it between his lips and flicking the lighter's starter. He says nothing, attempting to light the cigar, and once he does, he inhales sharply, then passes it to me. "Hold this."

He pulls on his gloves, the right, then the left, and the ring disappears beneath Italian leather and fur. "It was my brother's."

"I didn't know you had a brother." I puff on the cigar and watch the water, an iceberg materializing in the dark, one five times bigger than our ship.

"Yep." He finishes, and holds out his hand, taking the cigar back. "He died when I was in Japan. Got hit by a drunk driver when jogging."

I wince as I jump up and down a bit, trying to stay warm. "I'm sorry, V."

He shrugs. "You know how it is. Decades pass before you know it. Time fades everything." He sucks on the end of the cigar, then glances down at it. "Is this one of the Gurkha's? It tastes odd."

"I don't know. That's what they gave me. It's fucking freezing out here."

And that was it, two sentences that shared a piece of him I hadn't known. Two sentences in the middle of Iceland.

I open the first jewelry drawer and look over the rings. He hadn't been a big ring wearer. It was why the band—a cheap silver piece stamped with a pattern of sorts—had stood out to me. It hadn't looked like him, hadn't fit any of the fashion molds he so staunchly adhered to.

I find the band, exactly where it is supposed to be, in the first row. Pulling it out, I flip it over on my palm, surprised at how light it is.

I think of the Vince I know, a man so different from the wild and unkempt man on that image. And yet … this ring. I close my hand around it and push the drawer in. Turning slowly, I survey the room, looking for somewhere to hide the piece of evidence.

———

"You can't fuck her."

I turn at the statement, a glass of brandy half raised to my mouth. "Excuse me?"

"The girl from Detroit. The one that you kept adjusting yourself in the meeting for. You can't fuck her." John Montreal stands in the doorway of the library, his jacket hanging from one arm, his tie undone, face drawn. In this moment, he doesn't look like one of the city's most powerful attorneys. At this point, he looks like he's been run over by a train.

"I wasn't adjusting myself." I make a face, then tilt the glass back, taking all of it in one fluid shot.

"Please." He tosses his jacket on the bar and nods at Tony. "Give me two of whatever he's having. And then give us some privacy."

I smirk, watching the shots hit the bar top, the ice cubes quickly distributed. "You can't hang with me, old man."

"Hey." He points at me in warning. "Respect your elders."

It's funny since he doesn't have much age on me. Maybe ten years, max. Compared to Vince, he's practically my age. I say so and he shakes his head. "I've got at least three times the wisdom as you. You've got to factor that in."

I ignore that logic and push my empty glass next to his two, watching as it fills. "Thanks, Tony."

"You got it, boss." He wipes down the bar and leaves, ducking out of the back of the room and leaving the two of us alone.

I glance at John. "Why do I feel as if I'm in the principal's office?"

He takes a hefty sip of the first drink, holds the liquor on his tongue for a long moment, then swallows. "I'm going to cut your dick off if you don't keep your hands to yourself with her. She's fifty different types of liability, all rolled into that sexy body." He looks at me. "You understand?"

"It's not that there's anything illegal about what you and Vince did. Or that any part of it would void this will. But I don't have to tell you how bad it will look if this gets out. I don't want that to be his legacy."

"You think I do?" I sit on the closest stool and run a rough hand through my hair. "But I don't want it to be my sentence for the rest of my life either."

"You knew this. You knew, when you agreed to all of this, what you were signing up for."

But I didn't expect Vince to die so young. I thought I'd be old by the time he passed. And I didn't think I'd be tempted. That was the truth of the matter. I thought, for the rest of my life, that I'd be happy with occasional fucks with strangers that I'd never see again. I thought I'd be happy with a life that didn't involve love, or a relationship, or anything to that extent. I always had been before. I had never, not in the twenty-six years before I met Vince, had the desire for any of that. I had been, for my first two decades of life, cold and heartless. And I assumed I always would be.

But now, just five days after Vince's death, I've fucked a stranger and am twisting in the wind. It feels like an anvil is on my chest, pinning me to the ground, and the thought of hiding my sexuality for the rest of my life ... it kills me.

How did everything change so quickly?

I lean forward, my forearms sharp against the wood. "I don't know. Ignore what I'm saying. It's probably the grief talking. I just ... I need a few days to wrap my head around this."

"But you understand why you need to stay away from this woman."

I keep my head down, scraping my nails along my scalp, and wonder how much to tell him. On one hand, I could use the advice. On the other hand, my pride is taking one hell of a hit with this one. I finally look up and meet his tired eyes. "It may... be too late for that."

For a man trained to not react, he does a poor job. "It's been four hours, Marco. What did you do, trip her in the parking lot with your dick?"

I scowl. "No. It was—before that. Before I knew who she was. I met her on the street by our house. She needed a ride. One thing … one thing led to another."

"And you had sex with her?"

"Yes."

"Fuck me." He walks around the bar, grabs the first bottle he sees, and pours a generous helping into his glass. "You have no idea—"

"I have every idea," I interrupt. "Trust me. All I've been doing, since I found out who she was, has been envisioning the possibilities. You think I don't understand what's at stake?"

"So, she knows you're straight." He throws back the glass, his Adam's apple bobbing. When he sets it down, he smacks his lips and hisses at the burn, a quarter of the drink now gone.

"No," I say, correcting him. "I don't think she thinks I'm straight. I don't know… *fuck*. I don't know what she thinks. But she hasn't accused me of being straight. And, it doesn't matter. If it comes to that, we have the contract between me and Vince."

"And if she goes to the press, what then? What if she isn't his daughter, and she gets pissed, goes on tilt, and goes to the press? Or blackmails you?"

Blackmail. That's the main thing that has haunted me, ever since hearing her name. He's right. It's a valid concern. And, whether that was her intention all along or a big fat present that landed in her lap, it doesn't matter. She'd be blind not to see it. And what would I pay to keep this secret?

Ten million? Fifty million? A Hundred?

CHAPTER 28

AVERY

"I can't take any more, Andrei. I don't have jobs for them." I scroll through the list of women and feel sick to my stomach. Forty-two of them. Forty-two women, arriving in JFK in a week, with nowhere to go. "I don't understand how this happened. Is this Koruk's fault?"

"I don't know where the communication broke down. I just know I've got a stack of approved visa applications with next week's date on them."

Fuck. I need to be home. I need to be finding roommates and calling clients, finding forty-two openings that I can fit them into to. "Let me work on this."

"I'm sorry. I hate to throw this on you."

"I'll figure it out." I hang up the phone and push the thought of the arrivals out of my head, reaching forward and pressing play on the video. I watch the footage, Marco's words still ringing in my mind.

"Vince is—was—gay. Not gay like me, where I can manage to fuck a girl and come. Gay. I spent ten years in his bed. Ten. Years. I ate breakfast with him

every morning. Traveled the world with him. Listened to every story and chimed in on every decision. We went to orgies together, for fuck's sake. All male fuckfests. He was GAY. He wanted me, not...not this corn-fed hick."

I rewind and rewatch the video, a short clip where Vince Horace grips Marco's neck and leans over, kissing him on the cheek. He pauses, his face still close to Marco's, and there is a moment where the men lock eyes. Marco says something, and Vince smiles. They turn back to the crowd. I rewind the clip, press play, and watch it again.

I don't know what I'm looking for. It's the twentieth clip I've watched, and they are all the same. Two men: affectionate with each other. I can't find a torrid lip lock or a grope, but none of these events are places where I'd expect it. All of these clips are from stages, interviews, awards and fashion shows.

I close the laptop, pushing it away from me. I kick a foot free of the blanket and lay back, squishing the pillow underneath my head and looking up at the ceiling. I don't know why I'm still here. I was at the airport, had a ticket in hand, and couldn't get on the plane. I just stood there, like an idiot, elbowed and jostled by anxious passengers, all bottle-necking toward the gate. I couldn't do it. I couldn't get on the plane and run away with my tail tucked in between my legs.

I'm not Marco Lent's toy to boss around.

I'm not crazy.

And I'm not the sort to be scared off.

But... I'm also not willing to put my life in jeopardy. And I'm not ready for whatever wrecking ball he's threatening to smash into my business and into the lives of the women who trust me. If something happens to me, if police bust in and discover everything, they will be deported, I'll be shut down, and Ivan K, or some other asshole, will take my place.

I can't let that happen, yet here I am, still in this city, my stubbornness putting them at risk.

Is it wrong for me to want to know who my father is? Sure, Vince Horace is gay. But so is Marco Lent. And the soreness between my legs is proof that gay men can make mistakes. Gay men can be tempted. Gay men can have moments of insanity.

I roll over in bed, curl my knees to my chest, and think of tomorrow. I have no idea what I'll do. Maybe in the morning, this fight won't seem worth the risk. Maybe then, retreating will seem like a better option, and my stubbornness will—for *once* in my life—conveniently yield.

I close my eyes and think of him. His hands on my hips, his cock inside me. Thick. Filling me up. The lift of his torso as he brought his mouth to my breasts, pressed kisses along their curves and sucked a nipple into his mouth. So different from the man who had squared off against me in that conference room. I close my eyes and the need aches in between my legs.

CHAPTER 29

MARCO

"God, you're spoiled."

I turn in my seat and watch John step into the kitchen, his pressed suit and clean shave giving away none of his rough night, one that had involved way too much alcohol and stories of Vince that had made my cheeks hurt from smiling. Now, only my head hurts. I reach over and slap the stool next to me. "Sit down. Paul will hook you up."

The attorney settles on the stool, looking for a place to hang his jacket, and one of the attendants materializes. "Thanks." Pulling up to the island, he glances across the counter and nods to the chef. "Are you Paul?"

"Yes, sir. I'm making Mr. Lent a crab cake omelet, would you care for one?"

"That would be very nice, thank you."

"Get him a juice too." I lift my glass and catch the eye of the prep chef. "Extra beets."

"I don't like beets," John grumbles, leaning back as a napkin is placed in his lap.

"Yeah, but your hangover will."

Paul pushes forward a plate of sliced pears, each topped with blue cheese and wrapped in prosciutto. "For the meantime."

"Jesus." John reaches forward and lifts one from the plate. "You know someone *dry-cleaned* my suit and shined my shoes last night? And there was a guy in my bathroom this morning."

"You don't have bathroom attendants at your house?" I grin, and wince at the pain that stabs my temple.

"Go ahead and laugh. If I didn't have my bachelor lifestyle to protect, I'd move in." He eyes the chilled glass that is set before him, picking it up as tentatively as a child approaching broccoli. "You got a tablet somewhere? The background check on your girlfriend came in."

"They'll grab one." I chew through a pear and grab my own juice —an orange and carrot blend—ignoring his "girlfriend" reference. "Know anything about it yet?"

"I tried to open it on my phone, but the file was too big. My assistant didn't say anything about it."

I watch as Paul lifts the skillet and grabs a plate. "You haven't gotten anything from her attorney yet?"

"Nope." He checks his phone. "As of right now, they are still wanting to move forward. Maybe you weren't as convincing as you thought."

A tablet is presented, unlocked and placed before him. "Thanks."

He's got to quit thanking the staff. At this rate, they'll get used to it and his tongue will fall off from overuse. I say so, and he chuckles, not looking at me as he logs into his email. "You're a prick, you know that?"

I shrug, finishing off the last of my juice and pushing it forward. "We pay them well enough to make up for it." *I. I* pay them well enough. How long will it take for my mind to understand that Vince is gone?

"Huh." He peers at the tablet, his finger scrolling down a document.

"What?" I hold out my hand for the tablet.

He waves me off. "Wait a second. Let me finish it."

It's an agonizingly long wait, one I pass by taking a piss. By the time I return to the kitchen, the tablet is in front of my seat and he's eating, his fork scraping the china.

"What's the verdict?" I sit down and pick up the device.

"Your girl's a criminal."

"No shit?" I scan over the first page, which is a bunch of boring content. Height. Weight. Hospital of birth. I scroll down.

"Mostly underage stuff. Assault. Ran away from a prep school when she was fifteen. Petty theft. Looks like she has ties to some gangsters in Detroit."

"I didn't think gangsters still existed."

He laughs. "Really? The pretty boy with the heated socks next to his bed each morning doesn't know about the criminal underbelly of society?"

"Hey—" I say sharply, looking up. "Don't tell me you didn't like that. *Everyone* likes the heated socks. Those are Vince Horace cashmere, by the way. You could sell those on eBay if you're hard up for cash." And they're perfection, even if they fall apart on the sixth or seventh wearing. There is a reason no one buys the damn things, other than us. At two hundred dollars a pair, people have this ridiculous expectation of longevity. In socks. *Socks.* I don't get it. You're either rich or you're not. Either wear nine-dollar Gold Toes, or spoil your fucking feet.

I see the first arrest and stop scrolling. *Picked up on suspicion of prostitution.* "She's a hooker?" Oh my god. I got rolled by a fucking hooker and I fucked her without a condom. I've been sitting here, with a dick that's probably about to—

"No. Read on. She was *with* a hooker, got into an argument with some pimp and someone called the cops. It got cleared up at the station. Do you have any—oh, thank you." He takes the butter.

"Shall I butter your bread, sir?"

He hesitates, a piece of toast in hand. "Ah, no. Thank you. I'll do it."

"So, she's not a prostitute."

"Nah." He swipes a healthy amount of butter across the toast. "Unfortunately for us. I mean—if there's a case." When I glare at him, he laughs, holding the toast up. "What? My loyalty is to the estate, not to your—" He glances at the busy kitchen and stops the statement. "Keep reading."

Avery McKenna's second brush with the law was a year later when she was arrested for disorderly and lewd behavior. New Orleans. March, 2012. This time I read the notes before asking John. *McKenna was exposing her breasts to the crowd. Got into a verbal altercation with officer, then offered him sexual favors. Subject says she was joking.*

"God. How much more of this is there?"

"You gotten to New Orleans yet?"

"Yeah."

"Just one more. It's interesting." He pushes off the stool and comes to stand behind me, looking over my shoulder.

Seizure of cash. Two years ago. Looks like a traffic stop found… seventy thousand dollars in cash. They seized it until she could prove the source of the cash. *McKenna showed bank withdrawals equaling a sum greater than the amount, dated one month earlier, and the funds were returned.* "What's up with that?"

"I don't know. Drugs, if I have to guess. Whatever it is, it's good for us —something to lean on her with."

"Yeah."

"Keep scrolling down, to her assets."

I scroll down, seeing three parcel IDs. I click on the first one.

"What is ... an apartment complex? That's random."

"She paid three million for it. There's a second one that she paid almost five for. Apparently, she's in the housing business."

So, fund ... whatever the fuck she had called it ... that was a lie. I click on the third property, which looks to be her house. Three bedrooms, three bathrooms. Paid ... I scroll down. Two hundred and nine thousand for, six years ago.

The questions mount and Avery McKenna—Rolls Royce kamikaze, seducer of gay men, fighter of pimps, and real estate mogul—just became a lot more interesting.

I push aside the tablet.

"So, the bad news is, she's not broke. She's got the funds to fight us on this. And you know..." John sits forward, picking up a fork and turning to me. "It may just be easier to have a paternity test and be done with this, without having to get nasty."

"We order a paternity test and we're risking press, and giving her claim validity. She's got a fucking photo, John. Nothing else. A photo that looks vaguely like Vince."

He looks at me, and in those bloodshot eyes, I see a hint of fear. "It's more than vague, Marco. It looks a hell of a lot like him."

"He wasn't at LiveAid," I insist, and the lie feels sour on my tongue. I shove a bit of egg and crab in and furiously chew.

"You sure of that?" He fixes me with a stare, and we—I—don't pay this guy to cross-examine me.

"We're not doing the paternity test." I turn back to my plate. "And you'll hear from her attorney today. It'll be done. She'll be gone." I rip off a chunk of toast and avoid his eyes.

Behind me, there is the clearing of an ancient throat, and I turn to see Edward, who I swear to fucking God has a smirk on his face. "Mr. Lent, you have a guest at the front door. A Miss Avery McKenna."

———

"I can stay." John speaks in a hushed whisper, as we walk down the wide hall and toward the front parlor.

"You don't need to stay."

"I kind of do."

I ignore him, rounding the corner and striding down the wide hall, my dress boots clicking against the marble floor. On either side of us, Warhols line the hall. "Go. Go handle all of the things that need covering for me right now. I'll speak to her. I can handle this."

"Actually, you *can't* handle this, or we wouldn't be in this situation." He grips my arm and maneuvers in front of me, blocking my path. "We need to have an organized, united front, and we can do that through letters and documentation, and phone calls to her attorney. Believe me when I say that nothing good can come from the two of you having a conversation."

"I disagree." I reach down and rip his hand free of my arm. "Now, *go*. I'll call you this afternoon."

He stays in place and stares at me as if he can control me with just the force of a glare. Our footing is uneven, him and I, our relationship—sans Vince—still new. He is used to ten years of me being the subordinate who rarely speaks. But that is no longer my role and if it takes me physically throwing him out of my house to prove it, I will. Right now, I'm not entirely sane. Right now, I'm unraveling at the seams.

"Fine." He lifts his hands in surrender, his palms facing me. "I'll go. Just, for God's sake—don't touch her." He hesitates, steps back, then stalks off.

Edward waits, one hand on the door to the parlor, and raises a dignified brow. "Shall we, sir?"

"Yes." I bite out. "I think we shall."

She's sitting in the parlor, framed by original Monets, worth two million each. She's back in ripped jeans, combat boots, and a baggy scoop neck t-shirt with a tattooed version of Marilyn Monroe across the front. As I approach, she stands, one hip popped, and crosses her arms over her chest.

"I thought I told you to leave. To go back to Detroit."

"You did." She cocks her head to one side, and her hair is like it was the night I met her. Wild and untamed, in dire need of a deep conditioning treatment and a service in our salon. "And I didn't."

"May I ask why?"

"You could, but it would be redundant. You know why I'm here. And you know what it will take to make me leave." She shrugs. "I'm not asking for much."

"Just the blood of fashion's greatest man."

"Eh." She shifts her weight and scrunches up her face. "It's not that big of a deal. I've got plenty of it running through my veins."

Ha. I'd laugh out loud if I saw any humor in this situation.

She turns, twisting slowly to one side and surveys the room. "Nice digs."

Nice digs? I don't think our house has ever been described in that manner before. I purse my lips shut before an insult snaps out.

"So…" she smiles at me. "Can I get a tour?"

Absolutely not. She's probably casing the place, has some recording device stuck up her shirt, hugged by those delicious breasts. I bet she—

"Certainly, Miss McKenna." Edward steps forward, his haughty English accent almost warm in its delivery. "If you follow me this wa—" I hold up my hand.

"Absolutely not. What the fuck are you doing in here? Leave us alone."

"Miss McKenna." The old goat ignores me, as if he hasn't waited on my ass for a decade, as if he isn't dependent on my paycheck for his very—oh wait. He isn't. Thanks to Vince's generous will, the house staff will be getting two percent of his estate. Two percent of the pretax value of one billion dollars—I can't do the fucking math, but if you take that number, and divide it by twenty, I'm pretty sure that old Edward here has a bunch of fake breasts and champagne in his future. "Might I get you some tea? Or perhaps coffee?"

"Tea would be great, thank you." She smiles, he smiles, and no one here seems to remember that this is *my* house, and she's leaving.

He turns, and I snap my fingers at him. "Don't get her tea. Go… away somewhere. Leave us alone."

He sniffs, and I'll have to fire him. I don't understand how everything can go to shit the moment that Vince passes. Staff off the rails, a frustrating stranger in our house, an empire seemingly up for grabs … this isn't what Vince wanted. *Live well*, he said. Live fucking *well*.

This isn't well. This is anarchy.

———

She grips the teacup like a barbarian, and when she lifts it to her mouth, I see the chipped dark polish on her nails. Edward sets down a fresh napkin and a plate of blueberry scones, and I swear to God, if he offers her one more thing, I'm going to chuck the closest pastry at his head.

He straightens, does his little butler bow thing, and leaves.

"So." She sets down the teacup and reaches for a scone. "I was thinking that maybe we could negotiate." I watch her break a corner of the scone off and bring it to her lips. God, those fucking lips. All it takes is one look at them, one action by them, and I'm a raging mess of hormones.

I look away and pretend to brush something off of the arm of my suit. "Negotiate about what?"

"Well." She pauses to finish chewing. "I was thinking that you could let me have a paternity test, and I could keep your little secret."

"I don't have a little secret." I sit in the chair opposite her, the Wing-backs set far enough apart that I feel safe.

"Really?" She examines a piece of blueberry crumble before popping it into her mouth, and fuck me, she is aggravating. "I feel like you do."

"I feel like you're reaching."

My gaze follows her when she stands, brushing off her palms, scone dust falling to the carpet like glitter. She steps toward me, and I tense when she doesn't stop, one leg swinging over mine, her weight coming down as she straddles my lap. "I feel like you want to fuck me right now," she whispers.

She's right. I keep my forearms in place on the velvet, my hands hanging from the ends of the arms, and adopt as bored of an expression as I can manage. "You're terrible at reading people."

She looks down at me and tilts her head. Last time she was in this position, my cock was inside of her, stiff and thick inside hot perfection. My hands tighten on the wings of the chair and fight to not move.

"So … you're not hard right now?"

"No."

She places her hand on my chest, sliding down the cashmere sweater and toward my dick, which is a battering ram barely contained by slacks. I release my grip on the chair and trap her hand right before it gets to my belt. "Stop."

"Stop what?"

"Is this how you negotiate things in Detroit?"

"You're changing the subject."

"I'm trying to get you off my lap."

"Let's get back to our negotiation." She pulls her hand free of mine and rests it on the back of my chair, leaning forward, her face closer to mine.

The neck of her shirt slips over one shoulder and I see the strap of her bra. Red. Gold stitching. The same one from yesterday. I reach up and pull the t-shirt back into place. Her eyes meet mine and my self-control cracks, my palm dragging down the front of her shirt, cupping the fabric against her body, feeling everything I want to see. She inhales, and I want to yank up her shirt and pull down her jeans. I bet those panties are soaked.

I clear my throat, my hand settling on and tightening around her waist, pulling the fabric tight against her breasts. "I'll let you negotiate with me, if—" I lift my gaze and look into her face.

"If what?"

"If I can do anything I want, while you propose your terms."

Her face flushes, her breath catching, and she rolls her lips together while she thinks it over. Her eyes search mine, my hand tightens on her waist, and she nods, a quick tight jerk of acceptance.

I move my other hand to the waist of her jeans and pop the fly open. "Talk."

CHAPTER 30

AVERY

His hand grips my waist, his fingers caressing the skin through the thin material of the tee. I look down, watching his hand part the fly of my jeans. He drags the zipper down and the red satin of the thong comes into view. His eyes darken, his jaw tightens, and the pads of his fingers work down the lace seams of the panties.

Talk. I should be talking, presenting my case in a logical and intelligent manner. I close my eyes, lift my head, and try to find a thought process that doesn't involve nudity. "You don't think that Vince is my dad."

"No, I don't." He sounds so calm and in control. He slides his hand further, working it into the tight fit of my jeans. His fingers find my clit and he caresses it through the silk.

"So, then what's the harm in the..." oh God. My hand falls to his shoulder and I dig my nails into the soft fabric of his sweater.

"You aren't negotiating. You're asking a favor."

"Fine." I pull at his belt, my fingers clawing at the buckle, and he lets

193

the action slide. "Since you think it's a stupid idea, let me have the test. In exchange, I won't tell anyone that Vince Horace's boyfriend fucked me."

"Which time?" He slides his fingers further down, the firm pressure pushing silk against wetness. I don't know how he does it. With just a look, I'm damp. With a touch, I'm putty.

"What?"

He sits up suddenly and yanks my jeans lower, the new angle giving his hand more freedom. He works the panties to the side and pushes two fingers in. "Which time are you *not* going to tell them about? In Spring Lake, or right now?"

The cocky question, coming right as his fingers dip inside of me, rubs me the wrong way. My body caves in pleasure, but my mind struggles, pushing back. "No." I pull my hand back from his buckle and grab his wrist. His fingers stop moving, his eyes flicking to mine. I push on his chest and his hand goes limp as I push off his body and stand. "You're not fucking me." I don't know where the statement comes from or why, just now, I feel so resolute, but I do. *He's not fucking me.* Not right here, with his butlers standing on the other side of that door. Not right now, while I'm trying to negotiate something that affects my entire life.

It was a ridiculous decision, straddling him, attempting to use my feminine wiles to sway him. In that battle, I was a mouse coming to a dogfight, more likely to be devoured than land a blow.

I step back and his eyes smolder. He bends forward and picks up a fallen napkin, my stupid scone still half-eaten on a plate beside my chair. Keeping that gaze on me, he wipes his hand off. "Then continue with this proposal."

"That's it. I'll keep my mouth shut and you let me have the test. I'll get the results and go on my way." I pull my jeans into place and zip them up, working the button closed. What had I expected to happen? He said to *let him do anything* he wanted.

"I have to say," he muses. "This is not the reaction I expected you to have."

"Yeah. Me either." I pull at the neck of my shirt. "Is it hot in here? It feels hot."

He doesn't respond, and I turn away, talking too quickly at a time when I should shut up. "I don't want you to go to Detroit. Or to dig around in my business. But I can't let this drop. I can't. It'll just…" I let out a hard breath. "It'll tear me apart. The not knowing. I don't do well with not knowing things."

"He isn't your father. Trust me on that."

I let out a short laugh. "Yeah. No offense, but I don't trust you at all."

"That makes two of us." He finishes cleaning off his fingers and tosses the napkin to the end table, missing the surface. It drops to the floor and he dismisses it entirely.

I wouldn't trust me either. I've been sketchy as hell from the beginning, though it had been unintentional. I hadn't expected to jump in front of his car, hitch a ride, spend the night, and have sex with him—all without telling him who I was, or why I was there. And even today, showing up unannounced, doing this whole ridiculous straddle-him-with-cookie-crumbs-on-my-mouth routine—I'm surprised he's even having this conversation with me. I'm surprised he hasn't called the cops, booted me out into the street, and charged me with blackmail. Because that's what I'm doing, in some twisted way. I'm threatening to tell someone about Spring Lake unless he grants access to a paternity test.

Which I should have access to anyway.

Which I might get, if Andrei and I took them to court.

Is it blackmail if I'm just getting what is owed to me? Yeah. I think it

195

still is. And *owed to me* is a pretty freaking big leap, considering my weak-ass hypothesis.

"Here's the issue." He glances at his watch, then continues. "Your word doesn't mean shit. You tell me you'll keep your mouth shut, I give you a paternity test, and then you blab about my giant cock to GQ." He stands, reaching one hand into his pocket and pulling out a cell phone. "So, this is what we'll do. You'll sign an agreement waiving your right to any of Vince Horace's assets, and I'll give you your test. As far as you ever telling anyone about what happened in Spring Lake?" He shrugs. "Fuck it. We'll paint you as a prostitute with a rap sheet as long as my dick. I'm a fucking choir boy who's mourning the loss of his partner. No one will believe you. And if you do go public, I'll do what I threatened earlier and rip apart your life and send everything I find to the media." He types something on his phone, his head down, his dismissal as clear as a Times Square billboard.

Finally, he looks up. "You're a smart girl. I'm certain you'll see the right path to take." He slips his phone back in his pocket. "Now, if you'll excuse me, I've got a staff meeting to run that started ten minutes ago."

He doesn't wait for a response. He walks forward, his shoe brushing against the used napkin, and it spins on the floor. I watch him stride down the long room and wait for a backward glance, a final acknowledgment, something. I wait, then I'm left alone.

I press my lips together and fight the urge to scream. Instead, I stomp on the napkin, my boots loud on the marble floor, each jump damaging the delicate paper a little bit more.

I hate him. I hate, hate, hate, hate, *hate* him.

———

He's fast. By the time I walk four blocks over to the park, I have an email from Andrei with the contract from Lent's attorney. I open the attachment and scroll through the document, one that is lengthy and appears to cover every conceivable base. kill ten minutes hunting down something to eat, then call him.

"I don't like it." Andrei's voice is flat, and I can picture him, sitting at his desk and pulling at his earlobe. I move closer to the edge of a bench, a hot dog in hand, and pinch the cell phone against my ear.

"If I sign this document, have the paternity test, and I *am* his daughter then … I get nothing? I'm in the same situation I am now?" Not that my current situation sucks. Three days ago, loneliness, danger, and stale sex life aside, I was happy with my life.

"Well—" he sighs. "Here's the thing, Avery. You can fight anything. And *they* can fight anything. That's the bitch of the matter. And I know you've got money, but you don't have *their* kind of money. You go toe to toe with them in court, and they could stretch this into the next five years. So, it'll be a question of—if you are his daughter—how much you want to fight. And while there's a good chance that a judge might throw out whatever you sign, there's also the chance that they won't, and you have to stick with that decision. And being handed that verdict might cost you a couple mill in legal fees."

A couple million dollars? I don't *have* a couple million dollars for legal fees. And what I do have is hidden away in an account that the IRS— and any other governing body that ever feels the need to seize my assets—doesn't know about. Pulling out anything close to that amount to pay for legal fees would spark red flags I don't want to be raised. I take a bite of hot dog and work the food into the side of my cheek to speak. "What do you think I should do?"

"Well…I'm thinking it's better to know who your father is and *not* get any money, than not know who your father is." He pauses. "Am I right?"

Yeah, he's right. But I still hate to sign anything, to give Marco that victory. I say so, and Andrei laughs.

"I gotta say, Avery. I've never seen you get this worked up. He must be an absolute dick."

I let the comment slide, and think about Spring Lake, wondering how much of my anger is caused by what happened, and the hateful things Marco has since said. I don't know what I expected, but I assumed, after that night together, that there would be a small bit of affection between us, a familiarity that might smooth over our interchanges. Instead, he's an exposed wire, hot with electricity and one step away from lighting everything on fire. "So, you're saying I should sign this?"

"As your attorney, I'd never advise you to sign anything like this. But as your friend... yeah. I think you should. As I told you before, we could go to the courts and get a paternity test without this. But if he's threatening to dig into your life, I'm not sure that's a risk you want to take. And I know how you feel about the girls. I'm not sure that's a risk you want *them* to take."

It's not. I pinch off a piece of bun and toss it to a pigeon who looks like he's having a bad day. "I feel like I'm being screwed every way that I turn." *Him, standing me up, turning me around, his mouth rough against my neck, his hands knotting my hair into his fists. The bare, raw thrust of him inside of me.*

He sighs. "Just remember that a week ago, you didn't know who your father was, and I'm pretty sure, in your search for him, his net worth wasn't of any concern to you. Look at Vince Horace as if he's poor. Ignore the millions, and just see if he's your dad. 'Cause I don't think the millions, or billion, or whatever the fuck he's worth, is why you're in New York right now. You want to know who your father is. This is your chance to cross Horace off the list or circle his name. So, do it."

I set the hot dog on my lap and twist the cap off of the bottled water. "I'm beginning to think I don't pay you enough."

"For this shit?" He laughs. "You don't. But you overpay me for some other stuff, so we'll let it slide."

"Why, thank you."

"Now, go. Go see a Broadway show and take selfies in Time Square. Do all that tourist shit that Marcia loves. And text me once you make a decision."

"I think you've convinced me."

"You're signing the agreement?"

"I am." Two words that seem like a prison sentence.

"Alright. Find a notary, or head back to Montreal's office. Send me a copy once it's executed."

I nod, say goodbye, and hang up the phone. At my feet, the pigeon cocks his head in confusion.

"I know," I tell him. "I've lost my damn mind."

CHAPTER 31

MARCO

There is no staff meeting, but I needed an escape before I yanked her forward and bent her beautiful ass over that chair. I walk quickly down the main hall and step into the powder room. I lock the door, unzip my pants, and fist my cock. Hiss out a breath as I squeeze the rigid organ that throbs to the point of pain.

"You're so big," she whispers the words, and I'm lost to them, lost to everything but the feel of her body underneath my hands.

I want her on her knees, that look back on her face, awe in those features as she grabbed me with both hands. I shuttle my hand over my shaft, resting my weight on the pedestal sink, grunting with relief as the pain leaves at the contact.

"Please..." She groans the word and I yield, spreading her legs apart and pushing a finger inside.

I think of her laying before me, her hair loose and wild on the floor, her eyes pinching shut as I work in one digit, then two.

"I need more," she whispers out the plea and one of her hands find my cock,

her fingers wrapping around me, her grip starting to move, to squeeze and rotate and jerk.

The pressure builds, pushing at the base of my cock, and I jerk my hand faster, the orgasm sharp, as painful as it is pleasurable. I exhale, watching another shot of come, the sensation fading, my dick already losing some of its stiffness.

Fuck. I'm losing my mind around her. I went ten fucking years without being affected by women, ten fucking years of ignoring them and focusing on work—and now I can't be around her for five minutes without trying to get her clothes off. I had her in Spring Lake. Wanted her in that conference room. Almost, just now, forced myself on her.

I pushed her too far, trying to get her off in the midst of a negotiation. That was bad enough, my fingers sliding into her panties, circling her clit, pushing into her wet pussy. I went too far by assuming she'd let me do more.

I tuck myself back inside my pants, taking my time as I zip up the material and wash my hands. I pause and look up into the mirror, drying my hands. I wonder when I'll be able to look at myself and not feel dirty. I thought some of it would leave with Vince's death, but it only seems to be getting worse.

Reaching forward, I flip off the light and douse the small room into darkness.

———

Our world, without Vince Horace, continues to spin. I ignore the fact that it's a weekend, and spend an hour with each of our Creative Directors. I walk through the design floor and look through our junior designers layouts, checking on their progress. I assess orders, analyze our quarter, and review layouts for the upcoming ad campaign. Vince once bragged that his empire earns a thousand dollars a minute. He was wrong. It earns a hundred dollars a minute on average. Still, plenty to outfit us in diamonds and gas up the jet, just not enough to buy the fucking airline.

I sit in Vince's chair, make his decisions and run his company. I pull open his drawer, grab his favorite pen, and scribble my own name on forms, orders, and documents. I can feel him in this office, feel his hand on my back as I walk through the design bay, feel his squeeze on my shoulder as I sign bank forms and move millions of dollars from his name into mine.

I manage, through raw grit and determination, to not think of Avery McKenna. I don't think about the way her body responds so easily to mine, or how, when I cut her down, she managed to look both hurt and furious. I block out any thoughts of her dark brown eyes and focus on hemlines, advertising quotes, and financial reports. I look through the most recent catalog, past the red and gold lingerie set, and don't linger on the image, don't imagine the way the satin clung between her legs.

Just before five, my head a knot of tension and stress, I get a text from John. *She's here and ready to sign the contract. We're finding a notary now.*

I stand up, typing out my response as I move to the door and call out for Edward. *Keep her there. I'm on my way.* I send the text, hit the button for the elevator, and try and still the pounding in my chest.

———

She's changed clothing again, and I could design an entire collection around her unpredictability. A short corduroy skirt, printed stockings, and a sweater. She's got new shoes on, platform Doc Martens, and I have to pull my eyes from her legs in order to enter the room without running into the doorframe. I step into the office and pull the door closed, nodding to the both of them and ignoring the secretary that sits to her right.

Avery avoids eye contact, her gaze focused on the contract before her. Her frame is stiff, and I realize, in the set of her jaw and the fix of her attention on the page that she is mad at me. Maybe I should apologize, but honestly, at this point, the list of things to apologize for is getting a little long. I could have one of the employees type it all up, but it would cover three fucking pages.

She initials the bottom of a page and flips it over. Skims over the next, then does the same. The contract is a maze of words, complicated jargon designed to cover our asses five ways to Sunday. It contains, in at least three places, language about confidentiality, clauses that cover Vince's paternity but also my fuck up at Spring Lake. There is a reason John is the best, and I watch her pen glide along the paper and know this one will be airtight in court. If she thinks she can fight this later, she's wrong. If she thinks she can claim temporary insanity or some other feminine condition, she's wrong. If she signs on the last page? She gives us her soul.

Some of her hair falls loose from her ponytail and I almost reach forward and tuck it behind her ear. Instead, I pull out the chair to her left, settling into it, my legs stretching out and almost touching her. I watch her concentrate on the document. From this angle, she's beautiful. Which isn't to say that she isn't beautiful from other angles, but this one... the tilt of her jaw, the slight part of her lips, the way she moves them slightly as she reads. When her eyes dart to me, it is unexpected, and I'm caught unprepared.

She looks back at the contract and I watch as a pink hue darkens her cheeks. It reminds me of how expressive and responsive her body was, the bedroom lamp exposing every flush and tremble of her perfect porcelain skin. She turns the page and moves her pen to the signature block. Hesitating, she glances at John, and then at the secretary, who withdraws a notary stamp and places it on the table. I miss her eyes on me. I like them, even when they glare, even when they cut. I like the attention from her, and my need for it seems to grow with every interaction.

She signs her name. *Avery McKenna.* Her signature is more delicate than I would have expected. Prim and proper, from a woman wild and untamed.

She sets down the pen, slides the page over to the notary and looks at John. "Now what?"

"Now," John says, pulling open a side drawer and withdrawing a small box. "Now, we need to get DNA samples from you. We already have a blood sample from Mr. Horace's autopsy."

Autopsy. I hate that word, hate the thought of them putting Vince on a slab and cutting him open. I had resisted it, eight months of medical tests and MRIs and CAT scans more than enough evidence of the disease that killed him. But a primary heir can only do so much balking before suspicions are raised. So, I dropped it, and an autopsy occurred, one that showed exactly what all of his doctors already knew.

Thanks to that autopsy, we have a vial of his blood, one that may reveal an heir or shatter this issue. I glance at her and this time, she is the one watching me. She looks away.

CHAPTER 32

AVERY

Eighteen hours, that's all it will take. Eighteen hours, and I'll know if Vince Horace is a stranger or my biological father. I had expected a week of waiting, maybe two. But everything in this city seems to move quickly. I swab my cheek, they pluck a few hairs, prick my finger, and then cart everything away. Marco signs the contract, I am given a copy, and then we are outside, his car idling on the curb, the New York wind whipping his sweater flat to his chest.

He doesn't move to his car, he only stands there, his hands in his pockets, his head down. I look down the street for a taxi, taking the moment to scratch at the back of my knee.

"Would you like to go to dinner?" He glances over at me, the words almost lost in the growl of a passing Ferrari. That's something you don't see in my neighborhood. Exotic cars, or enemies playing nice.

"Not particularly." I see a yellow cab turn, two blocks away, and step forward, my arm raising.

He steps closer and his body shields the wind. "Not hungry?"

I sniff. "Not really interested in the company."

"I can behave." He wraps a hand around my arm, pulling slightly to catch my attention. "Stop hailing a cab. You don't need one."

I wave my hand more vigorously in the air and crane my neck around him, watching as the car comes closer.

"Let me take you to dinner. Please. I'll even apologize while we're there."

My hand loses some of its vigor and I drop from my toes, meeting his eyes. "You'll apologize?"

His mouth curves. "I'll give you the best you've ever had."

"Heartfelt?"

"Absolutely."

"Sincere?"

"What apology isn't?"

A lot. Most. Probably every one he's ever delivered. "You seem very confident about the quality of this apology."

"I'm confident about most things, Miss McKenna."

The cab passes, the driver not even glancing my way, and I drop my hand, giving up. "Fine. But I pick the place." I almost stomp over to the car, giving a cheery hello to the old guy, who holds open the door. He ignores me, and I make a face. Here I was, thinking that we had bonded over tea and scones. Maybe, he just likes to piss Marco off.

He closes the door, and I look around, realizing this is a different car. Same fine accents, but a rich brown leather interior instead of white. I tuck one foot under my butt and slide the seatbelt over my chest, securing it. The opposite door opens, Marco steps in, and I inhale before thinking, the scent of him as intoxicating as the first time I smelled it. Was it really only two days ago? It feels like weeks.

I wait until the driver gets in, then lean forward and grip the seat. "Chaykhana, please. It's in Brooklyn."

"Brooklyn?" Marco settles into his seat. "This'll be interesting."

Yes, it *will* be interesting. Chaykhana is owned by some Ukrainian friends of mine, husbands of girls I once brought over, and a strong link in the chain of communication that runs to the other side of the world. It's a place where I feel safe, one where I will have the upper hand, for one of the first times in this relationship. After signing that contract, I feel violated. It will be nice to see him in some discomfort. And if he's buying me dinner… one of my friends might as well benefit from it.

The Rolls pulls away from the curb and I tuck my hands under my thighs, the stockings tickling the back of my hands. "So… eighteen hours."

"Yep." He looks over at me. "Nervous?"

His tone is friendly and missing the cruel bite of before. Ever since I signed his contract, he's been different—a reminder of the man I met that first night, back when he didn't view me as the enemy. I miss that night, miss the playful flirtation that existed, the smiles that crossed his face. Has he smiled since? I don't think so. Lots of scowls. Lots of muttered curses, solemn glares, and the occasional cruel smirk—but no smiles. I swallow and lift my shoulders in a shrug. "Yeah. I'm nervous. Pretty anxious." I lean forward and turn off the closest air vent. "What about you? Contract or not, I can't imagine that it won't disrupt your life if the results come back positive."

"My life has been disrupted ever since I met Vince. I had no illusions that things would suddenly go smoothly just because he died."

I want to ask him so many questions. I want to know everything about Vince. Every memory. Every personality trait. Every success and failure. I swallow and keep the questions to myself.

When we pull up to the restaurant it's raining, a light drizzle that is

completely soundless inside the car. It's eerie, being so completely
shut off from the outside world. I miss my cheap Tahoe. Right now,
the rain would be peppering the roof, each drop a ding, a thousand of
them combining to create a calming cadence.

Marco leans forward, peering out the window. "This is it?" He sounds
wary, and I don't blame him. Chaykhana is stuck in between a tailor
shop and dry cleaner, the sign glowing red from the neon that
surrounds it. There are dingy white curtains that hide the interior and
a front display poster that advertises a *Buy One, Get One Dinner Free!*
special. It's a far cry from this morning's scone, the hot tea delivered
by the English butler, in the room that housed a million dollars' worth
of art.

"So… we're eating here."

"Yep." My door opens and his driver extends a gloved hand, an
umbrella held out, shielding me from the rain. I take his hand, stepping out and narrowly missing a puddle.

Alex and Vasyl greet me with big hugs, each squeezing me tightly and
smiling widely at Marco. They show me to a table in the back, one
tucked into the corner, and light a candle in the middle of it. They
seem to think this is a date, and when they bring a red rose inside a
thin vase, I wave them off. "This is business, Alex. Stop that shit."

"Ah." He pulls back the rose and claps a meaty hand on my shoulder.
"It's been too long. We miss your pretty face."

"I'll come back soon," I promise. "Maybe I'll get a place in New York,
come by and bug you every day." I grin, Marco scowls, and I could
spend the rest of my life making him scowl. I love the way it pinches
his features, the fire it lights in his eyes, the way his jaw tightens.

"Yes, you do that." Alex nods enthusiastically. "You know, my sister's
selling her place. It's just four blocks away. You should go look at it."

Marco almost speaks. I can see his mouth open, an objection forming,
then he stops himself.

"I'll get you a menu." Alex turns, moving his heavy bulk in between the tables, knocking over a salt shaker on his way.

"You wouldn't live in Brooklyn." Marco leans forward, his voice lowered. "I mean, if you came here. Tell me you wouldn't live in *Brooklyn*."

It is such an amusing response that I laugh. "What are you talking about? Why do you care where I live?"

"It's just…" He glances to the side. "It's not safe. For someone like you."

His misconception of me is so far from reality that I laugh. I almost wish he had come to Detroit with his "investigators" and walked through my neighborhood. His custom suit would have been ripped off before he made it two blocks. His watch, confiscated. His wallet, emptied. I live in a lawless corner of the city, one that cops ignore and anyone respectable avoids. He's cute, thinking that Brooklyn is dangerous. He's crazy, thinking that I wouldn't be safe here.

"You don't know anything about me." I smile at Alex as he sets down two ice waters.

He pulls laminated menus from underneath his arms and slaps them onto the table, his thick forefinger jabbing at the top section. "This here is the Buy One, Get One Free section. They're all good. I make that third one myself."

"Thanks." I smile up at him. "It'll take us a few minutes."

"I got some wine in the back. You want some? I just opened it an hour ago."

"Ah, no," Marco grimaces, and I find his foot and step on it.

"Let me guess," Alex hums. "A beer guy. That's you, right?"

I hide a smile behind a sip of ice water.

"Sure. Whatever your best is."

"I got a Russian beer you're gonna love. You too." He points at me. "You drinking, right?"

I lift my hands in mock confusion. "Seriously? You wasted breath in asking me that?"

He smacks the table in approval and everything on it shudders. "That's my girl." He grabs my shoulder again, and shakes it, grinning at Marco as if I've just found the cure for cancer. "She's a good one, this one. You agree?"

Alex's question hangs there, his eyes on Marco, waiting for a response.

"Uh... yeah." Marco bobs his head. "She's a good one." *A good one.* What am I, a prized steer?

"And pretty, too, yes?"

"Very pretty." Marco sighs.

"Hmmm." He lingers at our table and I glare at him. "I'm just saying. You're a pretty woman." He lifts his hands in surrender. "But I go."

I flip over the menu and ignore him, my peripheral vision revealing the moment when he finally turns and lumbers away.

"You're not pretty." Marco's voice is low, and I stiffen, lifting my gaze to him. "You're beautiful. Pretty ... for a woman like you. It's an insult."

I glance back at my menu. "He didn't mean it that way."

"I know he didn't, but it's still an insult." He picks up the laminated page and peers at it. "Now. What do you suggest I order?"

———

Our beers arrive, and I order for both of us, filling Alex's notepad with half the items offered. Marco doesn't argue, passing his menu back, a resigned look on his face. "Am I going to regret this invitation?"

"Probably." I twist off the lid to my beer. "But not half as much as I've regretted getting on a plane and coming here."

"Ouch." He examines the label of his beer. "That doesn't say much for my bedroom skills."

"Oh, please." I roll my eyes. "Your bedroom skills were fine. It's the clusterfuck that those bedroom events led to. That's what I regret." I reach forward, grabbing a lime wedge and squeezing it into the bottle. "I should have been honest with you about who I was." I look up at him. "I'm sorry."

"My bedroom skills were *fine*," Marco repeats dully. He sets down his beer, rests his elbows on the table, and rubs his forehead with both hands. "Oh my God. I knew it. I've lost my touch."

I laugh and throw the cap of my beer at him, the piece bouncing off his hands and falling on the restaurant floor. "Did you even hear me? I just apologized. And an Avery McKenna apology is…" I pause. "It's a big deal. A much bigger deal than the fact that you suck in bed."

He groans, his hands dropping. "God, and I thought I hated you before."

"Come on, now." I lean back as a runner puts down a steaming plate of veal pelmeni. "I can think of a few times the other night where you didn't hate me. And did you hear my apology? 'Cause it's not happening again."

"I heard your apology. Thanks."

He tosses out the short word as if it means nothing. Maybe he's over the deception, or maybe he wasn't that pissed off about it. Whatever the reason, I drop the subject and grab my fork, leaning forward and spearing a piece of pelmeni. He watches me, and I hold out the fork toward him. "Here. Try it. It's like a dumpling."

He surprises me by leaning forward, his mouth closing over the fork, the metal tugging a little in my grip. He sits back and chews. "Not bad."

"Oh, shut up. It's good."

I move closer to the edge of my seat and grab another piece. There is a stretch of companionable silence, and I look up after the bread is delivered, and catch him watching me. "What?"

"Nothing." He looks away, focusing on his beer. "I just can't believe I'm drinking something with a twist-off cap."

"I know. Sooo trashy of you."

He almost smiles, the corners of his mouth turning up in the smallest way possible, but I take the win and tilt my own beer back.

———

"Don't laugh." He dips the piece of chicken in the sauce. "It scarred me. I hired a psychiatrist just to work me through it."

"You're so full of shit." I twist off the lid on a fresh beer and toss it on the table. "There's no way she said that."

"She did," he insists, holding up his palm. "Swear to God."

"A tree stump. There's no way your mom made love to a tree stump."

"You think I'd make that shit up? It's called ecosexuality. I was stuck on a train and had to listen to ten minutes of her and Dad talking about it. You don't even want to know the different shit he's stuck his dick into."

I giggle. "I think I do."

"Well look it up." He shudders, and when he reaches forward, stealing a piece of my liver, I push the plate closer to him.

"You know…" I muse. "Maybe that's my issue. Detroit doesn't have

214

enough trees. I mean," I amend, "they *have* trees, they're just all in some public areas. Nowhere a girl can get some quality one-on-one time with one."

"Yeah." He drains the rest of his beer and catches Alex's eye, raising the bottle in the air. "That's your issue. Bam. Move to the woods. Problem solved."

"Doesn't she get splinters, though? I mean…" I scrunch up my face, imagining a scenario where a woman would rub herself against a stump. "It seems like the friction would cause serious—"

"Shut. UP." He points his empty beer at me. "I swear to God, shut up. You're giving me visuals I've paid a shitload of money to erase."

I smile. "Fine. Eat in peace. I'll just be over here, fantasizing about the massively hot session I'm going to have tonight with the ficus tree in my hotel's lobby."

"We're getting sidetracked from the point of my story."

"Oh right. That your parents are over-sharing free-loving hippies?

"No." He fixes me with a stern look. "The point is, it's not necessarily a bad thing to *not* know your parents."

"Oh puh-lease." I snort. "Your parents don't seem that bad. A little crazy, but still lovable." I'm mentally slow in all things parental, and even I can see the affection on his face as he'd told me about them. It was sweet, actually, the way his features had softened, his eyes warmed, and his posture had relaxed. Even when he was making fun of them, and ranting over their behavior … he loves them. It is both endearing and painful, all at the same time.

I dip a piece of bread in oil. "What did they think of Vince?" It's the first time I've mentioned him, and I don't look up, don't breathe too loudly, don't do anything to jostle the friendly atmosphere that is somehow, magically, existing.

"They only met him a handful of times. It was interesting. Interactions with Vince were always interesting." He picks up a fried shrimp and holds it between his forefinger and thumb, his eyes flicking from me to it as if weighing a decision. He puts the shrimp in his mouth, and I take a sip of beer and watch him chew, giving him time to figure out whatever he's saying next.

"Vince was a chameleon." He picks up a new shrimp, dunking it into a bowl of tomato sauce. "If he wanted someone to like him, they would. And he could talk *anyone* into just about anything." He eats the shrimp, then washes it down with the rest of his beer.

I feel something in that last sentence, some hint that I'm missing, but I can't, through all of the food and the beer, find it.

CHAPTER 33

MARCO

"Admit it." Avery holds the beer bottle by the neck and points a chipped fingernail at me. I need to get her home. The salon staff could have her in a perfect manicure within twenty minutes. "You liked that place."

"I didn't *mind* it," I allow, resting my forearms on the bar and leaning forward. "It wasn't the sort of place I would have chosen, but it was okay."

"It was *okay?*" She laughs. "God, you're such a pain." The bar is crowded, the televisions along the wall filled with Yankee baseball, and every once in a while, the place erupts in cheers. We've moved from Brooklyn to the Bronx, me letting her dictate the itinerary, and I'm certain she's trying to make me as uncomfortable as possible. It doesn't matter. I'm having more fun with her than I've had in years.

She doesn't remind me of Vince, yet there are enough minute similarities to give me pause. In the occasional gesture or angle, there is a small stab of recognition, probably more inferred over actual. You stare at someone four thousand days in a row, you start to see them everywhere. She lifts a hand, scratching at her neck, and her shirt sleeve falls, revealing a chunky watch. I reach out and grab her wrist.

She lets me have it, and I try not get distracted by the feel of her skin. "Nice one," I say, turning her hand over so I can see the face of it. It's big, almost the size of a man's. I remember us fighting over the face, Vince swearing that no women would buy it. He'd been wrong, and we'd sold thousands of them.

"I've had it a few years. Got it here, actually. At the store on Fifth Ave."

"I know the store." I think about what would have happened if we'd been there, Vince and I, on one of our quarterly visits. Would we have seen her? Yes. At least, I would have. I would have seen her in a crowd of thousands.

She pulls back her wrist. "It doesn't work very well." She works the clasp open and shakes it off her wrist, bringing it close to her face and using her other hand to turn the small dial at the side of its face. "It always runs slow. There." She sets the correct time and I take it from her before she puts it back on.

"Here. Allow me." I pick up the watch and work it over her hand, enjoying the excuse to touch her, to slide my fingers along hers. Too soon, the watch is in place, the clasp set.

"Thanks." She turns back and glances up at the television, checking the score of the game. It's official. I've completely lost my skill with women.

"You a baseball fan?"

"Yep." She points to the screen. "Look in the stands behind third base. First row. That's where my seats are."

I follow her directions, the section crammed with bodies.

"See the girl with the pink sweater?"

Her timing is good, the woman standing, hands cupped to her mouth, and screaming something at the players.

"Yeah. Your seats are near there?"

"*Right* there. That's Marcia. She's a friend of mine. And the skinny guy next to her is Andrei—my attorney."

"The guy who sent the letter to us?"

"Yep."

The camera angle cuts to the batter, and I don't get a good enough look at the attorney. "He's a friend of yours too?"

My tone sounds off, as if I am jealous. She doesn't miss it, and glances at me, her mouth curving into a playful smile. "The best kind of friend."

The best kind of friend? What the fuck is that supposed to mean? I look down at my beer before I ask the question, and force myself to put it out of my mind. She's fucking with me, she has to be. I felt her body, how tight it was when she settled down on my cock, the way she had responded when I'd slid my hands over her skin. She was raw and neglected, as hungry for the contact as I was. No way some prick lawyer in Detroit is banging her. No way he'd let her come to New York, on her own, for something like this. Any friend, any true friend, a fuck buddy or not, would have come along to help, provide moral support, done something other than sit in a baseball stadium, six hundred miles away, and ignore her.

"Tell me a Vince story." She sets down her beer and props her elbow on the bar, resting her chin in her palm.

I frown. "Buy his book. They're all in there."

"Bullshit, I read his book. I want to know a *story*." She reaches forward and pulls at the front of my sweater, and if I leaned forward, I could kiss her.

I sit back, lift my beer to my mouth, and promise myself, for the fiftieth time of the night, that I am keeping my hands to myself. "A story."

"Yeah. Something stupid."

"Hmmm." I probably shouldn't, yet I'm anxious to. "Fine. One story."

"A good one."

"They're all good." I grin, because they are. I have a thousand memories with that man, and every day by his side was a different adventure.

"Then start talking," she challenges.

I talk. I sip Heineken and tell her about Africa, the safaris there, and Vince's insistence that we stay with a local family in each town that we visited. "So, Edward—you know Edward, right? The ancient butler guy?" She grins. "So, he is staying at the Ritz, in our swank ass suite, and Vince and I are sharing a straw mat in some tent in the middle of the Serengeti." I reach for my phone, then stop, forcing myself to continue the story without showing her the photos.

"You're so full of shit," she accuses. "You could barely survive tonight without having someone wipe your mouth after dinner. No way you did that."

Fuck it. I pull out my phone, scroll through my albums, and then, with her leaning in, her hair tickling my cheek, I flip through the photos. Vince and me, shirtless, beside a dozen children, their smiles bigger than their faces should have allowed. Vince, his arm around my shoulders, a selfie taken with an elephant. Another shot, the elephant's trunk wrapped around Vince's torso, his hat askew, mid-laugh.

I look over and see her eyes, tight to the screen, the concentration in them almost heartbreaking. For me, they are bittersweet memories of an old friend. For her, they are lost experiences with a father she will never know. I want to reassure her, to tell her that he isn't her father

—that the man in these photos is a stranger, but I can't. I know things no one else does. I know that he *was* at that LiveAid concert. I know that that *is* him, in her photo, with that ring on his hand. And despite an unwavering certainty that Vince Horace is gay, I know that every man is susceptible, every man makes mistakes, and nothing is ever as it seems.

I flip forward, through our trip north, and realize how much I will miss him. For ten years, he's been my constant, my mentor, my friend. For ten years, he's been the one to call me out when I was wrong, applaud when I was right, and assure me, through all of my doubts, that we were doing the right thing.

For ten years, I didn't question the lie I was living. Now, with him gone, bits of me don't fit right, don't work right. A Marco Lent, with Vince alive, never would have made her sign that contract. A Marco Lent, with Vince alive, wouldn't be sitting here, in this bar, tempting fate.

Without him, I can see the paths I should take. I just can't seem to step forward and move down them.

I close my phone and hope that she doesn't move away.

As soon as my screen goes dark, she straightens, pulling her stool closer to the bar and grabbing at the fresh bottle of beer the bartender hands her. I don't know where she puts it. I don't know how she can drink so much and stay lucid.

Vince, from all the stories he'd told me, was a drinker. It ran in his family, and when a drunk driver killed his brother, that was the catalyst that caused him to step away from alcohol. While I'd often seen him with a drink, he'd never had more than two, the habit regulated with the stern manner of a drill sergeant. Sometimes I wondered what he had been like before. He'd told me stories of him and his brother, the parties, the adventures … in them, he seemed like an entirely different man—a black sheep versus a dogged workhorse.

"He worked hard." I felt the need to tell her that, after showing her so many photos of the opposite. "We played, but we also worked our asses off. He taught me that a fourteen-hour day was normal. He never went to bed without returning every email. And he had a fanatical obsession with quality." I take a long pull of beer and grimace. "God, the arguments we used to get in over quality. What you just told me, about your watch? If he'd been in this bar, and had heard that comment? He'd have left immediately, and taken your watch with him. He would have gotten in the car, and called every engineer in the company, regardless of the time. There would be meetings tomorrow, quality assessments, testing and discussions of watch recalls. Every employee in the company, down to the janitors, would have known that the Matilda watch ran slow, and some girl, in some bar, in the Bronx, was the one causing all of this work for everyone." I chuckle. "We would have been cursing you for weeks."

She smiles, and I bet she regrets asking me for stories. These aren't good stories, these are boring. I should have told her about the time we were free-diving off New Zealand and were surrounded by sharks. Or about Vince's quest to climb Everest, and his insistence that the executive team join him. I could have told her about our chili cook-offs against Ralph Lauren, or the time during the blizzard when we took an entire school bus full of children from the shelter into our house, and kept them there for two days until the storm passed. I could have told her any of those, and instead, I'm babbling on about what a control freak he was.

"Thank you," she says. "I know you didn't have to tell me that, any of that, but I appreciate it." She smiles, and this time, the gesture is steeped in sadness. I want to draw her to me, to hug her head to my chest and wrap my arms around her. I feel like she hasn't been hugged enough in life. My mother was a hugger. Before her fire dances and tree-induced orgasms, back when she spent days with checking accounts and withdrawal slips, she always had a hug for me, whether I wanted it or not. Those hugs are probably why, underneath my asshole exterior, a person still exists.

"You're welcome." She shouldn't be thanking me. I look away, watching a disagreement start between a couple on the other side of the bar, and think about everything I've put her through.

The room cheers and she glances up at the television, her body tensing as she watches a Yankee round first base and head for second. "No, no, NO!" The sadness leaves her face, replaced by energy, and she pushes on the bar top, her butt leaving the seat, and groans when he makes it safely to third. "Fucking outfield," she says to the guy next to her.

"Tell me about it." He leans toward her and I watch his gaze drag down her sweater's neckline. "You a Tigers fan?"

"Absolutely. Not that it seems to be helping them."

He laughs a little too loudly and my fingers tighten on my beer, thoughts of mothers and hugs replaced with decking this jackass off his stool. I should have sat on the other side, in between her and this prick. I lean forward and slide my palm up her thigh, my fingers scraping along the tiny butterflies printed on the tights. She glances down at my hand, then up at my face. "Hey."

"Hey." I reach between my legs and pull my stool forward, closer to her.

"Whatcha doing?"

I lean forward and rest my hand on the back of her seat, my thumb unable to resist sliding along the bare skin, exposed just above her skirt. I lower my mouth to her ear. "This asshole's trying to hit on you."

"Ah, is *that* what he's doing?" She smirks. "What would I do without you?"

I pull at the bottom of her stool, getting her flush to me, and give the guy a glare that has him turning back to the television. Pussy.

"You know, for a gay guy, you've got a big alpha male thing going for you."

"Yeah?" I keep my voice low, my eyes on hers.

"It's very attractive." The alcohol has mellowed her, softening those edges, weakening her resolve, and when she leans in, I am ready. Only, she doesn't kiss me. Instead, she just melts, her body curving into mine, and presses her head against my shoulder. "Let's go."

An excellent idea. I reach into my pocket for cash to pay the bill and she straightens, moving to her feet, her eyes back on the game. I count out some bills, pass the cash to the bartender, and turn to her. "Ready?"

"Yeah." She takes a few steps, her head still turned, watching a play, and then scowls. "Damn Yankees." She picks up my jacket and loops it over her shoulders, the oversized garment hanging off her frame, and it's a sharp contrast of refinement and punk. I watch her step forward, her curves peeking through the jacket, and I need a pen and paper, to sketch this design, turn it commercial, and class up every rich punk girl in the city.

She walks by me, moving through the crowd and to the door, and there is a moment when I wonder how I've lived without her.

———

I picture Vince, picture those clear and well-marked paths, and know I'm taking the wrong one.

Still, I step forward, carrying her in my arms, her hands linked behind my head, her head on my shoulder, legs hanging over my forearm. Moving into the house, I head for the elevator.

"Prepare the green suite. And call the kitchen. Get her something for her head, in case she wakes up during the night." I speak quietly, and the night attendant nods, then steps back, out of the way of the elevator doors. They close, and there is a moment of pause, just enough time for me to change my mind, to stop and step back off, get her out of my house, and to wherever she is staying.

I don't move. The moment passes, the car ascends, and I shift her weight slightly, getting a better grip. Her hands unlink, and she lifts her head, looking up and into my face.

"You're at my house. I'm taking you to one of the guest rooms now."

"Are you going to tuck me in?"

I frown in mock disapproval. "Oh no. I have people for that. My dedicated tuck-er-in-er. Raoul. He's excellent at it. He's got the pillow-fluffing down to a science."

She closes her eyes and the hint of a soft laugh sounds. "I'm too heavy for you to carry. You can put me down, I can walk."

"Quiet. You'll offend my masculine abilities." I'm not putting her down. Carrying her in my arms, her breath soft against my neck, her hand curling into a soft fist against my heart ... it feels like the best thing I've done in months. I'd carry her across the city.

The elevator doors open and I step onto the fifth floor.

There is a uniformed butler by the door to the green suite, and I recognize him, nodding as he opens the door, the room dimly lit by ambient light.

"Would you like a small fire, sir?"

I consider the idea and shake my head, wanting privacy over atmosphere, and to get her to bed as soon as possible. "No. Thank you. Please close the door behind you."

"Your room is all ready, sir. Should I dismiss the staff for the evening?"

"Yes. I'll call if I need anything during the night."

"Very well, sir. Good evening."

Good evening. I glance at the clock, doing the math, and am surprised that six hours has already passed. Tomorrow, we'll know. We'll know if Avery is a Horace, and if I am officially fucked.

I lower her onto the bed, and she rolls onto one side, then pushes herself upright. "Wow, I'm drunk."

"Yeah. If you're going to vomit, let me know now. I'll have a house-keeper sit watch over you."

She coughs out a laugh. "I'm not going to vomit. And I would think that you are joking … but you seem to have *way* too many people tripping over themselves with nothing to do."

"Vince liked a large staff." I kneel before her and work on the laces of her Doc Martens, sliding the first one off and setting it to the side. "I haven't had the time or desire to think about whittling them down."

"You know, I can take my own shoes off." She leans forward and watches me. "Been doing it on my own for almost… gosh. Two or three years now."

I smile, pulling up the tongue on the second and sliding it off. "Impressive." I rest my hands on my thighs and look up at her. "Then I guess you probably won't need me to undress you."

"Oh, I don't know." She flops back on the bed. "I'm starting to feel faint. And you know I have a propensity to faint."

"How could I forget?" I stand and swear on every rosary bead I ever grew up with, that I won't fuck her. I won't please her, I won't think dirty thoughts, I'll be the perfect gentleman that my once-conservative mother raised me to be. I step forward, looking down at her, and she flutters her eyes closed, slumping her head to one side.

"You did a better job of faking when you were in the alley."

"I can't hear you because I'm unconscious." She whispers the words out of the corner of her mouth. "Now you *have* to undress me."

"You pain in the ass…" I reach forward and roll her over until she is facedown, and she squeaks a little in protest. "I should have left you in the car."

She doesn't respond, and I find the zipper seam at the back of her skirt and undo the hook and eye closure. Her sweater has risen up a bit, exposing a thin strip of her back, and I can't help but swipe my fingertips over the space, a quick brush of contact that could be innocently accidental.

It's a short zipper, and I pull it down quickly, not giving myself time to think, or to prepare for the sight of her black cotton thong, disappearing into the cheeks of her ass, her sheer tights a barrier between my hands and her skin. I grab the sides of the skirt, working it over her hips, and she lifts her pelvis in an attempt to help my cause.

It doesn't help. It doesn't help *anything* when her back arches, her ass coming off the bed and offering itself to me, the perfect position for ass-gripping, pussy-pounding, penetration. I pull the skirt over and down her legs, concentrating on a small design in the bedspread, focusing on the point, and trying to ignore the most beautiful sight known to man.

I drop the skirt on the floor and she keeps her ass up, her chest still flat to the bed, and thank God for her butterfly-print stockings because I need every bit of help in keeping my cock under control.

Only now, I need to take *off* those stockings, leaving her in that thong. I look at the door, then the closet, and wonder if I should find her pajamas first. Something that I can immediately cover her with, the moment I take these off.

"I'm sorry," she mumbles. "I should have worn that kind with the garters."

"Trust me," I exhale. "I'm very glad you didn't."

She turns her head, peeking out at me through a mess of hair and bedding. "This isn't…affecting you, Mr. Lent. Is it?"

She bobs her ass in the air, and I reach out, stopping the movement, my hand gripping her ass and holding it in place. "Stop that," I snap.

She giggles, and I want to shut her up with my cock, her giggle vibrating along the shaft of my dick.

Instead, I reach up, working with quick, clinical motions, my fingers dipping under the top of the control hose, yanking it over that sweet delicious ass, and rolling it down her thighs. I have to push her flat on the bed to do it, my hand almost rough on her ass, and she yips in protest as she falls forward. She's lucky she's not my girlfriend. If she was, I'd give up on the stockings as soon as her ass was revealed. Right now, I'd have a hand on her back, another on my dick, and I'd be pushing inside, feeling her squeeze, putting my knees on the mattress, my hands all over her, and she'd be speaking in tongues within minutes. Butterfly stockings and schoolgirl Doc Martens deserve a hard, fast, fucking—the sort that shakes tits, swings balls, and causes a woman's pussy to explode around my cock.

Instead, I yank the thin nylon tights down, over her knees and skim the material past her calves, her feet lifting, ankles, heels, then toes, exposed. I drop the stocking, fix my gaze on the ceiling to avoid looking at her ass and find her body with my hands, rolling her onto her back.

She props herself up on her elbows. The sweater, fuck me to hell, is a cardigan-type, which buttons up the front, the cream knit stretched tight over her breasts, the expanse interrupted by a row of closures, and I can't tell from here if they are button-holes or snaps. Snaps would be my preference. In one hard yank, she could be exposed, and I could be one minute closer to being in my room, my cock in my hand, jerking off like a teenage boy in heat. I pull my gaze from the sweater and to her face, which is impossible to read. It's confident yet coy, the Siamese cat of seduction, and I feel like a catnip toy, batting between her paws, helpless to move away.

"Mind if I ask you a personal question?"

My eyes have somehow fallen to her panties, the high cut of them around her hip. I lift them back to her face before answering. "Sure."

"How many women have you been with?"

I should be unbuttoning her shirt. Lift hands, step forward, undo buttons. An idiot could do it, yet I can't. Right now, I can't seem to move. She pushes from her elbows and sits upright, sliding forward on the bed until her bare legs hang off its side, her feet bumping against my shins. I repeat the question in an attempt to buy more time. "How many women have I been with?"

"Yeah. I just didn't know if I was a one-time thing, or if you've been bisexual your whole life." I can see, in the break of eye contact, the quick downward glance during the comment, what the right answer is. She wants me to tell her that she's the only one. She wants to think that, out of every woman I've ever come in contact with, she was the only one I'd ever been sexually attracted to.

I know what she wants me to say, but I don't. I don't want to lie to her. At least, not any more than I have to. "I've always been attracted to women."

"Really?" She moves her hands to her sweater's top button and my dick pulses with the first twist of her fingers.

"Really."

"So...... then how many?" She moves her hands down and undoes the second button. More skin.

"How many have I had sex with?" I swallow in an attempt to clear my throat.

"Yes."

"A lot. Ten? Twenty? Something like that."

"How many men?"

She moves farther down the line of buttons, and the dip between her breasts, the curve of each, is exposed. She's not wearing a bra, and I notice, for the first time, the cling of the sweater, the fuzz of it hiding the shape of her nipples. I don't answer. Maybe I'll *have* to fuck her. Maybe I'll have to forgo my gentlemanly aspirations, forget the fact that she's had six or seven beers, and fuck her just to avoid answering this question.

Instead, I reach forward and push her hands out of the way. I undo the next button, my knuckles brushing across her cleavage. I keep going, my eyes strictly on the task, and I think about old lady saggy breasts to keep myself from getting hard. I twist open the last button and let out a hard breath. "There. Stay there. I'll get you something to wear."

I go to the closet, which is fully stocked in the latest Vince Horace collections. I move to the feminine side of the closet, flip through the undergarments, and select a red silk pajama set—the most modest thing I see. I walk back to the room and lay the hanger set beside her on the bed.

"So?" she asks, and she doesn't sound drunk anymore. She sounds interested. Maybe I piqued her interest by avoiding the question. Fuck. I should have just lied, quickly, and then told her I was ready for bed. "How many men?"

"That's a personal question, one I don't feel comfortable sharing." I step back and edge toward the door, in a manner that I hope looks casual.

"Oh my God." She covers her face with one hand and flops back on the bed, the motion causing one side of her sweater to fly open and a single, perfect, breast to be exposed. "It's bad, isn't it?"

It's beautiful. She's beautiful. The length of her legs. Her thighs. Her hips. The feminine curves. That pink nipple. Her delicate throat.

"Tell me it's not hundreds. Is it hundreds?" She moves her fingers and peeks through with one eye. "Please tell me it's not. We didn't use a condom, Marco."

"I know." I clear my throat. "I remember." Oh, I *remember*. It was my first time bare, my first time feeling how hot and silky it could feel, how the inner muscles grip and flex around my shaft and the sensitive head of my dick. I will never forget that.

"So… is it more than hundreds? Thousands?!" She drops her hands from her face and glares at me from her spot in the middle of the bed.

"It's not…" I speak when I shouldn't, move to reassure her when I should run. "You don't have to worry. I didn't—I haven't had sex with any men."

"What do you mean?" She hasn't covered up her breast, and I can't pull my eyes from it, can't stop myself from picturing it in my mouth.

"Nothing." I point to the pajamas. "Wear those. I'm going to bed."

"Stop." She sits up and pulls her sweater into place. "Wait. What do you mean you haven't had sex with any men? I don't understand."

BECAUSE I'M NOT GAY. I want to scream the words at the top of my lungs. Open the windows and scream them again, so that the entire city can hear. Less than a week since he's passed, and this lie is sitting on my chest like a boulder.

"You're drunk." I take another step toward the door and she's on her feet, standing in between me and the door, her sweater still hanging open, but the piece back in place, covering up all the parts I want to see.

"I'm not."

"Go to bed." I pick her up by her arms and move her to the side. The moment I release her, she's back in my way, as slippery as an escargot shell.

"You didn't have sex with Vince?"

"Though I think the chances of him being your father are ridiculously

231

thin, I still don't think it's appropriate for me to discuss our sex life." I make it almost to the door.

Her foot hooks out, her toes curled up, and she trips me, my hand whipping out to catch the dresser, a crystal lamp getting in the way and skidding across the surface. I swear, attempting to hop over her foot, and her hand clamps around my forearm. For such a tiny thing, she is strong, and we scuffle for a moment, glimpses of bare breasts swinging, and I stop before this entire thing turns into a Laurel and Hardy slapstick routine.

I feel as if my heart is beating at an unnatural pace. She's almost naked, her sweater hanging open, one of her legs still tangled in mine, in a stance that indicates martial arts training at some point in her life. I am on the defense, both physically and emotionally, my dick hard as a brick, my head confused, and my tongue loose.

"Talk to me," she demands, and it's the worst thing she can ask for. I can't talk to her. I can't talk to anyone. I have the rest of my life to look forward to this continuation of a lie. "Explain to me how you dated Vince for ten years and didn't have sex with him, yet you're trying to fuck me at every available opportunity."

"I'm not trying to fuck you tonight." I'm getting no credit for this. It's as if the universe doesn't give a shit about how hard I'm trying to behave.

She ignores the response and holds my eye contact as if she can literally see the truth in it. I reach down, peel back her fingers, and she releases her grip on my arm. I could run. I could get to that door before her, sprint through it, and slam it in her face. I could run, like a scared little boy who doesn't know how to have a conversation. It's tempting, and I look to the door without meaning to.

She straightens, her foot unhooking from mine, and when she crosses her arms, her breasts sit on her forearms as if up on a ledge. I look. No red-blooded man in the world could have kept himself from looking. "You're not gay."

"No." I can't help the word, which falls out on its own accord, but I don't regret it when it lands. I can't do this anymore, not with her, and I'm not certain how I will continue doing it with everyone else.

"Did he know?"

"Vince?" I choke back a laugh. "*Yeah*. He knew. It was why he picked me. Our relationship—despite what you may have seen in a magazine, was not a romantic one. He was—" I hesitate. "Almost like a father to me, but more like a friend. A very rich, very talented, very wise, friend."

"And you *pretended*." She has trouble saying the word, as if it is sticky in her mouth. "You pretended to be together."

I see the moment hope hits her face, her gaze snapping to me with the hopeful eagerness of a child. "He wasn't gay either? This was all a front? For the… for the fashion world?"

I know what she's doing. She's thinking that if I'm straight, and Vince is straight, then her mother isn't crazy, and at that concert, he could have pumped her so full of semen that she could have had three Averys. "No." I cut her off before her hope grows roots. "Vince was definitely gay. Ridiculously, whole-heartedly, helplessly, gay. Trust me on that."

She steps back and stumbles a little when she does, her weight hitting the closed door. "Then, what—" She sighs. "I—I don't understand, and I don't think it's because I'm drunk. I think this is a clusterfuck, and I don't know if you're lying to me, or telling the truth, but it doesn't make—"

"I'm not lying to you, but I can't tell you everything right now. We're a dozen hours from finding out if you're his daughter. If you are, I'll tell you everything about the situation. But if you're not?" I shake my head. "Then I've already told you too much. I shouldn't have told you *any* of this." I think of John, and the conniption he'll have.

She lifts her hands to her face, her fingers digging into her forehead and groans. "I wish I wasn't drunk right now."

I step forward, my hands sliding around the side of her waist, and I pull her toward me, her hands falling from her face. "Go to bed." I lean forward and kiss her on the forehead. "Go to sleep, and we can sort this out in the morning."

I shouldn't have kissed her on the forehead. It was too intimate, too tender, and when I pull away, she grips my shirt and keeps me in place. "Wait," she whispers.

CHAPTER 34

AVERY

He looks down on me, and I've never seen so much emotion in a man's face before. I tug on his sweater, and his eyes drop to my hands, then drag to my breasts, avoiding my face. Is he lying to me? I can't think of a reason for a man like Vince to have a fake relationship. He could have had a dozen boyfriends, could have had his pick of every gay man in North America. I also can't think of a reason for Marco to lie about it.

This close, I can see how thick his eyelashes are, the small wrinkles in the corners of his eyes, the perfect blend of features that now contort into a frown. "I can't—"

I lift my face to his and tighten my grip, pull him closer, and when he stumbles forward, I can feel the hard press of his arousal against my thigh. "You can't what?" I whisper.

"You're drunk." His hand slides from my waist to my hip, and he loops a finger under the side of my panties and twists the cotton around the digit, pulling the thong tight.

"So are you."

"I'm trying to be a gentleman."

I reach down and free his finger from my thong, pulling his hand up and placing it on my left breast. "Don't be."

"Avery…" he pleads, and his hand squeezes, the warm heat of his palm closing over my nipple. I lift on my toes, my hands clawing up his sweater and wrapping around his neck, and when his eyes drop to my lips, his other hand finding my other breast, it's over.

The dam of resistance breaks and the floodwaters churn. His mouth hits mine, and it's less of a kiss, and more of a claiming. I dig my nails into his hair, we make it to the bed, and I yank off my sweater and reach for his belt.

It's different, this time, from what it was in Spring Lake. Then, he was a bit of an asshole. A dominant, sexual, pleasure-delivering, pound-out-my-orgasm, asshole. Now, he is softer, more reverent. He kisses along my stomach, pulls down my panties, and takes his dear sweet time with his mouth. I come and he moves to my breasts, his move-ments patient, despite the stiff ridge of him bobbing against my inner thigh. He leaves me, pulls a condom from his pocket, and is back, my legs wrapping around his waist. His kiss is soft against my lips and I love the look on his face, the dark tightening of his features when he pushes inside me.

I could fall in love with him. The realization comes as quickly as my orgasm did, and is as blinding, my mind flipping through a dozen images of what I want. Him, in a tuxedo, at the altar. Him, my child in his arms. Him, with grey hair and a scowl.

He looks down, to the place where our bodies meet, and thrusts slowly, almost worshipfully, his hands on my hips, his eyes flicking back to mine. I hold his gaze, he stares back into mine, and in the eye contact, my second orgasm comes.

————

He sleeps naked, and I've never seen a more perfect specimen. I lay on my side, curled against him, my head on his arm. He is stretched out, his head turned away, his breathing heavy and constant, in tune with the noises of the city. I run my hand over his chest and look past him, at the window, the curtains now open, the room softly lit by the city.

If I fall asleep now, morning will come faster. The call with the results will come faster. The answer to the question that has pounded through my head for three days—finally delivered. Maybe that's why I'm fighting sleep. I'm afraid to get that answer, afraid of a situation I have absolutely no control over. I'm afraid of how I'm starting to feel about Marco. I'm afraid of what I felt last night, afraid I might be falling in love with him. Afraid that any future between us is impossible, given the circumstances that exist.

I feel sleep coming and I struggle against it, widening my eyes, forcing my gaze to move around the room, trying to stay awake. I'm not ready. I need to figure this out, need to wake up in the morning with some sort of a game plan. I need to arm myself, emotionally, for whatever outcome might come and figure…

————

There is a knock on the bedroom door and I feel the sheet move across my body, Marco's leg sliding in between mine, his hand wrapping around and pulling me flush to his chest.

"Go away!" Marco calls out, and his breath warms my neck, his teeth sliding along the skin, a gentle nip taken before he kisses the area. "Don't wake up," he whispers.

"Too late." I smile.

"Damn." He yawns against my neck. "I'd ravage you again, but I have a splitting headache right now."

I roll over and face him. "Poor baby."

"Don't give me that. You've got to be hurting too. You had more to drink than I did." He pulls the blanket higher, covering our bodies and winces at the sunlight, coming in through the open curtains. "I wonder what time it is."

I stretch forward, crawling far enough to reach my phone on the bedside table. I look at its display. "It's ten."

He grunts in response.

Ten o'clock. Three more hours until we hear the results of the test. I unlock my phone and look for a missed call, or a text, or an email. *Nothing.* I turn my head. "Will you check your phone? Just in case they called you?"

"Yeah. But my phone died in the night." He doesn't move, but raises his voice and speaks in the general direction of the ceiling. "Kmart, I need a butler." He pauses, and before I have the chance to ask him who the hell he's talking to, a voice responds, the sound seeming to come from all directions.

"Calling a butler." The voice is highly precise and modulated, the sort that comes from a robot.

I laugh. "What is *that?*"

"It's the virtual butler," he said. "We named her Kmart. We had to pick a name that no one would say in natural conversation, unless—"

"Excuse me. I didn't catch that command."

He grimaces. "See? When you say her name, it causes her to listen. It's like the Alexa thing from Amazon, except we had the technology installed ages ago. In fact, she—" He glances to the ceiling, then lowers his voice to a playful stage whisper. "She's a little outdated."

"I have still not heard a command."

"Kmart, go away."

"Certainly. Your wish is my command, Master Marco."

I start laughing. "Oh my god. Tell me you didn't program her to say that."

He scoffs. "Of course, I did. She can learn your voice too. Here, watch this. Kmart, add a new user."

"New user." She intones. "For voice verification and learning purposes, please repeat the following sentences after me."

I shoot Marco a wry look, but wait, feeling as if I'm about to audition for a role of sorts.

"Vince Horace is the greatest fashion designer in the world. There is no rival to him. He makes all of the other fashion designers his bitch." She pauses, and my chuckle turns into a full-blown laugh.

"Repeat it," Marco urges and pokes me in the side.

"I—" I giggle. "I can't remember it."

"Kmart, repeat."

She repeats the ridiculous mantra, and I state it back, the repetition occasionally marred by a series of laughter. I roll my eyes at Marco and he smiles. "What?" He says, raising his hands in mock innocence. "That was all Vince. He's the one who programmed her."

I hope he's my father. The thought hits me so unexpectedly that I'm caught off guard, my defenses down, and I'm struck with the sudden pain of being reminded that I will never have the chance to *know* him. I will never know the man who named his virtual butler Kmart and required that all new users praise his talents to gain entry.

"New user recorded. What is your name?"

I start to say my name and Marco clasps a hand over my mouth, lifting his head and speaking to the ceiling. "Sexy Bitch."

"Sexy Bitch is already taken."

239

I laugh harder, the sound muffled beneath his hand and he grimaces. I work his hands free of my mouth. "Goddess Sugar Tits," I whisper, fairly certain that no one, in the history of the Vince Horace database, has ever been described that way. He peeks under the sheet at said sugar tits with an appraising look, nods in approval, then repeats the name.

"Welcome, Goddess Sugar Tits," the voice intones. "You are now saved in my database of users. Is there anything that I can assist you with?"

"No thank you," I call out, and a tone sounds, indicating her exit.

"Goddess Sugar Tits," he repeats, pulling the sheet down, exposing my breasts. "I like that. Though, we may have to restrict the use of her in mixed company." He leans over and presses a soft kiss on the closest nipple.

A knock sounds and he pulls up the sheet with a regretful look.

"Should you hide?" I whisper.

"Fuck no." He relaxes back against the pillows. "Come in," he calls, and the bedroom door opens. It's a person I haven't seen yet, dressed in the all-white dress suit I've come to recognize as the house uniform.

"Good morning, Mr. Lent." If the man notices me, he doesn't react, his hands clasped before him, his tone one of complete respect. He's young, mid-twenties, and has the build of a gymnast. "How may I help you this morning?"

"I need a charger for my phone. Clear this floor of all staff, except for the salon and dressing room and let the kitchen know we'll be down for breakfast shortly."

"Certainly." The man leaves, closing the door behind him, and I roll to my side, sandwiching my palms together and tucking them underneath my head.

"Don't you get tired of everyone kissing your ass?"

He chuckles. "No, quite the opposite. I hated it when I first moved into the house. But after a few weeks, anything different became unacceptable." He glances at me. "Except with you. You've never kissed my ass. In fact…" he leans forward and presses a kiss to my cheek. "You've been a rather big *pain* in my ass ever since you first jumped in front of my car."

"Hey," I scoff. "A girl's got to get a man's attention any way she can in this city."

"Not a girl like you." He moves his kiss to my mouth, then rolls out of bed, finding the pajamas from last night and tossing them toward me. "Here. Let's get some breakfast."

"You don't get served breakfast in bed?" I grimace. "Wow. How positively civilian of you."

"We aren't cavemen." He emerges from the closet in clingy boxer briefs and pulls a T-shirt over his head. "Plus, it's a bitch to wait on items to travel five floors. You ask for butter, and you'll wait five minutes for it."

"Ah. The truth comes out." I stretch, then work my hands through the pajama top and pull it over my head. Scooting to the end of the bed, I look for my panties from last night.

"Here." He holds out a new pair.

"Thanks." I pull them on and sneak a glance at him. "Not to make everything awkward but…"

"You want to know where we stand." He runs a hand through his hair.

"Yeah. I mean… it's not like I'm trying to have a relationship conversation with you, but it seems like we've done a complete one-eighty since yesterday."

"Yesterday, when I was being a dick."

"Yeah. A *complete* dick." I squint at him. "Like, huge. Gigantic dick."

He nods and coughs out a smile. "I accept that." He sits next to me on the edge of the bed. "And you should know, first off, that I *am* a dick. Being one has been my MO for the past—" he grimaces. "Dozen years. And it was something that Vince liked. So, part of it is just habit. But the other part—" he sighs. "I've been pretending to be gay for a long time. And what I did with you in Spring Lake? That exposed me—and Vince—in an alarmingly negative way. And that exposure got worse, once I realized your potential connection to the estate. So, any cruelty I showed was a fucked-up attempt at damage control." He tilts his head, wincing.

"Plus, you're a dick," I add, and he smiles.

"Exactly. But I promise to be less of a dick, where you're involved." He reaches over and grips my knee, giving it a gentle squeeze. "I'm surprised you agreed to dinner last night, after everything that I've put you through."

I shrug, sliding my feet into the pants and pulling them up. "I think I went for the same reason that you started off being an ass. Damage control." I turn and look back at him. "If Vince is my father, we should, at a minimum, get along with each other." I pull my hair into a ponytail. "And… just to confess something? I'm relieved to hear that you and he were just friends, and not … more."

He rests his weight back on his hands, and his t-shirt stretches tight across his chest. "That's not too much of a surprise to hear."

"Yeah. I was a little creeped out with myself, after that first night, for sleeping with my potential father's lover." I snort. "God, I hate that word. *Lover.* It sounds so medieval."

"Yet you did sleep with me."

"Well." I lift a hand and gesture toward him. "You were rocking a pretty tempting package. And it had been…" I blow out a pained breath and plop down on the bed next to him. "A *while.*"

He studies my face. "That seems impossible. How do you not have half of Detroit under your spell?"

"Excellent question." I widen my eyes and throw up my hands. "Total mystery. Maybe it's my fourteen cats."

He groans and stands. "You don't have cats."

"Or..." I bring up my feet and sit cross-legged on the bed. "It could be my propensity to turn batshit crazy on the third date."

"You turned batshit crazy on our first date," he points out.

"Well." I shrug. "Sometimes, if the potential is high, I pull out that card early."

He strolls to the closet, and I admire the muscles in his legs. "While we're being friendly..." I call out.

"Yeah?" He reemerges, a pair of drawstring pants in hand, and unfolds them.

"What do you really think? Do you think he's my father?"

"Honestly?" He steps into the pants and shook his head. "I don't know. I don't think that you're ridiculous for asking the question." He gives me a sheepish look. "Despite the things I said before."

He walks over to where his pants lie, still in a heap from last night. Reaching down, he pulls out his cell, and his wallet, pocketing both. "But things were a lot cleaner when Vince didn't have a child." He avoids my gaze, moving to the bedside table and lifts his watch, checking the time. "I'm hoping you're *not* his daughter. It would make my life a lot easier." He glances back at me. "And yes, I realize what a selfish ass that makes me."

"It's okay." I shrug. "I hope that I *am* his daughter, and that would suck for you, so I guess we both want what it isn't good for the other person." I examine the bottom of my foot. "But... is it really going to suck for you? I mean, I signed that contract. Why do you care if he's my father?"

He says nothing, and the question hangs in the air. He works his watch over his wrist and I fight the urge to repeat the question.

"It's not just the money," he finally says. "I enjoy looking at you. I enjoyed dinner last night with you. And I really—*really*—enjoy fucking you."

"Oh." This is an unexpected turn of conversation, and I feel my cheeks warm with the telltale feel of a blush.

"When you signed that contract, it was the first time I thought you might be in this for something other than money or blackmail." He looks up at me. "That was a huge weight off my shoulders. And it changed how I felt about you. Which is ironic, since it probably made you hate me."

"It did," I agree. "But I got over that, sometime during last night's dinner."

"Look, I have a bunch of personal shit to figure out. Prior to meeting you, I thought I could continue with..." he waves a hand in the air. "All of *this*. But now..." He finishes with his watch and looks at me. "I'm suddenly realizing that I can't ever have my own relationship, my own life...not unless I violate my agreement with Vince. And I don't think that's what he intended, but that's how it feels. And I didn't expect to feel this way so soon. I thought..." he rubs at his jaw. "I thought I would have five or six years before I would be in this situation."

He shakes his head and looks away. "Just ignore what I'm saying. I'm not making any sense. Are you ready to go downstairs?"

"Yeah." I scoot to the end of the bed and stand, following him to the door and feeling even more confused than before.

———

Breakfast turns out to be a production, and I quickly understand why they didn't serve it to us in bed. The eat-in kitchen is massive, a large hearth at one end, the kitchen open to a large island that houses a cooktop on one side, and a half-dozen place settings on the opposite end. There are uniformed bodies all over the place, and I have a personal waiter, as does Marco. I feel some sort of demented obligation to justify everyone's job, and order four things off the top of my head, each request met with a pleasant nod, as if the pantry selection is unlimited and salmon benedict can be created as easily as a bowl of Frosted Flakes.

Marco raises an eyebrow at me. "Hungry?"

"Starved," I lie, and check the clock on the wall, dismayed to see that barely fifteen minutes have passed.

I scoot closer to the counter and receive a curious look from the chef, a dark-skinned man who flashes a smile and doesn't ask questions. While I watch, he chops apples and skins lemons, feeding them into a juicer. "Need help?" I offer.

Marco coughs, mid-sip into a cappuccino. "They don't need help," he snaps. "Tell her, Frances."

"It's true, madam," he says, in a cultured voice tinted in a French accent. "I have been waiting all morning to do something, and I'm afraid that you will look much better at it than I will." He winks, and Marco grunts in response. It's very lovable, the prickly nature he projects. I understand why Vince liked it. I feel, in watching his interactions, as if I am part of an exclusive club, one allowed to see the person behind the scowls.

His phone powers on and he picks it up, scrolling through the different apps, then shakes his head. "No news yet."

I nod and pull out my own phone, checking, for the fifth time, my own messages. Still nothing from Andrei.

245

"There are a few more hours left. Try to be patient."

Try to be patient. It should be easy. How did I manage thirty-one years so easily, yet these hours seem so interminable?

Marco wipes his mouth and stands. "I thought you could get dressed in the salon. Edward?"

The butler steps forward. "Yes, sir?"

"Take Avery to the third floor and have them help her with her dressing."

"Certainly." He nods, gestures to me, and I stay put on the stool.

"Help me with my dressing? Is that some code word for knocking me upside the head and burying me in the basement?"

The older man fixes me with a haughty look of admonishment. "I can assure you, Miss McKenna, that I would never be party to such things."

The man has no understanding of sarcasm. *None.* If I ever hire a butler, I'm going to get one with a wicked sense of humor.

"Just take her to the third floor," Marco says. "And try not to be a complete pain in the ass while doing it."

Edward nods as if accustomed to such abuse. "Very well, sir. I take it that you will be dressing yourself this morning?"

"Yes."

This is a ridiculous existence. The pendulum swings back and I almost hope Vince isn't my father. These people need help getting dressed in the morning? I heave myself off the stool and glare in Marco's direction and am rewarded with a smile, one that catches me off guard and reminds me how painfully good-looking he is. How could a person stay mad at a man like this? How could a woman keep her distance, protect her heart, and keep from falling under his spell?

I've got to get out of here—after we find out the news, and before I fall in love with him. A man like this could destroy my heart. A man like this will make every other man, every other kiss, and every other love, seem weak in comparison.

I yank myself away from that smile and follow the butler out of the kitchen.

———

It's a trek to the third floor, down a long hallway, through a short staircase, onto an elevator, and then out on the floor. Through it all, Edward says nothing. I attempt a conversation about the weather and get nowhere. I ask how long he's been in New York and get stony silence. He reminds me of my instructors at the prep school, an assortment of women and men who—if a knife was held to their throat—would still fail a personality test. I mention this to him, mention that I could set him up with a variety of hot young English teachers, should he have the desire for someone as dour and boring as himself. He doesn't respond, doesn't smile, doesn't engage, a reaction that only causes me to increase my efforts.

"We're going to be friends," I insist, struggling to keep up with him, his feet clipping briskly along the hall. "You don't know it yet, but we're going to be friends. People like me, you know? I'm a *very* likable person."

"Congratulations," he muses, his face slack with disinterest. He stops beside a double door and grips the handle, opening it with a flourish he probably practiced a gazillion times in butler school. "Here is the salon."

I step forward and pause, genuinely impressed. There is a long mirror stretching along one side, a counter before it, stage lights present, and three male attendants, each standing at their own chair as if at attention.

The first of the group steps forward, extending his hand and introducing himself, his eyes sweeping over me with the critical gaze of a seasoned professional. I blow an erratic hair out of my face and glance back over my shoulder, but Edward is gone.

CHAPTER 35

MARCO

I take my time in the shower, letting the hot water hit my back and think of last night. It's unfair to put all this pressure on her. It's ridiculous to expect that she, from just a few interactions, would have any feelings for me, and I have no reason to think about a future with her in it.

Yet, I am.

Something between us started, way back in Spring Lake, and intensified when she signed that contract, *something* that is taking over me. It's more than a physical connection and I'll be damned if I'm the only one who feels it. But maybe I am. Maybe I've gone a decade without spending more than a couple of hours with a woman, and now—with my first genuine interactions with one—my heart is too exposed, too naïve and young. I'm like a kid with his first crush. Maybe that's all this is. A crush. And, when she goes back to Detroit, I will survive it. I will go back to my life, back to my celibacy and forget she ever happened.

For right now, I have to shut off my brain. I need to back up and give her space. She's probably freaked out by me right now. I was talking nonsense in that bedroom. I spent the night kissing and spooning with her as if we were *something*, as if I had a right that extended to more than two adults gaining pleasure from each other. She's probably climbing out the salon's window and clattering down the fire escape, sprinting down the New York street in bare feet, her dark hair whipping in the wind. She'll probably run to John's office, file a restraining order against me and I'll never see her again without attorneys and security present.

"Fuck!" I pound my hand against the shower, reminded of the fact that —even if she *does* like me—what the fuck am I going to do? *Date* her? Tell New York's entire gay population that I'm straight? I've been on Oprah, for shit's sake. I sat next to Vince as he discussed homosexuality and how it is *not* a choice and how we shouldn't be afraid to share our feelings, to share our sexual preferences with the world. I sat on her stupid couch and was a hypocrite of the worst kind, an insult to their entire lifestyle, and I was that way with their golden boy. I did it for him, and I did it for me, and I did it for this billion-dollar fortune, and all of it seems *useless* right now. All of it seems like a waste.

I turn off the shower and open the door. Going to the closet, I flip through hangers and select a dark purple suit, the color almost black in its intensity. Vince had loved this suit. He'd called it the color of royalty. And it was. A color "fit for our lifestyle." I put the suit back and grab a charcoal gray one. Something drab and absolutely ordinary, one that would have made Vince click his tongue at me in disapproval. I grab my cell phone and dial John's number, holding it between my shoulder and my head and work the pants out of the hanger. "Tell me you've heard something."

"I haven't heard anything, but I'll let you know when I do. We'll be the second party to know. They'll call her attorney first."

"Well, she's here with me." I step into the pants. "She stayed here last night. And yes, it's complicated."

John is quiet for a long period of time. "Do you understand what you are risking by becoming emotionally involved with her?"

"I'm trying not to." I think of last night, my attempt to get her in pajamas, the torture of trying to be a gentleman, and the moment when she'd leaned into my body and looked up at me, her eyes begging for a kiss. In that moment, no threat could've kept me from kissing her. No risk, no assets, no life-changing situations. Her body against me, those lips upturned… I lost that battle the minute I followed her into the bedroom. Hell, I lost that battle four hours earlier when she stepped into my car.

"You're playing with fire."

"I know." I pull out a cardinal blue tie and toss it onto the island. "But currently, I don't give a fuck."

"Not giving a fuck can be very dangerous for Vince's empire, and for his legacy," John cautions. "She's *playing* you. She's seducing you and you're falling right into her trap."

"I'm not." I shake my head. "She signed the contract, she's not getting anything."

"Contracts don't mean shit if the party in them is affected. You don't think she could convince you to tear that up? You don't think she can convince you to give her something?"

He's right. "If I give her something, it will be my decision. She's not tricking me into anything."

I stop halfway through buttoning my shirt and speak clearly into the phone, making sure that he understands me. "This is *my* money. This is now my company and I will do what I want to do with it. Your job is to do what I ask you to do and to advise me if I need help in making a decision. I don't care if she's related to him or not, and I'll make my own decisions absent of any input from my dick. Don't tell me what my heart should do. You are not in charge of my heart. You are overseeing this estate. And you've known me long enough to know that I am not an impulsive or emotional individual. If I want to fuck her, I will fuck her. And if I want to fall in love with her, I'll fall in love with her. And I don't want to hear two shits of an opinion from you on it. Do you understand?"

"I'm on your side, Marco. I've been on your side from the beginning. Remember that."

"At the moment, my side feels kind of lonely."

"It's not. This ... we're going to get through this together, and I'll support your decisions. I just need to know those decisions so that I can do that. Okay?"

I don't know what the fuck he's saying this for. I'm keeping him in the loop. The only one who knows more details about the activity of my cock is my hand. Still, I nod. "Yeah, okay. I know they're going to contact her, but just…" I let out a breath. "Just call me if you hear anything."

"I will."

I hang up the phone and finish buttoning up my shirt. I close my eyes and wish that Vince was here.

———

I sit at my desk and look over numbers. Orders have increased and I email the warehouses and forward on the figures. It's not unexpected. We knew this would come with Vince's death. We've had time to prepare, have overstocked and prepped stores, increased staffing and advertising. Death, at least in fashion, is good for business. It's a bittersweet victory and I sigh at the compiled sales figures at the bottom of the report. It will be our best season ever and he is not here to see it and was too sick to oversee much of its implementation. At least the vision is his, the designs worked on eight months ago, back when he was obliviously healthy. The winter line, which unveils in September, will be the last one with his stamp on it. After that, every design will be from me, and our team of designers around the world, a team who has spent more than a dozen seasons under his tutelage.

The brand will be fine, and his vision will continue, with me at the helm. I'm ready. He spent ten years grooming me for this, and when it comes to fashion, I can make Vince Horace decisions with my eyes closed. When it comes to life, I feel much more lost.

"Master Lent?" Kmart speaks and I lift my head.

"Yes."

"Goddess Sugar Tits is waiting on the first floor." The name causes me to smile, and I stand up, closing the report and reaching for my jacket.

I move through the house and glance at my watch. Another two hours. I skip the elevator, taking the staircase, and when I round the corner she is at the front window, peering at something out on the street. I stop.

Yves St Laurent once said that what is important in a dress is the woman wearing it. She's not in a dress, but she's all that I see. She's beautiful. *Breathtakingly* so. Not that she wasn't before, but *now*. Her hair is darker, fuller, a cascade of waves along her back. She turns a little and I see a strapless cream leather bodice, and a wool A-line skirt, one I recognize from a couture collection we did three years ago. As she moves, it flairs out, and my eyes lift from it to her face. Her skin glows, her brows tamed and sculpted. Her makeup is subtle, but it's the first time I've seen her wear it, and it takes her natural beauty to a level that could stop a man's heart.

I step forward and she grins, gesturing down the front of her body. "What do you think?" She strikes a pose and I notice the peep-toe heels.

"I think I like your boots better."

"Yeah," she sticks out her tongue. "Me, too, but I wasn't going to pass on *free* shoes." She giggles, then stops, concern pinching those beautiful features. "I *do* get to keep these, right?"

I could spend every single day of my life dressing her, every day inspired by a dozen of her quirks to build a hundred collections. "You can keep them."

"I've got to say…" she tucks a strand of hair behind her ear. "I was making fun of the whole 'people helping you get dressed' thing, but…" she sways to one side and raises her hands in surrender. "That experience was pretty awesome. No wonder you look so hot. They do that for you every *day*?" She's so perplexed by the concept that I laugh.

"Yes." I wince as if injured. "To be honest, without my staff I'm a horrific elephant of a man. Please don't tell anyone."

She zips her lips and glances at her watch, a motion so quick that someone else might have missed it.

"Nervous?"

She makes a face. "It just feels like the hours are passing in slow motion."

From behind me, a phone rings, and her head snaps up. "Oh, that's my cell." She hurries forward, rummaging through her bag and pulling out her phone. She glances at it, then looks at me, her eyes wide. "It's my attorney."

CHAPTER 36

AVERY

The courier beats us there, and when we step into the office, he is waiting with the envelope and Marco's attorney. I step forward and knot my hands together, twisting the knuckles until they feel close to breaking.

"Okay." The attorney clears his throat and gestures to the courier, who tears open the top of the envelope and pulls out the contents.

"Your copy, Miss McKenna." He passes me the papers, and turns, offering a second set to the attorney.

The report is several pages long, all typed, and my eyes zero in on the words at the top of the page, highlighted with an orange marker.

NOT A PATERNAL MATCH.

Marco's hand closes on my shoulder, his eyes reading the page, and I turn into him without thinking, my hands clutching at his shirt, a sob welling up from somewhere deep in my chest. I'm *crying*. I can't remember the last time I cried, but it was before boarding school, and over something insignificant. Now, I feel the ache in my chest, as raw and painful as death. And that's what this is, isn't it? The death of a possibility. The only real possibility I've had so far.

Marco's arms wrap around me, and he's so strong. His grip, his chest. It is a hard press of comfort, softened by the kiss he places on my head, the sweep of his arms over my back.

"Huh." The attorney's voice sounds odd as if he is confused, and I turn my head, still clutched to Marco's chest, and look at him. "Marco. Look at this."

I step toward him, my eyes trying to follow the point of the man's finger, but keep flitting to the top. NOT A PATERNAL MATCH. Will those words ever stop repeating in my head?

"It says…" Marco takes the page and looks at me. "It says that Vince isn't your father, but that eleven of the fifteen markers match."

"Which means, what? The test is wrong?" Hope sparks, and I fight like hell to keep it under control.

"No. There's a note here, referencing the markers." He moves closer to me and points.

The high number of matched markers indicates that the tested individual is likely a close relative of the actual father, and most likely a father or brother.

I don't understand.

Marco glances at the attorney. "Could you give us some privacy?"

"Certainly."

I sit down in the closest seat, the paper held in both hands, and reread the sentence. The door closes and Marco leans against the edge of the desk. "Avery."

"I don't— I don't—"

"Avery." He leans forward. "Listen to me."

I look up from the paper.

"I think that Vince's brother may be your father."

That hope flares again, tempered only by the expression on his face, one of regret.

"Do you have that photo?"

I glance back at the paper, *most likely a father or brother,* then numbly reach for my bag and move around the contents until I find the photo. I hold it out.

"Look." He holds up the photo, his finger pinned to the man's chest. "Look at the ring on his finger."

I look, see the ring, then shrug. "Yeah. So?"

"I have that ring. Vince used to wear it at times. He told me it was his brother's."

"Who is his brother?"

He sighs. "His name was James, and he died about twenty years ago, hit by a drunk driver when he was jogging."

Died. I have expected it, knew that there was something wrong with Marco's delivery of the news but still… I still feel a bit of peace at this news. "So…" I point to the photo. "That isn't Vince? It's James?"

He nods. "I think so. He's wearing the ring, and the photos I've seen of him—they had a very strong resemblance to each other —James was just a couple of years older."

Yes. I suddenly remember the book, the photo of the two boys next to each other, their likeness uncanny. Other than that photo, and a few isolated mentions, there had been little else on his brother. "So, Vince wasn't at LiveAid. *James* was."

Marco says nothing.

"Right?" I press.

"Well—Vince *was* at LiveAid. I guess they both were. I didn't tell you because I didn't think there was a way that he could have slept with a woman." He grimaces. "I didn't think, and I didn't want—"

"You didn't want to risk your fortune." I finish. "Not until I agreed to give it all up." I look back down at the photo. "And the ring? You noticed it in the picture before?"

"Yes." He nods. "I recognized it the first time I saw the photo. And I didn't tell you then, because I was a greedy and self-serving bastard, and giving your idea credibility didn't work for me."

"You made me feel stupid," I whisper, my fingers tracing over my father's face. James Horace. I have a name. A name I can use to find out more.

"I have a way that might, in some small way, make up for that." He picks up my bag and passes it to me. "Come back to the house with me. I can't bring your father back, but there's something I can show you."

————

I step back into the house a different woman. Without realizing it, I had given myself some sort of mental ownership of the house, had envisioned myself living in it, lording over it. Now, I'm in my rightful and permanent role—just a guest, a relative of the man who once owned it.

Marco takes me to a service elevator in the rear of the home and the doors creak open with a shudder. We step on, and it's crowded in the space, our shoulders brushing against each other. "This isn't a tomb you're taking me to, is it?"

"Not exactly." He presses the button labeled B. "I'm taking you to the archive room."

The archive room. I perk up, and the doors open to a concrete hall, the air cooler down here. Marco waits for me to step off, then gestures to a set of black jackets hung on hooks before us. "Grab a jacket. It gets chilly down here."

I don one, the size a little big and zip it up, appreciating the warmth it provides. Marco opens the top drawer of a desk and pauses, looking down at the contents.

"What?"

"I—"his words break off and he lifts out a pair of red gloves, holding them in his palm. "I always thought it was stupid, his insistence that we wear gloves down here. I told him that these items would outlive all of us. And now... fuck me if I can't *not* put them on." He returns the red gloves to the drawer, reaching down and withdrawing two white pairs—one pair which he passes to me and one pair which he dons.

He closes the drawer carefully, then looks at me, his face tight. "Come on."

We are stopped by a large steel door, a keypad set into the wall beside it. "The code is 87224." He presses the number in, then hesitates before turning the handle. "No one knows that code, other than you, I, and the archivist."

I nod, and when he swings open the door, I step up and into the room.

It's beautiful, like every room in the house I've seen. There's a long wooden table to the left, one with overhead lights that shine down on its surface. Two club chairs to the right, set in front of a projection screen. Bookcases line the walls, and each one is filled with binders, their labels perfectly aligned with one another. There must be a thousand of them and I step to the closest, a light illuminating the shelves, and read through the first few titles.

January 1981 - March 1981

April 1981 - May 1981

June 1981

July 1981

August 1981 - September 1981

I pull the last binder out and open it, each page dedicated to a photo, an explanation typed beneath the image. I look at a young Vince, standing with a model, and lean in, examining his face, allowing myself to see the minute differences between his face and the image in my bag. I look at the caption.

Vince Horace with 19-year-old model Candace Whitmore, in Miami. This photo was taken before the Candelabra show at Lux platform on South Beach. The design she is wearing is from his 1981 Fall collection, and was titled 'White Tunic'.

I look over to Marco. "Where's the album from LiveAid? Have you looked at it?"

"I haven't looked at it yet." His features twist in a handsome wince. "To be honest, prior to this point, I was afraid of what I might find." He steps forward, his chin lifting, eyes scrolling over the shelves. "What was the date?"

"Mid-July. 1985."

"Here." He rises on his toes and pulls at a binder I would have had trouble getting to. He passes it to me and I take a deep breath to clear my chest.

"Take it to the table." He points, and I move, my thin gloves tightening on the ornate leather cover, the book heavy, my anticipation—and fear—tight. What if there are no photos? What if there are only photos of Vince? Or what if Marco is wrong, Vince wasn't there, and there aren't any photos from Live Aid?

I set the book down on the table and Marco reaches up, adjusting the overhead light. It shines down on the book and I open it, then hold my breath.

Photos. So many, but none that I want. Photos of Vince by mannequins. Vince by fabric. Sketches cut from design books and inserted into the book. There is as much focus on the clothing as the memories, and I flip through the pages faster, my panic rising.

"Wait." Marco stops me, right before I flip past a photo of Vince, by a Volkswagen bus. He points. "That's James' car. Or, was his car."

I stop, leaning forward and examining the photo first, looking for anyone else in the frame, any hint as to the van's owner. Then I move to the caption.

Vince Horace, just before leaving with brother James Horace, to travel to Philadelphia for the LiveAid concert. The concert was a dual-venue benefit for famine in Ethiopia.

I stare at the words until they blur. It's right here. Black and white. James was there and so was Vince, though that part no longer matters, in terms of my paternity. I turn the page. Vince, in a small town, some stop along the way. Vince, in a thrift store, pulling out garments from a discount rack. Vince, eating a hamburger on the hood of the van. There are no photos of James and I growl in frustration.

"Be patient." Marco's hand settles on my shoulder. "There will be more. In this room, there's always more."

I try. I flip slower, read more captions, and a dozen photos later, am rewarded with a single photo of James—by himself—leaning against the van, a gas pump in hand. He's looking at the camera and smiling. He's long and lean, wearing tight jeans and a sweatshirt, one with a logo on the front. He looks just like my photo—the same tan skin, scruffy chin, and wild hair. I pull on the end of my hair, now sleek and straight, thanks to Marco's beauty team. In the photo, he's got one hand tucked in his pocket, his shoulders a little hunched, as if shielding himself from the wind.

"What did he do? For a job?"

Marco shakes his head. "I don't know. Vince said he always found a way to make money. Plus…" he turns to me as if suddenly remembering something. "He owned part of the company."

"Part of what company?"

"Holy shit." He reaches into his pocket and pulls out his cell phone, making a face when he sees the screen. "The service sucks down here. Just a minute." He moves to the wall and lifts a phone receiver, looking at his cell phone and punching in a number.

"This is Marco Lent. Can you grab John for me?"

He waits, and his eyes meet mine. He says nothing, and I glance back down at the photo.

"John. How much did James own of the company?" He nods. "Okay. No, I understand. Verify it for me, will you? I'll tell Avery." He hung up the phone and a smile stretches over his face.

"What?" I'm following enough of the conversation to understand that I've probably inherited something.

"James, before he died, owned five percent—best John can remember —of Vince Horace. When he died, he left that, and his house, to Vince, seeing as he didn't have any other family or—" he nods to me. "Children."

"Meaning?"

"Meaning that you have a right to that five percent, which is worth somewhere around thirty-five million dollars when you exclude all of Vince's personal assets from the estate. Plus the house."

That last part, even more than the money, catches my attention. "You still own his house?"

"Yep." He grins. "And you've already been to it. Spring Lake."

"Shut up."

He raises one palm. "Swear to God."

"The house in Spring Lake, that was James' house?"

"Yep. You can get rid of the naked statue in front if you want."

I look down at the album, moving my gloved hands over the image. "You don't have to give me anything. I signed that contract and—"

"That contract involved the possibility of Vince being your father, not James."

"It doesn't matter. That isn't what I came here for." In my peripheral vision, I see him approach, feel the heat of him as he stops next to me, his hands on his hips.

"I know it isn't."

"This." I turn to the next page, don't see James, and flip back, pressing a finger on the photo. "This is all I need. An answer. A history."

"I know."

He doesn't know. He doesn't know what it feels like to not have a family or to have two adoptive parents who regretted their decision. He wraps one arm around my shoulders, bringing me closer to his side, and I accept it.

He doesn't know, but he's trying to.

He flips the page forward. Does it again. Again. I lean against his shoulder and watch shots of the entrance to the event. Photos of the crowds. A shot of Vince as he walked through the crowd and turned back to the camera, gesturing him forward. I linger over a photo of five topless girls, paint smeared over their chests, flashing peace signs to the camera. There are more photos, one of Vince holding a joint

265

and laughing, and Marco stays on that one for a long moment. "This." He taps the picture. "This is the man I knew."

We finally get to a photo of the two of them, their arms around each other, cups in hand, raised in a salute. Side by side, I can see the differences in the men. James is bigger, more developed, his face fuller, gaze more confident. Vince is the trendier of the two and is looking up at his big brother with a grin, his hand tightly gripped to his shoulder. I remember now, a scene from the book—one where Vince had told his brother first, before anyone else, about his homosexuality. In this photo, I see how close they were. It hurts to see, the sibling connection that I never had, the love between them. I might have had that love with him if he'd known I existed.

"I'll get you copies of all of these."

I nod, too overwhelmed to respond. I turn the page and there, in full color and glory, is my mother.

She is dancing, her arms swinging, her skirt flaring, a crowd around her, their hands raised as if about to clap. She looks beautiful and wild, her hair spinning through the air, her mouth open in a laugh. On the edge of the crowd is James, and he is smiling, his focus on her.

"That's my mom," I say quietly.

Marco leans closer. "I can see it. She's got your fire."

She's got your fire. I think of the woman I met and how different she had appeared from this woman. I think of her small home, the child tugging on her arm, the stress and weariness that had lined her face. She had seemed so ordinary. She had been so disappointing, and I feel a pang of guilt at how quickly I had judged and discarded her. I look down at the caption.

Unidentified woman, dancing at the 1985 LiveAid concert, just before a bonfire.

Unidentified woman. My mother.

And look—" he points out James. "He can't keep his eyes off her. Just like me, with you."

I blush. "Oh please."

"I can't." He leans forward, and the fingers of his hand tighten around my back, pulling me forward. He kisses me, and warmth spreads through my chest from the contact. When he pulls away, he's smiling. "I've got something else you're going to love."

CHAPTER 37

MARCO

"Okay, I'm done." She reaches over and pulls the remote from my hand, pausing the screen. "Let me have something more to watch later."

"You sure?" I turn and glance over the boxes, the hundreds of DVD cases glimmering under the theater's discreet lights.

"I'm sure. I'm gorged." She crawls along the couch and into my lap, curling into my chest, her arms sliding around my neck. "Thank you."

I'm not sure what she's thanking me for, but I'll take it. I pull her tighter to me and lean forward to kiss her. "You're welcome, Miss Horace." I pause. "Hmmm. I'm going to have to get used to that name."

She laughs. "Yeah. Me too." Her phone beeps and she picks it up, glancing at the screen, then tosses it down. "Ugh."

"Work?" I slide one hand along her bare legs, from ankle to knee, and dip slightly under the hem of her skirt. "Someone's funds need to be managed?"

"Something like that." She looks at me. "I need to go back home."

I hate that sentence, hate the idea of her leaving and us losing this moment of connection. What if I forget how to be human? What if she forgets whatever it is, about me, that causes her to smile? What if she comes back, and we are strangers again? I move my hand higher, passing it over her knee, and maybe I can distract her with sex. "For how long?"

"I don't know." She studies me, and I wonder if she can see my fear. "I've got to figure things out."

Shit. I hate that sentence even more. *Figuring things out* sounds bad. I slide my hand down the slope of her legs, the skin warm beneath the wool skirt, and stop when my fingers hit silk. Her legs part, just a hands width, and I take advantage of the opening. I watch her face, and fuck, she's beautiful. Her eyes soften when my fingers gently roll over the silk. Her mouth hangs a little, a sigh of breath escaping, and I watch her body flex. "The thing is…" I say carefully, watching her closely. "I have some of my own things to figure out. Things that involve you."

She holds her breath when I slide my hand further and I cup her through the panties. I can feel her dampness, feel the easy give of her body when I curl my fingers against the silk. "Things like what?"

"Like if you like *this*…" I use my thumb to circle her clit, the silk still between us, the contact causing a murmur of pleasure. "Or *this*… better." I nudge her panties out of the way and use my forefinger and middle finger, pushing them inside of her, the sudden entrance causing her eyes to pinch shut, her pelvis to lift, her knees to fall open.

I'm in love. I'm in fucking love with this woman. She has the blood of a Horace, the temperament of a lion, and the sexual proclivities of every fantasy I've ever had.

"I need more," she gasps, arching against me and clawing my chest for attention.

I'll give her more. I'll give her everything. I pick her up in my arms, steal a kiss from those lips, and swap our positions on the couch. In three quick moves, I am inside of her—my hips rocking, our kiss messy, her breath gasping, body squeezing me. She pants my name and I slow my thrusts, go deeper, take a moment to pull at her bodice and free her breasts.

I look down at her and, in the moment before I kiss her, I almost tell her how I feel.

———

She can't leave yet. I just found her. I swallow the thought and watch her twist her hair into a knot. She abandons the action and leans forward, wrapping her phone charger around her hand.

It's painful, watching her pack and knowing that she is leaving. It's even worse so when the process is so short, the act done in minutes, her new clothes stuffed into one of our duffel bags without a second thought. I lean against the wall and watch her, my mind flipping through a hundred ways to try to delay her exit. I reach into my pocket and close my hand around the ring I still need to give her.

She zips the bag shut and looks at me. "I think that's it. Are you sure about the plane? Cause I can just grab a fl—"

"I'm positive. Think of the plane as yours." I step forward and pull out James' ring. I've put it on a silver linked chain, one I pulled off an Atocha coin that Vince had, the intricate links pairing nicely with the band. "Here." I undo the clasp and hold it up, fastening it around her neck.

She looks down, lifting the ring and turning it over, examining it. "Wow." She glances back at me. "I have something of my father's. That's—that's pretty cool." She is affected by it, her voice cracking on the last word, and I suddenly hate myself for holding on to it for these last few days. I shouldn't have cared about the chain. I should have,

271

the minute I put two and two together on her paternity—run upstairs and grabbed this first.

"You'll have a lot more than a ring, once the paperwork goes through. There's a storage unit somewhere in New Jersey that is filled with his items from Spring Lake."

"Yeah, but…" She loops a finger through the ring and tugs on it. "This was in the photo. It's special."

She steps forward and kisses me, the action catching me by surprise, and I grab her waist, pulling her closer and deepening the kiss. I want to beg her to stay, but I don't. I kiss her, release her, and watch James' ring settle in the dip of her cleavage.

———

I walk down the long table, each ad page blown up and laid out on the glass. I stop beside one and shake my head. "Not this one. Use the shot from the park instead."

Vera moves the piece away and launches into an explanation of the ideology behind the winter campaign and the corresponding social media effort. I nod, my eyes catching sight of the next display ad, a girl from behind, in knee-high riding boots, walking along a track, toward an oncoming train.

I think of Avery, of her sprint across the Spring Lake highway, the silver on her boots flashing in the sun.

I think of her, standing at the other end of that conference table, her eyes meeting mine, the challenge in them.

I think of her leaning over the cramped table at that Ukrainian restaurant, and when she laughed so hard the table shook.

I look away from the displays and walk to the window, the clouds low and hiding the streets below. I glance at my watch and don't understand how a single day away from her can seem so long.

"Mr. Lent?" Vera moves closer. "Would you like to see the demographics report from the latest campaign?

"Yeah." I turn away from the view and focus on the woman's face. "Please."

She moves to the laptop, pressing a button and bringing a PowerPoint presentation to life. I stare up at the screen and wonder what Avery is doing.

CHAPTER 38

AVERY

"I'm asking you to work with me," I beg the scrawny blonde. "It's two weeks, max. You'll barely know she's there."

"I don't trust Russians." Kata sneers at the woman behind me, and I move in between them to block the view.

"What's she going to do, steal from you? You've got a lock on your bedroom door. Use it." I cross my arms and give her my sternest look. "Matilda already said it was cool, so I need you to play nice or I'll find a graveyard shift and put you on it."

The blonde explodes in a string of Ukrainian, and I know enough of the words to understand that she's cussing me out.

"Hey—" I interrupt. "HEY!" I point at her. "Stop that. I've never asked shit from you, other than this. Be fucking grateful for once and work with me. Remember what it was like when you landed. She needs a place to stay, and I don't have any more room in Herman Gardens."

I have placed twenty of Andrei's surprise arrivals. At this rate, we'll all be eighty before I find housing for the rest of them. I push open the door and pause, something inside the apartment catching my eye. "Bruce," I call over my shoulder.

"Yeah, boss?" The man appears, big and hulking, and Kata takes a step back.

"Tell Eddie to keep the newbies in the hall, and come in with me."

"Come in?" Kata shakes her head. "No. This is my private—"

Bruce shoulders through the place and she jumps back with a curse. "What's up?" He looks at me.

"Those sneakers by the door. Check her room for more."

"I bought those!" Kata protests and I follow him toward the left bedroom and past the brand-new Nikes lying on the carpet. He swings open the door and flips on the light.

"Motherfucker." I curse at the stack of boxes along her far wall, then look over my shoulder at her. "Are you serious right now?"

"I bought them," she protests.

"In men's sizes?" I open the top of the box, glancing down at the two-hundred-dollar Mizunos. "Jesus, Kata. Do you know who you're stealing from?"

She flips her hair over one shoulder. "Matt likes me."

"I'm not talking about fucking pimple-popping Matt." I grit. "I'm talking about Matt's boss. Frankie Martello. Heard of him?"

She shrugs. "Yeah. He's come in before."

I put my palms together, pressing my fingers against my lips and try to explain this in the simplest way possible. "He'll cut your toes off." I step forward. "If he doesn't rape you first."

"They're shoes," she protests.

"It's not about the shoes. It's about respect—which you don't have for

276

me, and you sure as shit don't have for him." I look around the room, every surface covered with items. Forget the shoes. I think she's been stealing from every store in Detroit. "This is what we're doing. Bruce, stay with her and watch what she packs. She's bringing what she brought here and nothing else. If it looks new, it's staying. Kata, you've got—" I look at my watch. "An hour to pack up everything."

"Pack up everything for what?"

"You're going home. We'll get you on a flight to JFK tonight and then on to Boryspil."

"No." She shakes her head rapidly, her eyes wet, lips tightly pressed together. "Please. I give it all back."

One year over here. One year and you'd think it was a lifeline.

"I'm getting you out of here because you broke the rules, but also so you don't get hurt." I meet Bruce's eyes and he nods in understanding.

When I pass by Kata, she grabs my arm, begging me to stay, and I twist free of her grip. Stepping into the hall, I look at Eddie. "Let's take everyone for lunch and come back in an hour."

———

If I ever have kids, I'll rock the hell out of class field trips. I lean against the shuttle bus and pass out Tigers tickets to the forty-two newbies as they depart. Once done, I turn to hand Eddie, Bruce, and Marcia theirs.

"What the fuck?" Marcia complains, reading the seat number on it. "Why can't I sit with you guys?"

"Because your Russian is better than the guys and I'm paying you three hundred dollars to help me out." I count out a fifteen hundred bucks in cash and hand it to Eddie. "This is for snacks. Try to keep Marcia happy."

"I'd be *happy* in your seats," she pouts, pushing her arms into a club-house jacket with a fuzzy collar.

"Yeah, me too." I look at the girls, who mill around the bus, a chorus of Russian voices filling the air. "Just don't lose anybody." I glance at my watch. "I have to call Frankie about Kata. I'll come find you guys in the fifth inning and check in."

As the girls pass, they lift their hands, and I high-five a dozen of them before they are gone, a cluster of color and energy. Eddie and Bruce nod at me, their faces solemn and serious, and I smile despite myself—the grin widening when I see Marcia's glower. She sticks out her tongue at me and I match the gesture. She reaches out and affection-ately pinches my arm. I look down at my phone and take a deep breath, any lightheartedness replaced with anxiety as I scroll down my address book and click on Frankie's name.

I've been in this situation before. The last time, I didn't handle it right, making the call before I had the girl out of town. That girl got roughed up so badly, she'd had to spend three days in the hospital before she was healed enough to fly home. I keep photos of her on my phone, and show them to each batch of newbies, pairing the display with a stern warning about breaking the rules. And yet, there's always, out of a hundred, one know-it-all bitch.

Now, with her on a plane, it'll be too late for Frankie to do anything. He'll be pissed, but I'll make sure the stolen inventory is returned tonight and will waive my fees for the next month. I'm banking on that gift, plus my exposure of the theft before he found it himself … hoping that will cushion any fallout.

Lifting the cell phone to my ear, I lean against the shuttle bus and wait, listening to it ring. Looking up to the sky, I wonder what Marco is doing.

———

"And this James guy—your dad—he owned part of Vince Horace, Inc?" Andrei lifts a loaded hot dog to his mouth, cupping a napkin underneath it to catch the mess.

"Yep. It went back to the company when he died, but Marco is signing it back over to me."

Andrei glances at me, his mouth full but his brows lifting. I wait as he chews, the giant bite washed down with a sip of beer. "Awfully nice of him."

"Yep."

He wipes at his face with a napkin. "I thought he was an asshole."

"Well," I stretch out my legs, "he was in the beginning. Or…" I pull my sleeves over my hands. "In the middle."

The edit goes completely over Andrei's head, who focuses on his hotdog, another bite managed before it falls apart. "Fucking bun," he mutters through a mouthful of food.

I say nothing, watching the big screen as the camera pans over the crowd.

"So, what are you going to do with all your money?" He sits back, his elbow bumping me.

"Find a better lawyer."

"Yeah, yeah, yeah. I've heard that before." There is the crack of a bat and we both lean forward.

"Foul." I sit back. "I'm thinking about leaving Detroit."

"No shit." He looks over at me. "Why?"

I'm not ready to say it, not ready to even admit it to myself. I'd spent four days in New York. Four days with him. It wasn't long enough to make any sort of decision. And now, back home, surrounded by everything I know—it seems like a dream. A crazy, seductive dream.

Dreams aren't real. People don't fall in love in days. Lives don't change overnight.

Yet, mine did. I found my father. Inherited a fortune. Slept with a billionaire. Lost my heart.

"Hey." He elbows me. "What are you thinking about?"

"Nothing." I reach down and lift my beer, hiding my face with it as I take a sip.

"You can't just *move*," he points out. "I mean, shit. I've got a stack of visa applications that are stretching into next year."

"I know."

"Plus…" he lifts his hands and gestures to the game. "You can't abandon the Tigers to go lounge in a bikini on a beach."

I smile. "I'm not abandoning anyone. And I might not go. It just depends."

"Depends on what?"

He's so fucking dense. I swear, if Marcia was next to me, she'd have sniffed out my indecision and labeled the source of it within three minutes. I've dropped hints for four innings and all Andrei cares about is the logistics of the assets transfer.

It's probably for the best. I'm not ready to defend my actions yet, not sure how to explain my feelings for Marco—feelings that are probably not reciprocated, at least not at my extremist level. It's as if, with him, my heart has forgotten how to protect itself, running forward and nose-diving into him with the enthusiasm of a Golden Retriever puppy.

I stand up and stretch. "I'm going to go up to the nosebleeds and relieve Marcia for a bit."

He nods, his eyes on the pitch. "Tell her to grab me a pretzel on her way down."

"Pure romance, between the two of you."

"You know it." A strike hits the glove and he leans forward to watch the final pitch.

———

I step over an air mattress, then another, making it across my living room in four giant steps.

"Miss Avery?" A quiet voice comes from behind me.

"Yeah?"

"My bed…" the girl sits up and points to the bottom of the air mattress, then makes a whooshing noise.

"Okay." I open the cabinet below the sink and pull a roll of duct tape out. "Use this." I toss it across the room, almost hitting a pink-headed girl whose name I don't know yet. I hold up my hands in apology and she shrugs.

"Okay." I let out a breath, my eyes moving over the room, which holds six girls, between the air mattresses and the sectional couch. I've got another three girls in each guest bedroom, plus one in mine. My phone vibrates against my butt and I reach back, pulling it out and glancing at the display. My heart skips at the New York phone number. I move through the kitchen and step into the garage, pulling the door closed behind me.

"Hello?"

"Hey." Marco clears his throat. "It's Marco. I'm calling from the house line."

"Oh, thank God. I wasn't sure if it was you or my other boyfriend." *Other boyfriend.* Why did I say that? We aren't in a relationship. At least I don't think we are. I've dissected our awkward conversations a dozen times and have convinced myself that we're either on the verge of getting married or new business associates who accidentally slept together, on three separate occasions.

"I hope it's not too late."

I flip on the lights, illuminating the stairs down to the garage, and sit on the top step. "No, it's fine."

"I saw you on TV. We had the game on in the kitchen."

"I'm surprised you remembered where my seats were."

"It's easy to pick you out of the crowd."

I smile, enjoying the thought of him looking for me. "I didn't realize you were a baseball fan."

"I'm not. I'm an Avery fan. And, to be completely honest..." he pauses. "I may have had one of the employees watch it for me and pause the video when a shot of you came up."

I laugh. "Oh my God. You just crushed the romance out of that action."

"But it's much less creepy," he points out.

"Yes." I nod. "A *tad* bit less creepy."

"I miss you."

My breath catches, the confession so unexpected. "You do?"

"Yes."

I should tell him that I miss him also, that I've thought of him at random times, and spent half the day wanting to text him. I don't.

"And, right now ... I think you should get naked."

I laugh and look around the garage. "I can't get naked right now."

"Well, this is going to be really awkward if I'm the only one touching myself."

I smile. "Shut up."

"I'm serious. Edward is glaring at me right now like I'm doing something wrong."

"I can't get naked," I whisper. "I have company."

"Male company?"

"No." I pull at a loose thread on my pajamas. "Sadly, no."

"Want some? I can be there in two hours."

I picture the reaction from twelve Russian girls, half with zit cream and mouth guards on, if Marco walked in. "Not tonight. Besides," I tease. "Don't you have an empire to run?"

"My empire seems…" he sighs. "Pointless without its king."

"You have to be the king. Isn't that what you wanted?"

"I'm not sure what I want. That's part of my problem."

"What's the other part?"

"It's more of a who. It's this brunette. She's got a mouth on her that I can't stop thinking about. Pale lips I want wrapped around my cock."

"Wow." I breathe. "It's like you don't even know when you're being offensive."

He chuckles. "Oh, most of the time I know."

A long moment passes, and he sighs into the receiver. "I want you to come back to New York. There are decisions to make, paperwork to sign, positions to be fucked in."

I smile. "I can't come back right now. Things are complicated with work right now."

"So, quit. Close up shop and become a woman of leisure. I've got a staff of twenty just dying for an extra ass to kiss."

He still doesn't know about my work, doesn't realize that I've got four hundred—now four hundred and forty-two—girls depending on me. He thinks I can close up shop and eat deviled eggs all day? He's crazy. This conversation is crazy. I need to forget about New York, forget about him, and go back to my life.

"I do miss you. Just you. Not that delicious mouth, or any other part of your tempting anatomy."

Does he? Could he? I lean forward, the concrete step hard through the thin flannel of my pajamas, and rest my elbows on my knees. "I miss you too."

Crazy talk. But it feels, in a ridiculous way, honest.

———

Five more days pass. Three calls from Marco. A quitclaim closing of one Spring Lake mansion. I sign paperwork in Andrei's office and he hands me a Vince Horace ring with three silver keys on it. I hang the keys on a hook in the kitchen and wonder what to do with them. I open the door and smile at the Chinese delivery guy.

He extends the first set of bags and catches sight of the girls in the background, his smile widening, one hand lifted in greeting. I hear a giggle come from behind me and set the bags down, turning back to take the second batch. "Thank you," I pass him the tip and swing the door closed before any of Cupid's arrows hit their mark.

There are more bags than usual, my normal delivery enhanced by my additional houseguests. Guests which, by Wednesday, should be out of my house and in hotel rooms, my negotiations with a local motel finally leading to a resolution that will get me through the next few weeks until a batch of my current girls leave and things return to normal workforce levels.

Wednesday. Surely, I can make it two more days without killing one of them. Last night, an argument over what to watch on television had led to a screaming match that took twenty minutes to resolve.

"Out of the kitchen!" I wave at the girls. "Eddie. Help me out here."

Eddie moves into the kitchen and nods at the girls, arguing with them in Russian. I move quickly, setting out the Styrofoam containers, feeling the bottom of each and moving all the hot packages to the stove and sticking the cool ones back in the bags. I quickly peek into each box on the stovetop, confirming they all contain food, then grab the bag with the cash-filled containers and jog downstairs, flipping through the takeout boxes and checking their contents. I open the Tahoe and toss the bags into the back, then lock the doors. The doorbell rings and I lift my head, a fissure of panic hitting.

I haven't interacted with the cops in a long time, but moments like this—when the cash isn't hidden, when it is in my home and my living room is filled with a dozen fresh arrivals—I worry about moments like this. Pocketing the key to the Tahoe, I jog upstairs, hoping to beat Eddie to the door.

I open the door to the kitchen and hear Marco's voice. Moving through the crowd, I come to a stop next to Eddie. "Marco."

Eddie guards the door, his arms crossed over his chest, and I push him out of the way. Stepping out on the front porch, I pull the door closed and look up at Marco.

He looks good. White pants. Skinny tie. Button-up shirt, rolled half-way up his forearms. I forgot, in the last week, how beautiful he is. I forgot how he can just tilt his head in greeting, and look like a cover model.

I swallow, well aware that I haven't showered in two days. "Hi."

"Hi." He glances at the closed door. "Who's the beefcake?"

"That's Eddie. He's…" I try to think of a description for Eddie. "He's a babysitter right now, but he's also security for me."

"Why do you need security?" His face darkens, and he steps forward as if to throw a protective blanket over me.

"Yo, Miss Avery." The door cracks open and one of the girls sticks her head out. "You have more toilet paper?" Seeing Marco, she does a double-take. "Hello."

He says nothing, and she swings the door wider, propping herself against the doorframe in a seductive pose that effectively demonstrates the excessiveness of her cleavage. "You bring more food for us?"

"Did I what?"

"No. He didn't. Just go inside." I call for Eddie and she rolls her eyes in annoyance. I gently shoo at her and ignore the spark of jealousy that comes when her eyes take another tour of him. Jesus, did I do this? Salivate over him like he was a raw piece of meat?

Maybe. Probably. Then again, I had been a little busy fainting into his arms and drooling all over his car seats.

Eddie appears, glares her into submission, and we are, once again, alone on the porch. I glance at the street and see a late model Escalade, parked at the curb. "Whose wheels?"

"The airport's car service."

I should probably invite him in. Only, inviting him in involves a lot of women and explanations. "So…" I cross my arms over my chest and look up at him. "That was—"

My shoulders hit the brick, his mouth on mine, his kiss hot and greedy. I grip his shirt, feel his fingers in my hair, his hips against mine, our tongues working in hot concert, pants of breath taken between frantic kisses.

How have I gone my whole life without this? I kiss him and fight to not think about him leaving. I kiss him and forget about the girls, the job, the money. I kiss him and all I want, for the next hundred years, is this. Him. Us. Family. Security. Love.

I think I love him.

A car drives by, slowing, and I think of us, under the spotlight of the porch, and pull back. Look into his face and appreciate the glazed look of arousal in his eyes. I did that. I glance at his car and think of my house—packed to the rafters with unwanted guests. "You can't stay here." I see the look on his face and hurry to explain. "I mean—I'll come stay with you if you get a hotel room. I just don't have any room for you here. I'm literally sharing a bed with a Russian cocktail waitress right now. But I can have Eddie watch the girls and sneak out to your hotel room for the night." I slide my hands under his shirt, tracing the divots of his abs with my fingertips.

"Then, let's go. Pack a bag and I'll have you naked on a bed within twenty minutes."

"Well..." I shift my weight, the welcome mat damp against my socks, and think about the cash. "There's something I have to do first."

———

"I don't understand." Marco looks at the cash, the pile dumped out on the Tahoe's tailgate. "Who does this belong to?"

"The girls. Not those girls." I nod toward the house. "Different girls. It's payroll for the week."

"I thought you worked in something with funds."

290

"I do. Their funds. I take it from their employers, and package it up and distribute it to them."

"This seems...illegal."

I line up the bundles and take a moment to count the stacks. When I finish, I reach for the first stack and stuff it in a Ziploc. "It is. Kinda. I mean—the entire process is illegal, but *my* portion of it isn't necessarily *illegal*—it's more that I'm contributing to someone else's illegal activities. Mainly, I'm passing on under-the-table income to the girls and knowingly assisting in tax evasion. But that income *is* being taxed, just as additional profit to their employers."

"And this is how you earn money—this is your job." There is a playful shout from inside and he glances at the door to the house.

"Well, I don't normally have a house full of girls. That was a logistics error." I complete the task and move to the floor, bringing the bagged cash with me as I roll underneath the SUV.

"And the guys giving you this cash, they're criminals?" From my spot on the ground, I can see his shoes, the shadows cast by them as he walks beside the truck and stops.

"Yeah." I stuff bags into the compartment, moving more quickly than I usually do, ready to be done with this conversation.

"And that big guy in there, he protects you." His shoes bend, the heels lifting, and he crouches, one hand coming forward and balancing his weight. I look at his watch, the diamond-littered dial glittering in the dark.

"Yes." I don't mention Bruce. He seems alarmed enough by Eddie.

His legs move and suddenly, he's on the floor, sliding under the vehicle until he's beside me.

I wince, covering my mouth with one hand. "That floor is filthy." I pick at his blue shirt with my hand. "And this looks expensive."

"It doesn't matter." He looks up at the bumper, at the stacks of cash lined up. "Won't these fall out when you drive?"

"Like this, they will." I grab the last few bags and stuff them in the bumper, then roll the compartment up, hiding the cash, and lock it into place. Looking over at him, I widen my eyes. "Pretty impressive, huh?"

"I guess." He looks up at the engine, and from this angle, I can't read his expression. "Can't you do something else as a job?"

I don't want to get into it, don't have the time to explain how I got into this job, or the emotional obligation that I feel for these women. "This works for me. Right now, at least." I know I can't do this forever. If I ever have kids, I'd have to quit. A family would be a giant liability that could be used against me, their safety at risk any time I pissed someone off.

"Okay." He leans forward and kisses me. "I will reserve judgment for now. I've never been with a bad girl before and Criminal Avery is making me really fucking hot."

I reach over, my hands dusted with engine grime and smear a line of black across his cheek. "Good. Because Grease Monkey Marco is pretty damn sexy." I pull at his neck and kiss him, then roll out and away from him. "Now. Let's find a hotel room without a dozen Russians in it, and work out every fantasy I have."

He makes it out from under the vehicle and brushes off his shirt. "Do I have to go back through the kitchen?" He looks properly concerned, given the attention paid to him on his entrance. You'd think the women had never seen a red-blooded male before. Eddie had been irritated by their fawning, Marco had taken it with an almost bored acceptance—a reaction that made me realize he's probably spent his entire life being drooled over.

"No, you don't have to go back through that." I reach out my hand and hit the garage door opener. "Let sneak out this way."

CHAPTER 39

MARCO

She drives her Tahoe like it's a Lambo, and we peel through streets that look like a war zone. I see huddles of homeless, sitting against closed storefronts, shopping carts in tow, and wonder how anyone is homeless with abandoned homes everywhere.

She is so alive. That's an odd thought to have, but it's how I feel around her, as if she teems with energy. Each moment is unpredictable, each interaction a different experience, her presence a rainbow of color in a world filled with gray. When she left New York, it was as if I saw the monochromatic color of my life for the first time.

She looks over and smiles at me, and I try my hardest not to beam back at her like a love-blown idiot.

————

Avery steps out of the bathroom, a towel wrapped around her body, and I fight a war to keep my mind in the game. Fumbling with a little bottle of lotion, she squeezes a glob onto her hands. When she rubs them together, all I can think about is how my cock would feel in between those slick palms.

I sit up higher on the bed and pat the spot next to me. "Let's talk for a minute."

"Hmmm." She crawls onto the end of the bed and plops on the pillowtop without any concern for sex appeal. "Sounds serious." She furrows her brow at me, and I smile despite myself.

"Your work is too dangerous."

"It's not." She pulls a pillow free of the stack and rests her head on it, her eyes on mine. "It was early on, but I have good relationships with everyone now."

"And what happens when someone wants your job? What's to stop some thug from killing you and taking everything?"

"That's a risk in any job."

She's not that stupid. I can see the lie in her eyes, and if she thinks she's going to continue in this profession without a security team around her, three bodies deep, she's crazy.

I tell her this and she growls. Tells me a story about how she got into this business, and why it is important to her. I watch her talk, see the fire and energy in her eyes, and love her even more for her protective passion for this portion of the streets. But she has to stop. I'm not losing her to one of these gangsters, or to jail.

I change the subject, pulling her into my arms and confessing about Vince, about the agreement I signed ten years ago, and Vince's reasons for wanting me as his boyfriend. I tell her about his legacy, and about all the rallies I've attended, speeches I've made, and lies I've told. I tell her everything, and hear—through my own words—how awful it all sounds.

"It's not awful." She pulls away from me and repositions us, crawling up my chest and straddling me. "You made a business decision. It was a win-win for both of you."

"Only I feel like I'm losing, right now."

A smile cracks her features. "You just inherited an entire... empire. You aren't losing anything."

I could give two fucks about the empire. Maybe it's because I have it, but this last week—every piece of it has felt tainted. Every piece is worthless without her. I avoid that thought process and run my hands over her thighs, appreciating the look of her without underwear, the soft brush of her hair against my stomach when she tilts her pelvis.

I slide my hands under her towel, grabbing her ass and squeezing it hard, her eyes lighting up a little at the rough contact. She reaches back and wraps her hand around me, and I forget my next thought.

———

"So... why Detroit?" I step over a fallen branch and hold out my arm, helping her over it.

She shrugs, moving back toward the park's walking path, quickening her steps to avoid the crowd of kids we had gone around. "It was a city I could disappear in. When I left school, this was the city that sort of adopted me. I made friends, found a place to stay, and never left."

I watch her as she dips, grabbing a Frisbee off the ground and flinging it in the direction of its owner. "What would it take for you to move?"

She glances at me. "I don't know." She looks down the path. "I'd have to figure out what to do about my work."

"I think you should move to New York."

She stops and turns to me, the wind whipping her hair across her face, and she turns into the breeze to stop it. "Why?"

Because I love you. I want to say it, but I can't. Instead, I give her as much of myself as I can. "I don't want to lose you. I can't—" I meet her eyes. "I can't think of moving forward without having you in my life."

"And what about Vince?" She asks quietly.

"Vince…" I look around, stepping closer to her and lowering my voice. "Vince once told me that it was nobody's fucking business what we did with each other when we were alone."

"So, you'd keep me a secret?"

"No. *Fuck* no." I wouldn't do that to her. After the last decade, I wouldn't do that to anyone. "I can tell the truth about you without telling anyone details about Vince and I. He was right. It's not their business. I loved him like a father and a friend. But they don't have to know that. And you…" I have to stop. I can't… I close my eyes and say it anyway. "I love you in an entirely different way."

"You do?" She is thinking, I can see it in the pinch of her eyebrows, the saw of her teeth across her bottom lip.

"Yes."

"Like a… love-hate way?" She peeks up at me and I see the twitch of her mouth, the attempt to suppress a smile.

"No."

"Like a love-your-boyfriend's-niece kind of way?"

I growl, deep in my throat. "No."

She steps closer and tilts her head, looking up at me with pure filthy innocence. "Like a love-goddess-sugar-tits kind of way?"

"Like a love-my-future-wife kind of way."

She stops. "Wow," she whispers. "That's a big way."

"It is." I reach up and rub the back of my neck. "Too big?"

She grins. "I like big. I like big..." she moves flush against me, her hands sliding down the front of my shirt. "And long. And..."

I trap her hand before it makes it all the way to my crotch. "And... you're trying to distract me with sex."

She wrinkles her nose at me. "I am?"

"Yes."

"I think you're the one who started talking about penises." She doesn't love me. It's okay. I'm a fuckin' baby kitten when it comes to this stuff. Of course, I became attached. Of course, she is flippant and going back home, and only interested in orgasms and jokes. I can handle it, even if I sound like I can't. I—

"I love you too." Her nose stops that wrinkle, and she speaks as confidently as the girl who once dove in front of a Rolls Royce.

"You do?"

"Yeah." She raises on her tip-toes and brushes her lips to mine. "But I'm not leaving Detroit without a plan."

I'll get her a plan. I'll get her a plan so perfect she won't be able to say no to it. I'll get her anything she wants in this world, just to hear those words again.

CHAPTER 40

Avery

SUMMER

"It's a sweatshop."

"It's not a sweatshop." Marco crosses his arms and fixes me with his sternest look. "It's a factory. One that will abide by every single government regulation that exists. Fair wages. Fair hours. Reasonable overtime."

"I'd still be bringing them over here and…" I hang my head. "I don't know. It feels like a sweatshop."

"It *should* feel like an ex-Nike factory." He turns me around, making me face the building. "You've got to use your imagination and picture something different."

I try. I squint really hard at the giant square building and try to imagine something. "Nope." I turn my head. "Maybe a giant statue in front would help. I got one at my house. I can get a shipping quote to move it."

"We aren't moving the statue," he deadpans. "My girlfriend loves that statue."

I snort, and turn back to the building, rubbing my hands together in an attempt to stay warm. "Can we go inside?"

"We own it." He brings out a set of keys and dangles them in front of me. "So, yes. We can do whatever you like."

"You bought it?!" I groan and swipe at the keys. "Well, now I *have* to like it!" I stomp toward the building, glancing over my shoulder and pointing to a low-slung stretch of buildings to the side. "What's that?"

"Housing," he calls out, flashing me a cocky smile and jogging to catch up.

"I already have housing," I grumble.

"Well, now you have more."

I stop at the front door and flip through the keys, all clearly labeled. Finding the right one, I shove it into the lock and turn the deadbolt, the door swinging open with a loud screech. When we step in, the lights flicker on.

It's empty. I'd envisioned giant machines, production lines, and conveyor belts. But there's nothing. We step out on a ledge and look down on a cavernous room. "I hope you didn't pay a lot for this."

"I should have taken you to a factory first. Then you could envision it. Just… trust me. In six months, this room will be a beautiful, productive space."

"And you'll be able to employ four hundred girls."

"Yes." He pulls me toward him and places a kiss on my forehead. "We will employ your girls. There's a commercial kitchen here that will feed all the employees. They can work there or in the cafeteria. There's a laundry and uniform facility for the employees. We'll move our HR and accounting departments from New York to here, and the housekeeping crew for the offices and plant alone will be massive. Plus, packaging and shipping and receiving..." He smiles. "Don't worry."

"And you'll use locals too?"

"Yes." He tugs on my hair. "Stop worrying. Almost all of our full-time employees will be local. We're promising the city fifteen hundred jobs. This is good for everyone."

I look down on the plant floor. It seems too easy, though—in actuality —it is anything but. Marco is moving an entire factory for this, closing their Italian plant and moving everything to Detroit. I don't want to know how much that is costing him, though he swears that he will save money on production, once everything is said and done.

"So... six months." I look over at him. "And then I'll be out of the money business."

"No." He glances at his watch. "As of... right *now*, you are out of the money business."

I push off the railing, objections firing, and he cuts me off before I get a word out. "I've spoken to Andrei. He's going to work with Matt and have him handle things until the transition to the factory occurs.

Matt. I think of the ex-Special Forces agent, a handsome fortress who has shadowed me ever since Marco visited Detroit and found out about my job. Matt can certainly handle himself, and I've closely watched his interactions with the girls in the last six weeks. He is good to them and understands what I'm attempting to do. Still, "I'm not ready. It's only been—"

"Avery." Marco looks at me solemnly. "Your job, and your clients are dangerous. You've been lucky so far, that no one has seriously hurt you. But now, dating me—I've exposed you to an entirely new sort of risk. Someone could kidnap you for ransom. Your *clients*—" he gestures in the general direction of my neighborhood. "They could kill you for exiting this business. You are inconveniencing them by pulling this workforce out. And you are taking that risk, because of me. I understand that. I hate myself for telling you to do it, but I can't go another day and worry about you. You're too precious to me."

"They don't even know I'm dating you," I argue. "Nobody knows." We've bent over freakin' backward to keep this secret, agreeing to put six months of separation between Vince's death and any publicizing our relationship, out of respect to his legacy.

"I don't care." He folds his arms over his chest. "I'm not risking it. I'm done, Avery. I'm done with anything that puts you the slightest bit at risk. And maybe that makes me an asshole, but I don't really give a f—"

I silence him with a kiss, and he drops his arms, wrapping them around me and pulling me against his chest. He deepens the kiss and I finally pull away, laughing. "You *are* an asshole, but I understand."

And I do. I've lived recklessly ever since I ran away from the McKennas. I haven't had anything to lose, and have made risky decisions because of that. It's nice to be valued. When he says that he can't lose me, and I see the worry that fills his eyes...it gives me something I've never had—the feeling of being worth anyone's concern.

I tuck my hand under his arm and turn, standing beside him and look out on the factory floor. "So..." I muse. "This is the future home of Vince Horace."

He leans over and kisses the top of my head. "Now, let's get you packed and move into ours."

CHAPTER 41

Three months after my move, and I still feel like a guest. Maybe that's normal when you are constantly waited on hand and foot. I roll over in bed, glancing at the news, and watch the two women open the curtains, put away Marco's clothes from last night, and set the paper and a hot cup of coffee beside me. "Here." I sit up. "Gimme."

She passes me the cup, and I scoot back until I am leaning against the headboard, sipping the Columbian blend and waving at them as they leave. Way too many staff. We've had several discussions over this. But Marco doesn't have it in him to fire anyone. Behind that obnoxious and high-maintenance exterior, he's a gigantic softie. Plus, whether he'll admit it or not, he likes the constant attention. I'm not entirely sure he could survive without the ability to clear his throat and have someone trip over themselves to assist him.

There is a knock on the door, and I look up to see Edward, standing stiffly in the doorway. "Miss Horace, your guest is requesting to be brought up."

I wave a hand forward. "Go for it."

"Good, 'cause I'm here." Marcia pokes her head out from behind

Edward. "No thanks to this guy, who thinks that you two are the freaking royal family." She breezes into the room and launches herself on the bed, the blankets poofing out around her weight.

Edward sighs, one of his deeply disappointed ones, and I hide a smile behind my next sip of coffee. "Thank you, Edward. I'll keep an eye on her from here."

"Please do." He exhales again, then turns, pulling the door closed.

"You'll keep an eye on me?" Marcia snorts. "What am I, a toddler?"

"Not much different from one, actually." I reach for the remote and turn off the television. "Sleep well?"

"Are you kidding?" She rolls over and crawls up the bed toward me. "One guy offered to tuck me in. Andrei about ripped his ass off."

I smile, her English still wonky at times, and kick my feet free of the covers. "You should have taken him up on it. Hell, *Andrei* should have taken him up on it. It's actually a pretty glorious activity."

"It is?"

"Yep. They heat the sheets and serve you a cocoa and cookie midnight snack. Then, once you are tucked in, they give you a hand and scalp massage."

"You full of shit." She holds up a hand. "Wait. Never mind. I was delivered dental floss on a silver tray this morning, so—yeah. I believe."

"It's crazy, I know."

"It's damn cool, actually. I mean, Andrei's is okay...but we ate dinner last week out of a KFC bucket. This..." she raises her arms. "This is the life."

I grin, because she doesn't even know the half of it. She's excited by dental floss on a tray. She doesn't know that tonight we're taking the jet to Bimini. The yacht's there, stocked and ready, to take us through the Caribbean. It's my thank you to Andrei—and her—for picking up my slack and for working with Matt on the transition. I can't wait to see her face when she sees the boat. It's excessive in every sense of the word.

"Come on." I set my coffee down on the tray and slide off the bed, pushing my feet into slippers. "Let's go downstairs and find our men."

CHAPTER 42

MARCO

LATE FALL

Versace once said that fashion shouldn't own you. He said that we decide who we are and that we express ourselves by the way we dress and the way we live. I respected Vince for many things, but am ashamed of the way he allowed his image to rule his life. I'm ashamed of the way I contributed to that image, and how I gave up my own self-respect in the process.

It's time to tell the truth, as best I can, while still respecting his wishes.

I look at Avery, standing to the side, behind all the cameras and crew, and see her gaze move to mine. She nods, and I know I don't have to do this. I know I can continue hiding her from the world and from the press. But that's not fair to her, and it's not fair to us. It's been seven months since Vince's death, and I can't hide her a moment longer. Not when I plan to propose to her tonight.

The lights come on, blinding my view of Avery, and I look to the woman, sitting across from me—the *GQ* terror. I had Paulie call her, with thoughts that this might bring things full circle.

I don't expect this will be easy. She won't like my vagueness in the areas of my relationship with Vince—but that isn't what this interview is about. This interview is about my new life, the company's new American factory, and the woman I've fallen in love with. If she presses me, I'll tell the truth—that I loved Vince, but love Avery in an entirely different way. If need be, I'll quote the king himself: It's none of their fucking business what our relationship entailed.

In preparation for the media storm this interview will create, we've made a few arrangements. The first was an exodus from her past—a process that started with a visit to Kirk and Bridget McKenna, who turned out to be a very polite, semi-retired couple, who still, seventeen years later, have no interest in parenting. Avery made her amends with them, wrote them a check that paid off their lakefront mansion, and walked out with a confidentiality agreement that guaranteed that the world would never know the connection between Avery McKenna and Avery Horace. While I didn't think the check, nor the confidentiality agreement was necessary, Avery seemed to need the closure of an official 'parting of ways' so I kept my mouth shut and kissed her when she returned.

Her name change was filed in California by John months ago, and the decree sealed by the court for reasons of privacy. If someone digs hard enough, they'll hit the truth, but California has over five hundred Avery McKennas, so they'll research until their eyes fall off before they realize they're in the wrong state.

Her Detroit apartments and home are now in trusts and filled with legitimate, tax-paying residents, who come in on Andrei's work visas and are employed by Vince Horace, Inc.

I think she's happy, but I'm terrified that it's not enough, that I've forgotten some task, some piece of her heart that is left unfilled. She's completed every part of me. I just want to do the same for her. I reach my hand in my pocket and touch the ring box, verifying its presence.

"Mr. Lent." The journalist smiles and I force myself to return the gesture. "Let's begin."

EPILOGUE

MARCO

ONE YEAR LATER

My wife needs to be spanked. *Especially* in moments like this, when she's teasing the hell out of me, in shorts that should be illegal, bending forward and picking up her beer. She straightens, looks over at me with an innocent expression. "What?"

She knows *what*. She knows that I'm going on three days without sex, fighting an erection that she's been accidentally brushing her hand over all afternoon, and am about two seconds away from throwing her over my shoulder and taking her into the VIP bathroom for some one-on-one time.

I look away, focusing on the pregame announcer, and ignore her when she settles into the seat next to me. She pulls a shopping bag onto her lap, and pulls out a new Dodgers hat and jersey.

This is another reason why she needs a strong smack, right across that delicious ass. She's annoyingly consistent in her dislike for anything pinstripe. She's taken the hatred up with almost cheerful exuberance, donning the colors of any opponent. Our closet—previously sectioned by designer and vintage, now has a rack filled with cheap polyester shirts, gloves, jackets, and hats. I swear—the jersey she's pulling on right now? We have that one already.

"It's Granderson." She pulls her head free of the neck. "He was just traded in from the Tigers."

Ex-Tigers players get extra attention, including the ones on the Yankee roster, who she goes easy on in her nightly taunts of any player in pinstripes. I can't keep track of these people. I don't know how she knows them all, their stats and team histories. Though, I guess a forty-man roster is nothing compared to her four hundred girls, all whom she knows by name.

She glances down the row of empty seats. "Remind me who we're meeting?"

"A couple from LA. They own a lingerie company that's interested in using the Detroit factory."

She brightens. "Dodgers fans?"

"I'm not sure. The guy took me up on the tickets, so I'm guessing so."
Past the two seats for them, the rest of our tickets are being used by a
combination of house employees and their partners. Surprisingly
enough, upon distribution of Vince's estate—a million going to each
employee—almost everyone stayed on. So, it's still a house filled with
ninety-percent gays, a ratio that Vince would be happy about.

"Mr. Lent?" A deep voice speaks from beside me, and I turn, moving
to my feet and shaking the man's hand. "Trey Marks. It's a pleasure."

I introduce myself and meet his wife, a gorgeous brunette who climbs
over the seat and settles down next to Avery without reservation.
They start discussing LA without a moment's pause, and I shrug at
Trey. "That was easy."

"Kate's never met someone she couldn't get along with."

A trio of boys thunder down the stands, stopping at the wall and
calling out to the players. I watch as Avery reaches in her bag, pulls
out a handful of balls, and carries them over to the boys.

*"Eat this." My mom holds out a stick of some sort, all but poking Avery in the
nose with it. "It increases fertility."*

*"Mom," I warn, pulling her bag from the trunk and passing it to the closest
uniform. "She's not going to eat that stick."*

"Well, you don't have to just chew on it, Mr. Fancy Pants," she huffs. "You can mix it up in a smoothie or something."

"Thank you, Mrs. Lent." Avery takes the stick with the solemnness of someone who actually plans to gnaw on wood.

"Let's not scare her off the day before the wedding, okay?" I reach for the stick, and Avery holds it out of reach.

"You do plan on having children, don't you?" My mom peers up at Avery with the calculated analysis of a velociraptor eyeing its prey.

"We do." Avery smiles at me, and I think of last night, the way she had tasted in the shower, her breath fogging the glass as I'd taken her from behind. We'd moved from there onto the floor of the closet, in too much of a hurry to make it into the bedroom. My knees had dug into the thick rug as I'd thrust inside of her, her skin still pink and warm from the shower, her soft cry of pleasure making me come too quickly.

I had made up for that in the bed, the sounds of the city coming through the open window, her legs spread, my mouth on that hot pink skin, fucking her with my tongue, sucking gently on her clit, holding her down with my hands until she came against my mouth. Her taste, her sounds, the tight grip of her body around my fingers ... I had crawled up her body and pushed back inside of her. Bare cock inside wet pussy. Her juices and heat squeezing my shaft, her tits bouncing from my thrusts, her eyes fierce and loving on mine. I had come again, filling her with my come, and prayed in the final thrust before I pulled out—for babies. Lots of healthy, fat babies.

Three months since the wedding, and I can picture her with a crowd of little bodies around her, holding up their hands, calling her name. I pray for boys, because if she ever has a girl … I'll be toast. I'll never say no, and worry over every moment. I'll watch her fall asleep and count the moments until she wakes up. I'll give her everything in this world and try to build a second, just to give her that too.

Avery looks over at me and sticks out her tongue, passing a Sharpie to the closest boy, and then gesturing to the players, coaching the kids on who is most likely to sign. She crouches to pick up a fallen ball, and I watch the hem of her shorts ride higher, exposing the buttom curve of her ass.

"I'm not going to be able to concentrate on the game, with you wearing those."

"You designed these. You know that, right?"

I study the dark denim critically. "They didn't look so short on our models."

"'Cause your models don't have curves. Next time, bring me in."

I would, except I'd blow a gasket if she dropped her clothes in the middle of the fitting room, the way our models do. I'd rip out every designer's eyes, wrap her in fabric, and go broke from the lawsuits. I reach out and pop the top button of the shorts. "Take those off."

"Take off that pinstripe shirt, and I will."

317

"*This feels like a negotiation opportunity.*" *She hates me in pinstripes. Which is why, upon receipt of our season tickets, I went slightly crazy in the design hall, tasking the team with an entire wardrobe of game-friendly attire.*

"*Nope. I lose all of your negotiations.*" *She cocks a brow at me, her confident expression instantly putting me on guard.* "*I was thinking more of a trade.*"

"*A trade?*"

"*Yep. I've got a different shirt for you to wear.*"

"*I'm not changing shirts.*"

She pouts, an exaggerated gesture that only makes me more suspicious. "*But I had it <u>made</u> for you?*"

"*By the designers?*"

"*No. By NextDayShirts.com. I used a coupon. Saved <u>forty</u> percent.*" *She drawls out the discount amount in a way she knows will drive me crazy.*

"*Sounds horrendously pedestrian.*"

She snorts. "*Oh my God. Stop. You grew up in IOWA, for God's sake.*" *She opens a drawer and bends over, pulling something out of the back, my thought processes stuttering at the full ass cheeks displayed.*

"Here it is." She turns, holding up a dark navy T-shirt, the empty back of it facing me. It looks cotton. Unisex. Painfully bland.

"That better be Yankee blue," I deadpan.

"It's not." She beams. "Now, are you going to wear it?"

"Fuck no."

She stomps. "Wrong answer. You don't get to see the shirt until you agree to wear it."

"Give me that." I snatch the shirt out of her hands, and she shrieks in response, battling me for it. I get it away from her, and turn it over, holding it up and reading the display.

FUTURE DAD OF A DETROIT TIGER

It had the Tigers logo, the words arching over and below it, the Tiger wearing a pacifier and bib. My heart, in the moment it took to read the words, stops, stutters, then beats a hundred times faster and bigger.

I look at her, and she smiles. I look back at the shirt and my vision blurs with tears.

319

"Interesting shirt." Trey passes me a beer. "Will this be your first?"

"Yeah." I let out a breath. "Just found out today. I'm still in the can't-believe-it-yet phase. We're going to the doctor tomorrow."

The doctor. As soon as Avery had mentioned that, my fear had begun. What if something is wrong? What if something happens to Avery? In the moment I considered that possibility, I almost wished she wasn't pregnant. I almost wished we could go back, chop off my baby-making-ability, and guarantee that she was safe from at least *that* danger.

Almost. I watch her refereeing a rock-paper-scissors game, pulling off her baseball cap and handing it to the winner, and have never loved anyone more. She turns away, waving to the kids, and I picture her with our child in her arms.

She walks toward me, and I rise, gripping her waist and pulling her against me. I bend down, kiss her, and then whisper in her ear, "I love you."

She wraps her arms around my chest, her mouth nuzzling against my neck. "I love you too. Especially in Tiger blue."

———

AVERY

6 YEARS LATER

"Must I?" Edward sniffs in disapproval, his face long, features bland.

"YES!" She jumps to reach him, her ponytail bouncing, the water balloon outstretched. "You have to do the first one, 'cause you're the *oldest*." She whispers the last word and glances around, to make sure that no one hears.

"Very well." Edward takes the hot pink water balloon from her outstretched hand and turns, his back rigid, his dress shoes moving forward, to the edge of the pool. "And now?"

"Now," she steps up next to him, her floaties bumping into his pants. "Now..." she says carefully. "You reach back and frow it!" She gives him a careful demonstration, her hand empty, the imaginary water balloon landing somewhere in the middle of the pool. "But try to *hit* someone."

"Like this?" Edward slowly reaches back his arm, his face absolutely devoid of emotion, and then, with surprising speed and agility, flings the water balloon forward, hitting Marco dead center in the middle of his chest.

I burst out laughing, watching as Marco looks down from his seat on the edge of the pool. His eyes narrow and he reaches into the closest bucket and grabs a handle of balloons.

"YES!" Vina cheers, jumping up and down, the tutu of her bathing suit bouncing. "You got Daddy!" She spies Marco's action, and extends a stern finger. "No! No hitting G-pa!" She squeezes in between him and the edge of the pool, holding out her arms as if to protect him. Only, given her short stature, she's only defending him from the thigh down. "He's OLD!" she screams, and then her eyes widen, one hand clamping over her mouth as she peers up at him. "I didn't mean old-old," she whispers up at him.

Edward steps back, away from the pool, and clasps his hands in front of him. I watch him closely, and can see, in just the tiniest twitch of facial features, the edge of his mouth lifting.

She's broken him. From the minute she was born, I saw the beginning of the crumble. He insisted on fetching her bottles, on examining her bibs and nappies before use, on sanitizing her toys constantly. When she started to talk, insisting that he was her grandfather, the crack in his veneer widened into a cavern.

I feel something behind me and turn, seeing Marco's foot hook my waist and pull me toward him. I allow the move, the warm water of the pool splashing against the side as he maneuvers me between his open knees. He leans forward, wrapping his arms around me and presses a kiss on my shoulder. I watch as our daughter sternly gives instructions to the opposing lines of four-year-olds, a moment of composure in place until all hell breaks loose, brightly colored water balloons flying between the two rows of children.

"I wish Vince could have seen this. Your dad, too." He squeezes me.

"The sex grotto, turned into a water-balloon battlefield?"

"Yeah." He chuckles against my neck. "But also, our life. The changes."

I twist in his arms and look up at him. "Do you think he'd be happy?"

He nods, and I see the hint of sadness that tints his eyes. My husband is getting older. There is now silver in his hair, crows-feet that appear when he smiles, and a peacefulness that has dampened his scowls. They still appear, frequently enough, but don't have quite the same venom—their effect still devastatingly sexy when they hit.

He scowled a lot during our first year together. After that interview, one where he left Vince's playboy legacy intact, and confessed to falling for me ... there was strong backlash from the gay community. Stores were picketed, there were boycotts, and sales struggled. We lost the support of one of Vince's strongest markets, and Marco struggled with the guilt of being a fraud.

But over the last five years, he has channeled that guilt into charities. The Vince Horace Memorial Hospital, set up two years ago, is directly funded from Vince Horace, Inc. While it serves any needy individuals and families, it has six inner-city centers set up for the mental and physical well-being and care of gay, lesbian, bisexual, and transgender individuals. In addition, money is funneled every month into runaway centers for gay youth and equality litigation and support.

He's still a fraud. There are still only a handful of individuals who know the truth—that his relationship and love for Vince was strictly

323

platonic and not passion-filled. But I think, behind the long hours, press avoidance, and big donations ... I think Marco has begun to forgive himself. Vina has been, in large part, to thank for that. She burst into our lives and took over every part of it.

I watch her adjust her goggles, her tiny brow creasing in concentration, her palms pressing against the front of the eyewear to stick them into place. She pinches her nose with one hand and leaps into the air, cannon-balling into the pool, the resulting splash barely noticeable.

I remember earlier today, when we walked down the block to buy the balloons, and she danced between the snow flurries, ducking away from each one in an impossible attempt to not get hit. She is a lucky girl. I wonder if she will ever realize it. I've taken her to Detroit, taken her to the bad areas and showed her the way that so many in our world live, but she doesn't understand. In her four-year-old mind, it's normal that she can have a pool party in December, or order an ice cream sundae from a chef in her kitchen, or walk down a runway in Paris in her own pajama line.

She's spoiled. I can see it, and I fear it. I keep telling her *no*, but every part of this world screams *yes*.

"Stop worrying." He pulls off his shirt, the front of it wet from Edward's attack, and tosses it aside, moving me forward and sliding into the water beside me. "I can feel you worrying."

"I'm not worrying." I let him pull me into the deeper water, my arms and legs wrapping around him. "I just..."

"She's fine. She has the summers at Spring Lake to keep her in line."

"Right." I fix him with a look. "A mansion on the ocean. Tough life."

"Without any staff," he reminds me. "Nobody to pick up after her, or fetch her things, or catch us doing anything naughty..." he slips his hand down the back of my bathing suit and grips my ass. I laugh and squirm away, my legs floating through the water before he brings me back.

"Mommy!" My name is a command, stern and disapproving, and I turn to see Vina, sitting astride a floating unicorn with an inflatable spiked collar.

"Yes?" I hang on to Marco's neck and look at her.

"I have a present for you." She splashes over, the unicorn in danger of tipping, and hands me a water balloon. Leaning forward, she crawls into my arms, and I let go of Marco to give her some room. "Don't leave, Daddy! Sandwich."

"I got you." Marco pulls me back into him, her soft tutu squishing in between our bodies, her wet head resting on my shoulder. His arms tighten around me, and I feel as if my heart will break.

This. It's all I ever wanted, but it's so much more than ever I thought it would be.

Her hand reaches down, finding mine, her tiny fingers pulling my water-balloon-gripping hand into the air, and when she cuts her eyes to her father, a mischievous grin lighting up her face, I understand what she wants.

"I love you, Daddy," she says softly, patting his arm.

He meets my eyes, and I see the innocent happiness there, the love that has no idea of what is to come.

"I love you, Vina," he says hoarsely, and presses his lips to the top of her wet head.

"I'm sorry," I mouth, then swoop my hand up and down, the full balloon bursting on the top of his perfect, salon-created, mess of hair.

Water splashes, he curses, and her shriek of delight fills the air in the moment before he dunks me under the water.

I hold my breath and open my eyes, taking a moment in the stillness of the water to admire the muted and blurry image of them, his laugh, her giggle, the closeness and connection they share. I swim around them and come up for air beside them, and right before I break the surface, it feels like the seams in my heart will rip.

Love, in this moment, has no boundaries. Vince, James, Andrei,

Marcia, Marco, and Vina ... they've taught me that. I am finally loved. I am finally happy. And I finally, in the wet and messy embrace of their hug—understand the meaning of family.

Want to be notified when Alessandra Torre's next book releases?

Click Here or visit NextNovel.com!

AUTHOR'S NOTE

Hidden Seams marks the finish of my sixteenth novel. Sixteen! I remember, so clearly, when I finished my first. The heady power of reaching The End. The anxiousness to publish. The terrifying fear of rejection. Now, things are different. I have a career, one that doesn't hinge solely on the success of one book. That security allows me to be bolder, to explore storylines that interest me, and to take risks.

This book was born from a variety of places, and is one of my riskier concepts.

The idea—a straight man who pretends to be gay—was my husband's, and this is the first idea of his that I've ever written. He offers me ideas like a prostitute dishes out hand jobs. They come from anywhere, at any time. Some are amazing, and others are terrible, but with all of them, I sort of nod and write them down, with no plans to ever write. And that's because a story must come from inside ME to have any legs. I have to be able to picture the characters, and put myself in their lives. Except ... this idea sort of stuck with me. It pestered me from its spot on the notebook list. I actually picked up the computer and wrote the first five chapters of it about six months ago—then had to set it aside to work on a different novel (The Ghost-writer). But it kept niggling at me.

Then, I had a drink with a girl in a bar. A Russian, who was here on a work visa. Does this sound familiar? It should, if you didn't skim over most the novel. The more we drank, the more we talked, and the more I found out about the people she worked for, the places she stayed, and what her experience has been like so far in our country. She was the basis of many of the characters in this novel, and the inspiration for Avery's job.

Marco was a different beast, and I had trouble with his character until I ended up on the tail end of an *Archer* marathon. If you've never seen the show, it's about a spoiled-ass secret agent who is ridiculously selfish in every sense of the word. And I loved him. I don't think you're supposed to love him, and I may be the only person in the *Archer* fan-base who does love him—but I did. I loved him, and I stole so many Archer tendencies in my creation of Marco.

Please excuse any fictional liberties I took with the story. Please understand that these are flawed characters, and their views and actions do not reflect my own opinions or history. I hope you enjoyed a peek into their world. I hope you loved their chemistry, and their battles, and their love—as much as I did.

I owe a moment to the individuals who helped me with this novel. Thank you to my husband, for the idea and inspiration, and your continual patience with my writing schedule. Thank you, Tricia Crouch, for being my biggest cheerleader and beta, and for all your input, advice, and help. Thank you to SueBee and Wendy Metz, for reading early versions of this and giving me your feedback, warnings, and advice. Thank you, Janice Owens, for an incredibly fast turn-around and your gazillion helpful comments and catches. Thank you, Madison Seidler, for always making time for me, and for molding and improving this story into something that readers will actually want to read—and for letting me send it to you in pieces! And thank you Perla

Calas, for your proofs and feedback, and for fitting me in at a time when your schedule is so hectic.

And thank you to the amazing bloggers who read, review, and promote all my novels, including this one. It's been an incredible five years, and I have all of you to thank for it. And the biggest thank you to the readers. Thank you for your support. Thank you for picking up this book. And thank you for recommending it to others.

Until the next novel...

Sincerely,

Alessandra

DELETED SCENES

Fun Fact - originally, Avery was a journalist and Marco was a make-up wearing man, living a double life. Sound confusing?

Maybe it was. It also lead me to a dead-end, which is why I tossed out about forty pages of content and started fresh - though I did keep in the car accident.

Want to read the original content and beginning? Click here!!

ABOUT THE AUTHOR

Alessandra Torre is an award-winning New York Times bestselling author of sixteen novels. Torre has been featured in such publications as Elle and Elle UK, as well as guest blogged for the Huffington Post and RT Book Reviews. She is also the Bedroom Blogger for Cosmopolitan.com. In addition to writing, Alessandra is the creator of Alessandra Torre Ink, a website, community, and online school for aspiring authors.

If you enjoy Alessandra's writing, please follow her on social media, or subscribe to her popular monthly newsletter, where she hosts a monthly giveaway, along with writing updates, personal photos, and more.

www.alessandratorre.com
alessandra@alessandratorre.com

ALSO BY ALESSANDRA TORRE

Looking for another sexy read?

Love in Lingerie. When two best friends run a lingerie company, the only thing hotter than their product is their chemistry.

Hollywood Dirt. (Now a Full-length Movie!) When Hollywood comes to a small town, sparks fly between its biggest star and a small-town outcast.

Blindfolded Innocence. (First in a series) A college student catches the eye of Brad DeLuca, a divorce attorney with a sexy reputation that screams trouble.

Black Lies, the New York Times Bestseller. A love triangle with a twist that readers couldn't stop talking about. You'll hate this heroine until the moment you love her.

Moonshot, the New York Times Bestseller. Baseball's hottest player has his eye on only one thing—his team's 18-year-old ballgirl.

Tight. A small-town girl falls for a sexy stranger on vacation. Lives intersect and secrets are unveiled in this dark romance.

Trophy Wife. When a stripper marries a rich stranger, life as a trophy wife is not anything like she expects.

Love, Chloe. (First created for Cosmpolitan.com) A fallen socialite works for an heiress, dodges an ex, and juggles single life in the city that never sleeps.

Some suspenseful Alessandra Torre novels:

The Ghostwriter. Famous novelist Helena Roth is hiding a dark secret – her perfect life is a perfect lie. Now, as death approaches, she must confess her secrets before it's too late. An emotional and suspense-charged novel.

The Girl in 6E. (Deanna Madden, #1) A sexy internet superstar hides a dark secret: she's a reclusive psychopath.